Duggins' Demise

David Seanor Brierley

Disclaimer

This is a work of fiction and any resemblance to any person living or dead is purely coincidental. The places, characters and names, events and incidents mentioned are a product of the author's imagination

2QT Limited (Publishing)

First edition published 2018

2QT Limited (Publishing)

www.2qt.co.uk

Cover design & Typesetting by Dale Rennard

Printed in Great Britain
Lightning Source UK Ltd

A CIP catalogue record for this book is available from the British Library

ISBN 978-1-912014-08-8

Dedication

Duggins' Demise is dedicated to Trevor Howard Marshal, a long-term friend now sadly missed by all who knew him.

Acknowledgements

To Catherine Cousins and the wonderful staff at 2QT Publishing, a huge thank you for all your help, patience and encouragement. To Gary, struggling through tears more than sweat, to put my handwritten manuscript into some sort of sense and to all the people who had faith in me and in putting my work into print. Thank you all most sincerely.

Chapter 1

Hi, I'm Christopher Hart, Chris to my mates. In our gang there is me and my mates: John Richards, Gary (Bin Dipper) Singleton, Ian Hogan and Roger Kidd. Add Frances June McKay (Frankie), a girl, and we are a gang of six. We were in our last twelve weeks of school before starting a new life called 'work'.

My home consists of Mum, Ann (Annie) Hart, one-time bus clippie who, after marrying Dad (Wilf) became a mother to me and my sister, Joan. Joan is nearly nineteen years old and working as a hairdresser in town at the exclusive Silver Salon. Dad is always at work as a bus driver. If he isn't at home, he's at work.

Dad met Mum after he had been working as a bus driver for a few years. As he put it: 'This young lass appeared at the boss's office. The boss, Bill, shouted out, "Wilf, can you take this young lass out and show her the ropes?" That was our first meeting that went on to become a partnership for life.'

'What you called, then?' Dad asked.

'Ann Hyder,' Mum replied.

'OK, Annie, jump aboard this bus. It's a quiet first trip. You'll soon get the hang of it.'

If there's one thing Mum has a pet hate about it's being called by the nickname 'Annie'. On the other hand, all the clippies – including Mum – called Dad 'Lenny', and he seemed to like that. It's a term of endearment, he would say.

Things progressed and Wilf started walking out with his 'Annie'. Twelve months later Annie quit her job at the buses and became Mrs Hart. The only time Wilf called Ann the correct way was on their wedding day. After that it was back to, 'Where's my Annie?'

They've lived in the same house since they got married twenty years ago, just a small two-up two-down with a front door that opens onto the street, Vine Street. At the back we have a small garden with a lawn. We wouldn't have had that but for Mum putting her foot down.

'Lawn for me and the kids, the rest for your vegetables.' Veg – and what veg! Carrots, potatoes, beans and sometimes lettuce, but that is more likely food for the bugs. Every time we go to pick a lettuce, it is crawling with bugs, slugs and snails. Our garden is at one side, next to Mr Wilks. Dad said Mr Wilks had a lovely garden with a nicely cut lawn and flowerbeds with roses, but since his wife, Madge, died nearly eight months ago it's not getting the same attention.

Right down at the bottom of our garden where Dad has his shed and compost heap (phew, what a stink) there's a gap in the fence, then you go down the grassy embankment onto the railway. Well, I say railway. There's an old railway coach just dumped. It's been there years. Dad said it's a clerestory coach[1], but to me and the gang it's where we meet up. Joan is my elder sister. Well, she's my one and only sister. To the gang she just cuts hair. (She cuts the gang's hair.) Ted Harker, that's her boyfriend, he says,

'My blonde bombshell, where is she?' Under my breath I say,

'Right next to you, dumbo.' Ted is like a lapdog. When they go out he's always fussing over her. He's not like one of the gang, rough and tough.

Dad is always saying to Joan,

---

1. A clerestory coach is a railway carriage with roofline windows, circa 1880-1920. Railway carriages are often called coaches (passenger carrying vehicles).

'You can do better, you know. There's plenty more fish in the sea.' But no, our Joan has made her mind up: Ted's the one.

'Just because he comes from the posh side of town he's no better than us,' Dad says. 'And it's not posh where Ted comes from anyway.'

Joan will then bite back.

'Mr and Mrs Harker don't live in a two-up two-down terrace like we do. No, they live in a big semi. You're only jealous, Dad.'

'Oh, no, I'm not!'

'Oh, yes you are. Let's leave it at that, Dad. I've made my mind up and Ted's the one for me.'

Ted Harker works at the local factory, Windle and Son, a small engineering firm. I suppose it's nearer to where we live than anywhere. It backs onto the bus garage.

'So Ted,' Dad says to him, 'I can keep an eye on you, lad.' I suspect Dad sees him only once a week, and then in passing.

'Joan,' Dad calls out, 'I'll be on the 8.30 service from Washery Road so if you're down at the bus stop and want a lift, Jenny's my clippie. You know the rest.'

'OK Dad,' Joan replies crisply.

Joan travels for free on Dad's bus down into town.

'It never happens to me,' I challenge.

'Well, school's just down the road. You don't have to go to town, do you?' Dad calls back.

'No, Dad.'

'But when you go down town at the weekends – and sometimes with your mates, they nearly always travel free, don't they?'

'OK, Dad. We're saving a lot and it's costing the bus company money. How's that work?'

'Use your brain and think about it, son. They say you lot are getting a good education but I can't see it, can you, Annie?' Dad laughs. Mum just looks at Wilf and then carries on with what she's doing.

Mr Wilks lives next door. He's quite a tall man but he's stooping a bit with age. As Dad said shortly after Madge died,

'He'll let himself go, just you wait and see.'

'Not if we look to him,' Mum replied.

Henry and Madge have been good to us over the years, so Madge going was a shock to us all. She had gone to town on one of her weekly trips to the shops but never came home. The police had called at ours because they couldn't get a reply at number 131 next door. Ours is number 129. Mum told them that Mr Wilks would be in his shop down the road. Mr Wilks sells anything and everything, like the Mr Blue paraffin (and what a stink that stuff makes) that Dad always has me carrying home for his shed. He says,

'It helps to keep me warm in winter.' *So why do I have to get it in the summer?*

Mr Wilks sells rat traps, mole traps, mousetraps, nails, screws, light bulbs: you name it, he sells it. Mum directed the police to Mr Wilks' shop. Then twenty minutes or so later she went down there herself. She told Dad later that Mr Wilks was in a hell of a state. Mum closed the shop and brought him home. Madge had gone to town on one of her trips, got off the bus and collapsed. She was rushed into hospital but died in the ambulance. Madge was only fifty-eight years old and Henry had just turned sixty. He used to say that when Madge got to sixty they were going to put the shop up for sale and retire. But sadly for Mr Wilks, that's not going to happen.

On the day of the funeral not many attended. I had to be smartened up. Joan and Ted, Mum and Dad and a few of his friends attended, then they all came back to ours. Talk about a house full. But Mum did it for Henry and he seemed to like that. I certainly did. Sandwiches, a nice bit of cake and some fizzy drinks, with something a bit stronger for the grown-ups.

Since Madge passed away, Mum's been helping out at the shop two or three days a week, just to help Henry. He tries to get to the wholesalers twice a month in his rusty old van. Most of the time it's parked behind the shop. That's just as well. When he starts it up clouds of blue smoke appear as the engine coughs and splutters into life.

'I see you're using Mr Blue paraffin again!' came an anonymous shout from across the back of where his van was parked one morning. Henry gave a wry smile and off he went, engine spluttering, bodywork groaning, down the road.

'If you don't go to the wholesalers once a month you might miss something,' Henry stated.

'Like what?' Mum questioned. 'A spare engine for a space shuttle?'

'No, but there's always something new.'

'Yes, more for you to try and sell to the likes of us!'

***

'I'm ho-ome!' That was my usual cry.

'I can see that,' Mum said.

'What are you doing?' I asked.

Mum sighed.

'Oh, I'm just looking at some old photos.'

'Who's that, then?'

'Who's who? Well, that's your father.'

'But it doesn't look anything like him.'

'I know. That picture was taken when your dad was in the Royal Air Force.'

'Doesn't he look skinny?' I scoffed.

'No, slim. Your dad was slim,' Mum insisted.

'What did Dad do, fly Spitfires?' I made the actions and loud noises of a plane.

'No, he was ground crew, helped to keep the planes in the air,' Mum said proudly.

'What, a load of blokes holding the aeroplane off the ground?' I joked while flexing my muscles.

'You're just being stupid now, Chris. Go and find something to do. Better still, nip down to Wilks' store and get a green bar of soap. Don't forget, a green bar.' Mum firmly emphasised the 'green bar'.

I turned to leave. Mum was still engrossed in the old photos.

'Did you say green soap?'

'Just ask Henry for green soap. Tell Mr Wilks Mum asked for some green soap. He'll know what it is.' Mum sounded a little frustrated.

'OK, I'm on my way.' With that, I left the house.

Frankie was coming along the street towards me.

'Hi, Frankie,' I said. 'What are you up to?'

'I've just been to Cherry's shop for a couple of teacakes for my mum. Where are you going to?'

'Wilks' shop,' I replied, 'for some green soap for Mum. Don't ask me why, I don't know.'

Frankie is a *girl*. Yes, a girl. Frances is her real name, Frances June McKay, but to the gang she's Frankie, a slim, red-headed and fiery girl.

'What are you doing later on?'

'I don't know. What are you doing later on?'

'I don't know. What are you doing?'

I don't…' We could have played this game of word tennis all night!

'I'll come over after tea,' Frankie suggested.

'I think Ian's coming over as well,' I said. I say 'over': he only lives in the next street. Number 3 Windward Street. There was only him and his mother. His dad, as Ian said, 'buggered off' when Ian was about six years old. Ian had a lot of hand-me-down clothes, mostly from me, or I should say via Mum. What I was wearing three months ago becomes Ian's 'new' jumper, trousers and coat. The only things he doesn't get, other than my smalls, are my shoes. I have big feet and Ian only has small feet.

Ian is – well, Ian. Very tall, about five feet eleven inches, thin as a lath, with brownish, fawn-coloured hair. He always wanted his hair short but his mum was adamant.

'You keep your hair long, dear,' I've heard her say. Ian said he didn't want to look like Frankie with frizzy hair, as he called it.

Gary on the other hand, couldn't care less what his hair looked like, even more so his clothes. We called him Bin Dipper.

On the way to school he would meet us about halfway. He came running up behind us.

'Hey, Chris, Frankie, look what I've just found.'

We both knew Gary had a habit of looking in people's dustbins. Anything that people put waste into, Gary had to look.

'What you found today, then?' Frankie asked.

'It's this.'

'What's this?'

'I don't know, but it must have a use.'

'Yes, it did have a use, but something's broken off. See, there,' I said, pointing.

'Well, I might be able to find another use for it,' Gary said hopefully.

Frankie said,

'Throw it away.'

'But I can't.'

'Just ditch it now,' I said.

'But...'

'Now!' I ordered.

The piece of junk, for want of a better word, was discarded by a pile of rubbish that had been put out for collection by the bin men, or Gary would retrieve it on the way home from school.

To look at Gary, you'd think he had been living in a dustbin himself. Yes, but he's always clean, he's just scruffy, untidy, dishevelled. His father has his own business, rag-and-bone. I suppose that's where Gary picked up the habit of thinking there's always a use for something that other people have discarded.

They used to have a horse and cart going around the streets collecting bits of scrap metal, rags, old clothes, bones and tat. I never saw any of the collected stuff in their yard but then they do have a big black dog called Rover constantly on guard. I expect Rover gets all the bones! If we had nothing to do on a Saturday, we would sometimes go with Gary and his dad around the streets. They would shout,

'Rags and bones, any old rags and bones,' almost singing. If people came out with anything it would go straight onto the cart, and a donkey stone[2] was handed over as payment.

John always likes to give the impression that he's a cut above the rest but he hadn't a clue what donkey stones were for except

---

2. Donkey Stone; traditionally a small piece of stone about the size of a bar of soap, brown in colour, used for cleaning the doorstep outside or usually just putting a clean line around the edge of the step.

for keeping donkeys and horses hooves clean. He's a bit of a chubby lad, about five feet tall, with black hair with a parting just the way his mother likes it. Even twelve weeks before we left school he was eyeing the girls up. Frankie thought he was a bit of a ponce – that's the phrase she used.

I never really knew what John's father did for a living. They had moved away from our side of town to the posh side but his mother said he should stay at our school, Vernon Street Modern. She considered that John was getting a good education there and his father didn't have much say in the matter. But his dad used to bring John every day in the car, or a van, or on a motorbike. The trouble was, he seemed to be a bit of a wide boy with his dodgy dealing. John could turn up in anything but one thing's for sure: he never came by bus!

Roger is part of our gang, but we only see him once in a blue moon.

'What's a blue moon?' John asked.

'I don't know, John.'

'Then why say it?'

'Well,' I replied, 'you don't see a blue moon very often and we don't see Roger very often, do we?'

'So if Roger turns up it'll be a blue moon, eh, Chris?' John was truly puzzled.

'Just shut up, John,' Ian spoke out. 'Stop trying to make something out of nothing.'

'Anyway, John, if Roger turns up have a look at the moon it might be blue. You never know!' and we all had a laugh except John.

***

We live at 129 Vine Street and on the other side of the street at 116 live Mr and Mrs McKay and their daughter, Frankie.

They've lived there about as long as we have. If you carry on along the street on our side, you come to number 131. That's where Mr Wilks lives. As the street goes round to the left, on the right-hand side is a piece of spare ground that has four garages on it. Behind the garages is a high brick wall at least three feet higher than the tops of the garages, with broken glass set into the mortar. My dad told us from an early age that there was a tiger in there and, being young, we believed him. Anyway, one day we decided to see if there was anything over the high wall.

'Right, Ian, as you're quite slim and tall, I – or should I say *we* – have decided that you are our man to climb onto the garage roof and look over the wall. But make sure you don't make a noise. We don't want to attract attention to ourselves, especially with you on top of the roof.'

'But why pick on me?' Ian protested.

'I've just explained why. You couldn't send Frankie on a mission like this.'

'Why not?'

'Well, for starters, she's a girl!'

'So what about you then, Mr High and Mighty?' Ian was sounding desperate now.

'I can't go. I'm the gang leader!'

'Oh, all right, then, I'll go.' Ian finally and reluctantly caved in.

'Right then, Ian, there's a hump of earth by the last garage. Use that to climb onto the roof then go from one garage to the next until you reach the last one. We'll make sure the coast is clear. The last one is where Malcolm Brown has his car, the one that Dad was telling us about. When Malcolm was showing his wife their new car she got in it. She was under the impression that she had put the car into reverse and released the handbrake, put her foot on the gas – but the car shot forward, not backwards. Then crash! Oh no! Oops! Took one of the car doors clean off and bent the other one, put a dint in the bonnet and bent the bumper. Old Man Brown wasn't impressed.' I enjoyed telling this tale and I told it well.

'Where's the car now?' Ian quizzed.

'He has to keep it in front of the house,' I said.

'So the car that's sticking out of his garage is nothing to do with him, then?' asked Ian.

'Well, I don't know, but we'll use the garage next to his. It's about the same height and the brick wall is the same height. OK?'

Ian climbed up.

'What can you see, Ian?' I asked. We all wanted to know.

'Well, there isn't a tiger, just a load of old car tyres. Hang on, I'm slipping. I'll just get a better foothold. OK, I'm right now.'

'So what else can you see?'

'There's an old car, rusty – in fact there's more rust than car!'

'What else?'

'That apple tree in the corner, the one we're always trying to pinch apples from. And there's a lawn but it's more weeds, very overgrown. But still no tiger. Oh, hang on.'

'What you seen now, Ian?'

'There's a big ginger cat coming over.'

'Is it a lion?'

'I don't think so. If it is, they've got a new, smaller breed. Hang on, there's somebody coming out of the house.'

'Who is it?'

'I don't know, but *she's* more like a tiger! I better get down. Oh, too late. She must have seen me from her kitchen window.'

The tigress shouted at Ian,

'You there. Get down! Get down! I'll send for the police. You're trespassing. Get down now!' She gestured with her arms, flapping like a demented hen.

Ian stepped back from his vantage point, missed his footing and went crashing through the garage roof. Not the garage that he had first used as a vantage point but the one next to it, Mr Brown's, the man who was repairing his nearly-new car.

It wasn't the fact that Mr Brown had just cleaned his glasses, then recleaned them, thinking he had wiped them with an oily rag. It wasn't the fact that on the wooden wall of the garage there was a shiny piece of tin. No. The reason why it suddenly became very light in the garage was that, at the same time as Mr Brown hit the exhaust with his hammer, Ian crashed through the garage roof and thud – he hit the bonnet of the car. That was another dint in the bonnet.

Ian rolled off the bonnet onto the garage floor on the opposite side to Mr Brown. Oblivious, Mr Brown carried on working, hitting the exhaust with his hammer, unaware that Ian had put a hole in the garage roof, making it brighter and easier for Mr Brown to see – and at the same time doing more damage to his car.

Ian managed to scramble out of the garage, but as he walked past Mr Brown he made a rash comment.

'It's a nice day. Looks like the sun is going to come out.' He hurried away. Mr Brown just grunted and carried on working on his car.

'Let's go, Frankie. Ian, we'd better go. I wouldn't like to be around when he finds out he has a big hole in his garage roof and another dint in the bonnet of his car.' I was moving away.

'Where shall we go?'

'Round to mine,' Frankie said. 'We can watch from there. Let's see what he'll do when he finds out.'

'OK,' and we all hurried off to Frankie's house.

We didn't have to wait long. A cloud of blue smoke belched out as the car burst into life. The car was backed slowly out of the garage into the sunlight. Mr Brown got out and went to shut the one remaining garage door. Only then did he notice that there was more light in the garage than usual. He turned and looked at the car. The car lights were not on. Then he noticed the new dint in the bonnet. He ran his hand over it. Suddenly the air went blue with the language that spewed from his mouth!

He turned and went back to the one half-open door, only to find a gaping hole towards the back of the roof. He kicked the one remaining door hard. It was only the fact that the door was still on its hinges that kept the entire garage from falling over! But it did sway.

'We'll have to see if we can make it fall down,' Ian said.

'We can't do that,' I replied.

'We could always say it fell down. I mean, it is leaning over,' Ian laughed.

'You've made it worse, Ian,' I pointed out.

'What do you mean?'

'Well, you fell through the roof.'

'If it had been a tin roof I would have made a noise but I would have just rolled off.'

'Yes, but you didn't. You went through it and dinted his car.'

'Well, I had to land somewhere!' Ian laughed again.

'It's a good job you rolled off on the opposite side to where he was working.'

'I know. I would have been caught red-handed otherwise.' Ian was having the last word.

Just then, as we watched, the car's bent bumper caught the door that was hanging off. As the car went backwards, the door became taut and suddenly the garage was no more. Just a pile of old timber, to the great dismay of Mr Brown!

'Well, Chris,' Frankie spoke up. 'He's managed to pull it down himself. We couldn't have done it. If it got out that we had, we'd have all been for the high jump.'

'Yes, but at least Ian did give him a hand,' I smiled.

***

That night when we were having our tea, first Dad then Mum wanted to know what had happened to Mr Brown's garage. I told them everything. Well, not quite everything: I didn't tell them about Ian falling through the roof or the damage to Mr Brown's car. I thought better of that.

'Still, it does seem strange that Mr Brown had a new car just over three weeks ago. Now he's got the same one but it has two dints on the bonnet, one bigger than the other, a front bumper that's bent and going rusty and just a pile of wood where a garage once stood,' Dad said when I finished telling him what we saw. 'I'll nip over to Mr Brown's after tea and see if I can help.'

'Help with what?' I asked.

'Well, I'll see if he wants anything doing. He might want his garage rebuilding. That I can't do, but there might be something else.' With that, Dad got up and went.

Then Mum spoke.

'Well, who's helping with the washing-up, then?'

As I was the only other person there, I said,

'Well, Mum, it looks like that will be me.'

'I just knew you would say that, son. So what do you want to do, wash or dry?'

'I'll wash,' I said.

'OK, but make sure you get the cups and the cutlery clean!'

'But I always do, Mum.'

Mum just looked on and smiled.

'I hate doing the pans,' I protested.

'Oh go on, then, I'll finish off,' Mum conceded.

Chapter 2

'Chris, Chris!'

'What?'

'Are you getting up? You're going to be late for school, and I want you to go round to Mr Wilks. See if he wants anything from the shops in town today,' Mum called.

'OK, Mum, I'm getting up now,' I replied, yawning.

'Your breakfast is on the table. When you've had it, go next door and ask if Mr Wilks wants anything.'

'Have I got to?'

'Yes, and be sharp about it too.'

'I'll go now, Mum.'

As I opened the front door Frankie was coming out of theirs.

'Where you going?' she shouted.

'To Old Man Wilks to see if he wants anything from town. I won't be long, then we'll go to school.'

'OK,' she yelled back. 'I'll hang about over here for you.'

I banged loudly on Mr Wilks' door. He must have been standing behind it because, as I went to knock again, the door opened slowly.

'What do you want?' Mr Wilks asked.

'Mum wants to know if you want anything from town today, as she's going in later.'

'Just a minute,' he replied.

I stood waiting, peering down his hallway, trying to see what lay beyond the grotty old hatstand. A flat cap and an old hat hung there limply. An old brolly hung below the flat cap, and leaning against the wall was a lot newer brolly. I could see it had white and pink markings on it that seemed to brighten up the hallway. Further down, on the right, a bright light shone through the slightly open door. Mr Wilks could be heard shuffling a few papers.

His house was just like ours but at home Dad had knocked through from the back living room to the front room. When Gran came a-visiting (not very often), Mum would make sandwiches and cups of tea and we would all go and sit in what we called 'the parlour'.

Mr Wilks finally appeared after what seemed like an age.

'I'm not getting any younger you know, Mr Wilks,' I said, but he didn't react.

'Here's my list. Not a lot this week.'

'Well, I expect I'll be around before the end of the week to see if you want anything else.' Still no response.

Mr Wilks thrust a bit of old writing paper at me and a crisp tenner.

'Have you just made this one, Mr Wilks?' I tried to joke. Still no response. 'OK, I'll give this to Mum. Can't hang around. I have to go to school. I'm going to get educated.'

I expected the same nil response. I was quite surprised when Old Man Wilks said: 'Life is education. You'll learn more in life than at school.'

With that I left him standing on the doorstep.

I ran in, slammed the list on the table with the money on top.

'It's a new tenner, Mum. Mr Wilks made it this morning. That's why I'm a bit late. Have to go. Frankie is waiting across the road. Bye, Mum.' As I opened the door to leave, a stiff breeze entered the room. The ten-pound note lifted and the grubby bit of writing paper with the list of things Mr Wilks wanted from town fluttered off the table and onto the floor.

'Mum, Mum!'

'What, Chris?'

'I can't stay, but the tenner is on the floor with Mr Wilks' list.'

'OK, I'll pick them up. Don't you think you could go a bit slower if you got up, say, twenty minutes earlier?' Mum teased. By the time she had finished her sentence I was out the front door and across the road to where Frankie was waiting.

'Are we going now?' she asked abruptly.

'Yes,' I replied.

'Why don't you get up a bit earlier? You know you have a few jobs to do in a morning before you go to school,' she questioned.

'I like my sleep too much.'

'Well, Chris, it's just a thought.'

Vernon Street School was about three-quarters of a mile away. It was a case of walking down our street to Zanzibar Street and over Millfield Road. This was the main road so you had to be very careful. The traffic never seemed to ease off, like on a lot of the roads around here. We always met up with Ian there.

All three of us crossed the road to go towards Vernon Street, but first we went to the corner shop. Most days we would call in and get something – a bag of crisps, a Mars bar. We had to be careful if Gary had caught us up. He would come out of the shop with something – pop, crisps, chocolate bars of any description – but money never seemed to change hands. More often than not, he also turned up with something that he had 'acquired' as he walked down the lane from where he lived.

After leaving the shop, we crossed over Maude Lane. Very few cars ventured this far, and the road surface proved it. There were potholes in the rough, gravelly surface and grass had started to grow in places. Through the garages there was an old rotting car dumped at one corner – no wheels, no engine, one or two of the windows broken. The back seats had been slashed. The driver's seat was just about intact. The front passenger seat was hanging through what at one time was the nearside door. Electric wires were dangling from wherever there was a hole. Bits of glass were everywhere. Someone had tried to extract what was left in the fuel tank, given up, put a rag into the hole and lit it. The fire brigade had dealt with it but now, as it had been fired, you couldn't tell what colour the car had been. The colour of rust now covered it.

Gary had told his dad a few weeks before about the car being dumped.

'*We could use it as a runaround,*' was Gary's first thought. His father hadn't taken it on board. Now there wasn't any point. 'I'll mention it again. No doubt Dad will come and take it away for scrap.' That was Gary's old man, always after something for nothing.

Gary is proud of his old man and said that when he left school he was going into 'The Firm'. 'My dad says I only need to know the three Rs.'

'What's that then, Gary?'

'Reading, Riting and Rithmatic,' Gary spouted carefully and confidently.

'Well, you can forget about the spelling part, or the writing.'

'Why's that, then?'

Well, you can't even spell "writing".'

'Yes, I can,' Gary insisted.

'Go on then, have another go.'

'Easy: *r-i-g-h-t-i-n-g.*'

'See what I mean? There's a 'w' in front of the 'r'. It's a silent letter. And where did you get the 'g' and the 'h' from?' I was taking the mick. We all laughed.

'So why is a 'w' there?'

'I don't know.'

'Well, then, you don't need it, do you?' Gary came back.

'OK, have it your way.'

'Anyway, Chris, you think you're so clever. What are you going to do when you leave school? What are your plans?' Now Gary was getting into his stride.

'I want to go into engineering, take on an apprenticeship.'

'That's OK, but you'll be earning peanuts 'til you're twenty-one and by that time you might be married to Frankie, or someone like her. You won't be able to afford it!' Gary could give a good argument.

'I won't be married. Frankie is Frankie. She won't want to marry me.' I dismissed the thought.

Frankie raised her voice: 'You're damned right, I wouldn't. We are mates, all part of the same gang. What do you say, Ian?'

'The only one likely to marry is poncey John.' Ian didn't want conflict.

By this time we had reached the school gates and there, as expected, poncey John was getting out of a different car to yesterday. This time it was an American Red Mustang.

'That's a fancy car,' I said. 'How long has your dad had that, then?'

'Oh, he's just borrowed it from his mates.' John tried to sound uninterested.

'What happened to the Jaguar you had yesterday?' I wanted to know.

'I don't know. It had gone by the time I got home.' John was a little defensive.

'So is Daddy picking you up tonight?' Frankie mocked. 'Or are you going home on one of them newfangled things they call buses? You know what they look like: they've an upper and lower floor. You go from one floor to the other up a staircase. There's a man at the front, he's the driver just like Chris's dad, and a man on the inside. You have to pay him and he will let you travel on his bus. They call him a clippie, just like Jenny is on Chris's dad's bus.'

John was not to be outdone.

'No, my dad said he would come and take me home,' he confirmed.

Frankie carried on.

'Will he be able to take me, Chris, Ian and Gary home as well?'

'I don't think so. We live on the other side of town.'

'You mean the posh side?'

'Well, you do have a point.' John had a feeling that Frankie didn't like him very much. This was reinforced when Frankie said,

'I don't know why you are in our gang! I expect it will only be for another six or seven weeks, then you won't want anything to do with us.'

I joined in the fray.

'There'll be me, Frankie, Ian and Gary. We'll all be living just a few streets away from each other. Roger we only see now and again, and John – I expect we'll only see him on odd occasions.'

***

That day we were going to see the man from the careers office. Our teacher, Mr Fellows, told us when we arrived in

21

class after assembly that when our names were called out we should leave the classroom in an orderly manner and go down the corridor to the headmaster's office to see the careers officer, Mr Hinchcliffe.

The teacher called out,

'Hart, you're the first. Don't forget, don't be cheeky, listen to what Mr Hinchcliffe has to say and answer his questions. That goes for you all. Now don't forget.'

I got up and walked out of class and down the corridor and knocked on the door to the office.

'Come in. And you are—?'

'Hart, sir, first name Chris.'

'Right, Chris, what would you like to do when you leave school in about six weeks' time? Go into the building trade? What about being a motor mechanic?' The careers officer fired off some quick questions then paused for breath. Now I could answer.

'I would really like to go and be an apprentice at Farrell Bridge Engineering. My dad was telling me there are some vacancies for apprentices. He took me the other day, and I think I might have got in already,' I said confidently.

'Don't worry, Mr Hart. I'll give them a ring and see what the position is. No doubt you have been successful. You should be hearing from them. Did you do a test at Farrell Bridge?'

'Yes, a bit of maths and English.' I kept my cool, stayed relaxed.

'By your reports, and from what the teachers say, you seem to be quite a bright lad so I think you will probably get on at Farrell Bridge.' Mr Hinchcliffe's comments were very encouraging.

'Thank you, sir.' I smiled, pleased as Punch.

'You can go now, Chris, but like I said I'll be in touch with Farrell Bridge Engineering to see how you got on. Can you send in Frances McKay, please? I would like to have a talk with her about her career.' I left the office on a high.

Frances duly arrived at the headmaster's door. Before she had chance to knock, the careers officer said,

'Come in, please. You are Frances June McKay. Ah, yes, my first girl. Now, what would you like to do when you leave school?'

'I would like to work in the local bank.' Frances was positive.

'As what, may I ask?'

'As a bank teller,' she explained.

'I see from your report from your form teacher that you are very good with figures. Why didn't you go to the local grammar school?'

'I didn't pass my eleven-plus. Maths and English, that's what I failed on, so I decided I would work hard and get good results here and now it looks like it's paid off,' Frances said candidly.

'Well done,' Mr Hinchcliffe replied. 'Well, I see that there is a vacancy at the bank. Would you be prepared to do a test for them to see if you have the right aptitude for the job, Miss McKay?'

'I would like that.' Frances suppressed a resounding 'Yes!' but couldn't stop a Cheshire cat grin.

'Then I'll be in touch with them to arrange one.'

'Thank you,' came the elated reply.

'Right, I'll get on with that straight away.'

Mr Hinchcliffe asked Frances to tell the teacher to send the next student down. The careers officer interviews went on all day. Gary went down in the afternoon. But...

'I told that geezer down there that I'm going working for the old man. I'm going to become a part-owner.' Gary gave it his tough, try-and-stop-me voice.

'Go on then, Gary,' I said. 'Which part of the horse and cart are you going to get?'

Ian spoke before Gary had a chance to: 'The back half.'

'We have a truck now,' Gary said proudly.

'I know. It was a joke, Gary, a joke.'

'We got rid of the horse and cart weeks ago. Dad said if we had a truck it would improve our image.'

'So now you're upmarket rag-and-bone men. You'll have to watch out around your way.'

'Why's that, then?'

'Well, you'll have a class act picking up classy crap!'

'We don't have crap,' Gary protested.

'All right then, rubbish!' Ian had the last word this time, but it was like water off a duck's back to Gary.

Roger went down just after lunch. He wanted to go into the police. That was cut and dried: his old man was an inspector down at the police station and Roger was going to follow in his father's footsteps, come what may. His interview was short and sweet.

John went down as Roger came back into the classroom.

'Now, John, what would you like to do when you leave school?' Mr Hinchcliffe had asked this same question of countless students.

'I want to go and work for my dad.'

'What line of work is he in, then?'

'He buys and sells things.'

'Like what?' Mr Hinchcliffe enquired.

'Anything.'

'But what?'

'Cars.'

'So he's a car salesman?'

'No.' John's monosyllabic answers did not impress.

'Does he buy and sell fancy goods, children's toys, clothes? Does he buy and sell food products? Is he a travelling salesman?'

'No.' John had him on the run now. Mr H. was losing it and starting to sweat!

'You don't seem to know what your father does, only that he buys and sells things. I'm sorry, but I can't offer you a job like your father has until I know precisely what he does.' The careers officer raised his voice a little.

'I've just told you I want to work with my father.' John leant forward.

'But you don't know, or you're not prepared to tell me, what he really does. So, Mr Richards, until you decide when you are going to tell me, I can no longer carry on with this interview. Please ask the next person to come in.'

'But, but—'

'I'll have a chat with you later when you decide to tell me what he really does for a living. Please leave now.' Mr Hinchcliffe was wringing his hands with frustration, trying to stay calm.

Ian was the last pupil to go down the corridor to see the careers officer. He seemed to be in there ages. The bell had gone for us to leave school and go home but Ian was still inside chatting to the careers officer. We wondered if Mr Hinchcliffe had expired in there.

Roger said he couldn't wait any longer, and left. He had to go tell his dad that Mr Hinchcliffe was going to get in touch with the police to see if Roger could sit an entrance exam. No doubt Roger's father would be able to pull a few strings.

That left just the four of us waiting for Ian to come out. Then we heard the creaking of the door handle followed by a click as the door opened slowly. We heard Mr Hinchcliffe say: 'Think about the things we have discussed. I'll be back in a couple of weeks, and if there is something you fancy then I'll try to sort it out. OK, Hogan, it's time you were at home – or at least on your way.'

Ian joined us for the walk home.

'So go on then, Ian, what have you decided you want to be when you leave school?'

'I don't know,' Ian replied hesitantly. 'He told me about lots of jobs. The trouble is, I don't really like any of them.'

'What jobs did he offer you?'

'Well, trainee bricklayer, working in a shop, working as a mechanic at Joe Walsh's garage, or there's an apprenticeship at the bus garage where your old man works, Chris.'

'That'll be a good job.' I tried to encourage him.

'It might be, but I don't really fancy that either. Also there's a job on the railway down at the loco sheds just off Queens Road, the other side of the station. Hinchcliffe said you never know but you might become an engine driver. I said I couldn't be an engine driver because my eyes aren't wide enough apart!' The gang laughed at that one. 'I told him I didn't know what I wanted to do, so he said he would be coming back in about a fortnight's time to have another chat to me. It seems I'm quite a popular chap.'

'No,' John stated, 'you're like me – can't or won't make your mind up.'

'What d'you want to do for the rest of your life, Gary?' I asked.

Gary said,

'You mean there's life after Vernon Street School when we finally leave?'

'Yes,' I replied.

On the way home we discussed what had happened at school and what jobs we were hoping to get, trying to help Ian and John make their minds up. John was still talking about doing the same as his dad. We all said he was a wide boy.

'What's one of them?' John asked.

'Somebody who doesn't care as to whether the stuff he's selling is nicked or legit.'

'My dad's not one of them,' John said thoughtfully.

'I think you will find that he is,' Frankie confirmed.

'No, he's not!'

'Well, have it your own way, then.' Ian put in his twopenn'orth.

'Why don't we go and see what's in that old mill, Mars Mill, down the bottom of Maude Lane?' I was feeling adventurous.

'What, now?' Frankie questioned. 'Don't you think it's a bit late? And you know what your mum's like – what all our mums are like – if we don't report in. And no doubt you will have to do some jobs, like taking the shopping round to Old Man Wilks.'

'All right then, we'll go and have a look round on Saturday morning. Agreed?' I was gang leader, after all. So we all agreed. 'Saturday morning, nine o'clock sharp. Don't forget!'

Chapter 3

Sun was shining through the curtains in my room. Mum and Joan were chatting away downstairs. There was no sound from Dad. He must have gone to work. I arose, got dressed and wandered into the bathroom. I washed, if you can call it that, brushed my teeth, then ran a comb through my shiny brown hair – shiny because Mum had insisted that I washed it the night before.

'Chris, breakfast, what do you want for your breakfast?' No reply. Mum asked again.

'Nothing,' I said.

'You have to have something,' Mum persisted.

'All right, then, I'll have a jam butty.'

'Orange juice or tea?'

'Orange juice, Mum. A cup of tea is for the old folk. You see them in the cafe in town sipping tea and eating something or other. Orange juice, please, Mum.' I liked to tease my mum.

Joan asked: 'What are you up to today?'

'We're all meeting up and going down to the old mill at the bottom of Maude Lane.'

'You won't get in there. There's a man with a big yellow dog.'

'Yellow dog? Is it a painted one?' I chuckled at Joan.

'You know what I mean,' Joan tutted.

'Ian had a ride down there the other day on his bike. He said he just rode into the mill yard, rode around. Not a soul about, the gates were wide open. So we, the gang and I, decided we would all have a look around there.' I was still eating my jam butty.

'You mean you're going to have a nosy.' Joan smelt a rat.

'Can I have a sarnie to take with me?' I tried to change the subject.

'What, corndog?' Mum asked.

'Well, if it has to be.'

'You're not having that tongue in your sarnie. That's for Sunday tea.'

'Why, is Gran coming round again?' I guessed.

'No, Joan's bringing Ted round. They are going to discuss their wedding plans.'

'I pity Ted,' I muttered under my breath. 'Poor Ted. See you, Mum.'

I went out through the front door and strolled over the road. Just as I was going to knock at Frankie's door the door opened.

'Hi, Frankie, are you ready, then?'

'Yes,' she replied. 'Where's Ian?'

'He's meeting us at the corner shop with Gary. Ian will be buying some grub. Gary will be giving it a good home. Sadly for Mr Cherry, the shopkeeper, his profits for today will dip slightly!'

We met up with Ian.

'Hi, Ian, where's Gary?'

'He's in the shop. I know he's getting pop but I don't know about anything else. We'll have to wait and see.'

At that moment Gary appeared.

'Let's go a bit quicker than normal,' he said.

'Why?' asked a suspicious Frankie.

'You know why, Frankie.'

'Have you never thought about offering the money for what you take, Gary?'

'Well, Frankie, if I do that then my street cred has gone.'

'What street cred? You haven't got any.'

'If I did have some I would have lost it.' Gary could always answer his critics. I took control: 'Come on, Frankie,' I shouted. 'Come on, Ian, Gary, let's go.'

Finally we set off down to Maude Lane. Maude Lane is a bit of a rough road, and wagons used to go up and down it. Now there's only the old mill at the bottom and nothing else. If you carry on past the mill the lane goes into Holly Hill Farm.

'Who lives there, then?' asked John.

Ian said: 'Green or Greenly. It's something like that. I've been up there a few times on me bike. Not much to see. He has a big white bull, though. In fact, last time I was up there old Green, or Greenly, came out shouting.'

I joined in: 'Ted and our Joan have been up there a few times too, but I don't know what they were doing up there! Can you imagine coming down here in a wagon, full of bales of cotton, bouncing up and down with all these potholes? You wouldn't be able to miss any. They're all over the road, and if it had been raining you wouldn't be able to see them. It'd be just like being on the big dipper at the seaside.'

'I wouldn't know, Chris,' Ian said. 'I haven't been away for years. Mum just can't afford it since Dad left us.'

'Well, it is, Ian,' Gary piped up.

'How do you know? When did you go to the seaside?'

'I haven't been, but I know what the lane's like.'

'How do you?'

''Cause I've been up and down this lane with me dad in the new truck,' Gary stated proudly.

'Why have you been up and down this lane in the truck?' Ian quizzed.

'Dad wanted to know how it felt.'

'What's wrong with the main road, like everybody else uses?' demanded Ian.

'I don't know,' Gary replied.

Frankie piped up: 'He will have seen some scrap somewhere on the lane and gone to pick it up, most likely.'

'Did you stop at all on the lane then, Gary?'

'Yep, on the way back up, just after turning round at the mill entrance.'

'So what did you stop for?'

'Oh, we picked up an old oil drum, all sticky with something.'

'Yes,' Ian said. 'Oil!'

Gary's epic saga continued: 'Couldn't tell you what it was. I managed to get it all over my hands and the top of my jeans where I tried to wipe them off. There was a couple of cans of paint. One had been opened and most of the white paint was over the grass, just a bit left in the tin. The other can hadn't been opened. It was so rusty on the lid you couldn't see what the colour was supposed to be, and most of the label had come away with the weather. How long they'd been there is anybody's guess. Dad found an old teaspoon on the truck dashboard and said, "This will open it, son, then we'll be able to tell what colour it is." The tin lid was soon prised off. Well, what colour do you think? Green, pea green! Dad said, "It's just right for your bedroom, son!" Dad doesn't have much idea about colour schemes. I said to him, "So you think that will go with the paint you put on the other week? I don't think so. Orange and green? No." Dad said, "We'll have to see what your mother says." That green paint is still in the back of the shed next to all the other old dinted rusty cans of paint that Dad has picked up on his rag-and-bone round.' Gary stopped at that point, to everyone else's relief.

Then it was Frankie's turn.

'So, Ian, if you want to know what it's like to ride on the big dipper at the seaside, just ask Gary if you can go on the back of his truck. Ask him if he will go down Maude Lane. Tell him you thought you saw something sticking out of the bushes or the long grass. He'll be down here like a flash. It'll be a bonus if you get something, and if you don't he'll mutter about it all the way home. He'll think that someone else got there before him. But you'll have the satisfaction of riding on the truck and the same pleasure as riding on the big dipper at the seaside. You'll be in a win–win situation.'

As we got nearer and nearer to the factory gates the lane got a bit wider, but in places you would have had trouble passing someone in a car. Brambles were growing all over the place – and nettles too, along with tall grass. Beyond the tall grass and brambles were thick, dense bushes, mainly hawthorn. I only knew about their name because I'd been out with my dad one day with our dog, Shelley.

The dog came with that name. We had wanted a boy dog but it turned out Shelley is a girl.

'Can't we change it for a boy?' I pleaded.

'No,' Dad replied. 'She stays.'

She's Mum and Dad's dog, really. They spoil her rotten. Anyway, we were out one day taking Shelley walking when she disappeared through the long grass and nettles then got stuck in the hawthorn. Dad had to go and retrieve her, just like dads do.

'Don't follow, son. You will get caught up as well. All three of us don't want to be caught up in the hawthorn.' Just then out popped Shelley, as large as life. Where did she come from? About twenty feet further up the lane!

Fifteen minutes later Dad finally managed to get himself out of the hawthorn, scratches all over him. The scratches on his arms were worst.

'So, son, you can see what I'm saying. Don't try and climb through a hawthorn hedge. Them spikes are really sharp. Now, where's Shelley?'

Shelley was sitting at the side of me, patiently waiting.

'Come on, Shell,' Dad shouted and off she galloped, long, spindly legs going everywhere except in a straight line. She's a poodle but it's very hard to tell; she looks more like a Heinz 57. But Dad loves her to bits. He has to: he's the one that she always wants to go for a walk with.

The entrance to the factory became a lot clearer as we rounded the slight bend in the lane that, by this time, had widened out so that the delivery wagons could take a swing and drive through the gates of the mill. In front of the gates the road was cobbled. In the days when the mill was in full swing these cobbles would be kept swept, and the mill yard as well, so that the horses that pulled the carts could get a grip on the cobblestones.

At the entrance there had been two large iron gates. These would have been painted black but now one gate was missing, probably gone on the back of Gary's dad's scrap metal wagon. The other gate was still there but the paint had flaked off in places, only to be replaced by green algae. This had started to grow in and around the right angles and joints of the iron gate. On the opposite side, where the other gate was supposed to be, just a big iron gatepost stood now, towering above the guttering of the gatehouse. The windows in the building were broken, some with no glass in at all, and the door was hanging off. It too was past its former glory. It was very hard to tell what colour the door had been. One thing for sure: it wouldn't stop a draught now! Inside, there was broken glass everywhere, bits of paper everywhere.

Ian picked up an old crumpled newspaper.

'What does it say?'

'It's the football results.'

'Go on, then, read out what it says.'

'Muncaster 2, Rec— Sorry, that bit's missing. Well, that's a long time ago.'

'Why do you say that?'

'Because Muncaster haven't had a football team for years. Dad used to support them, but they had to wind the club up years ago. They went broke. Nobody would go and watch them play. Dad said they were rubbish at the end. They should have signed up some new players.'

'You mean they should have bricked up the goalmouth. That would have stopped the other side from scoring!' Gary laughed out loud.

'I see you understand the rules of football, Gary,' Ian gloated.

'Just an idea, that's all,' Gary laughed again.

'What are those things over there for?' Frankie asked.

'That's part of the weighbridge.'

'Weighbridge? Where's that?'

'It's that big flat thing just outside the door. See there.'

'What was it used for?'

'Have a guess! Weighing things! Your dad will be used to these, Gary.'

'Dad tries to fiddle the one down at the scrapyard every time he weighs some scrap in, but *every time* he gets caught out. You would have thought by now he would realise you can't fiddle them,' Gary confided.

'Go on, Gary, tell us how it works, then.' Frankie was keen to learn.

Gary took a deep breath and said: 'Well, you drive onto the weighbridge, get your front and back wheels on that bit there, not your front wheels over there or your back wheels over there.' Gary was enjoying the centre stage and giving it lots of gestures. 'But all your wheels on there. Then the man in the weighbridge office pulls that lever there, and finds out by looking at that gauge and that gauge there how much you weigh.' He took a bow.

'But I know how much I weigh so I don't need to use it!' Frankie tried to be a bit witty.

'Not you. The truck you're in, or the cart that is being pulled by the horse.'

'Horse? Don't say it, Gary.'

'Then you pull off the weighbridge, go to where you have to be unloaded, perhaps over there, take off your load and on the way out go onto the weighbridge again and go through the same process. The man in the weighbridge will calculate the two weights and the difference between the both weights is how much you have delivered to the mill. He books it down in a large book they call a ledger. At the end of each week the ledger is taken to the admin office. They take the figures for the week and work out how much cotton and coal and other things have come into the mill. Have you got it, Ian, Chris, Frankie?' Gary's knowledge impressed the other gang members.

'I think so.' Ian nodded and smiled. 'How do you know about all this, then?'

Gary explained about the time he spent in the lorry with his dad and how the scrap was weighed in: 'Now you all know nearly as much as I know, right?' Gary grinned from ear to ear.

'It's a big yard,' John observed.

'It has to be,' I answered.

'Why?'

'Well, when you think of all those horses and carts, then it went over to lorries, they would have to be able to turn around. You look where Dad works down the bus garage: there's lots of open space down there. They need all that so they can turn the buses around and park them up. It's the same here. You have to be able to turn the horses and carts round. And, when they started to use lorries, they would have needed a lot of room to turn and back up under the hoist.' I used my transport knowledge to good effect.

Gary asked seriously: 'When they built the mill did they know they would end up using lorries?'

'What do you think, Gary? It was built over a hundred years ago. They'd only just started building the railways. There wouldn't have been any cars, buses, aeroplanes. Lorries were miles in the future.'

'Chris is a clever sod!' Frankie said to Ian.

Gary mumbled something else.

'Yes, you are so right,' Ian replied.

'What's that over there?' Gary was pointing to a wall about four feet high.

'I don't know, Gary. Let's go and have a look.'

Ian led the way. As we approached the wall, we could see the reflected sunlight dancing on the surface.

'It's the mill lodge,' I said.

'What do you mean?' Frankie asked.

'That's where they store the water to run the stationary engine.'

'Why do you need water to run an engine that's going nowhere?'

'There's always one, Ian.' I shook my head.

'Well, I am a *girl*. How am I supposed to know about *boys*' things?' Frankie emphasised 'girl' and 'boys'.

I looked at her.

'I'll try and explain. If we ever get into the mill, we might find the stationary boiler.'

We got to the wall and peered over.

'What did I tell you, Frankie? It's the mill lodge.'

'Why call it a lodge?'

'It's another way of saying keeping something.'

'I'm still keeping up with you,' Frankie said.

'Somewhere between this, the mill lodge and that building over there, that's where the stationary engine will be if it hasn't already been taken away and scrapped!' I pointed about forty feet away to a very tall building, nothing like any other building around the weed-covered yard. This was an imposing building, made out of stone like the rest of them but much more majestic. 'There'll be some pipes taking the water from here at the lodge to that building over there. See that chimney? That must be part of the boiler house. They produced steam to power the stationary engine that Frankie said went nowhere.'

'And what do you think lives in the water?' John piped up. 'Sharks!'

'You have a real vivid imagination, John,' Ian said.

John went on,

'Well, if it's anything like the high wall behind the garages, anything could be in the water.'

'I don't think there will be sharks, do you, Gary?' Ian looked for support.

'There's more likely to be bits of scrap metal lurking in the depths of this pond,' Gary said hopefully.

'It's not a pond. It's a mill lodge!' I growled.

'How deep do you think it is, Chris?'

'At least six feet, Frankie.'

Gary butted in: 'I'll throw a stone in over there.'

'What for? It's not going to come back up and tell you how deep it is, is it, Gary?' Ian jested.

Then John spoke up. He must have thought about it.

'Tell you what, Chris… If we had a good length of rope and tied it to a brick and lowered it into the water, let it sink to the bottom, then pulled it out, the wet bit of the rope would tell us how deep it is.'

'But you would need to have a tape measure, and as we don't have any rope, or a brick, or even a tape measure, it seems rather pointless!' Ian dismissed the idea out of hand.

Suddenly, out of the depths of the lodge, a very large fish rose and broke the surface.

'See, I told you, Chris!' John spluttered. 'Sharks! They have sharks in this pond.'

'This is only a mill lodge. It's probably a carp. They put them into lodges so that the mill workers that liked to do a spot of fishing in their spare time could come and fish in the lodge. And of course, at lunchtimes the workers would come and sit along here, and any scraps left over from their scran box would be thrown into the water. What should be waiting for it but these beauties?' I was an authority.

Just then Frankie dropped part of her jam butty. Instead of landing on one of the tufts of grass that were at the foot of the wall, it fell into the water. Before it had time to sink, first one then another dark shadow rose from the depths of the lodge.

'There must be hundreds of them in there,' Frankie said, amazed.

'Probably not hundreds, but quite a few.' I peered down. 'We'll have to bring our fishing rods down here next time we come.'

'Why, are we coming here again?' enquired Frankie.

'I expect so,' John and Ian spoke together as one.

'We'll see,' I said.

Chapter 4

'Let's go over there.' John was pointing to a large green door in the corner of the yard. 'I wonder what happened inside. Let's see if we can open it.' The door was slightly ajar.

'If you and Gary push on that one we just might be able to get in,' I suggested. 'Right, John, Gary, push. Ian, can you squeeze in?'

'Yes, I'm in. Hang on.'

With a crash John and Gary fell into the dark building. They resembled a pile of rubbish on the floor.

'If you had only waited. The door was only latched. Come on, Gary, John, get up. You don't know what you're lying in.'

'Well, the floor is dry.' Gary laughed.

'Yes, but you don't know what has run over it, do you?' Ian offered.

'What do you mean?'

'There's rats and mice living in these sort of places.' The two lads were up on their feet in a shot!

Frankie said: 'Where's the light switch? It's so dark in here.' Except for the chinks of light streaming through the few windows that weren't blocked off to keep the warmth in and the cold out, it was pitch-black.

'You don't expect to just go and switch the lights on? There aren't any. They're not going to close down and leave the electric on just in case someone like us turns up in ten to twenty years' time, so we can wander about in light?' John ribbed her. 'Think about it Frankie! Anyway, it's not *dark* dark.'

'My eyes are used to it now. I can make you lot out. It's just a bit greyish dark.'

Thud!

'So why have you just fallen over that on the floor if you say you can see?' John mocked Frankie.

'All right, so I'll have to be more careful. What's that in front of you, Chris?'

'That will be where the finished goods would be loaded onto trucks for delivery. You wouldn't want to make something then let it get damaged or rained on before it left the mill.'

All five of them stood on the loading dock.

'Now what, Chris? Where shall we go now?' Ian the intrepid explorer asked.

'There's only one way, and that's through that door there.' I pointed ahead. We could just make out a half-open door, a dirty door. No paint had ever touched it, or if it had it had been worn away by the countless hands that had opened and closed it every day.

'Where does it lead to?' a voice in the dark asked.

'I don't know,' I replied.

The door creaked loudly. Having swung backwards and forward over the years then been left alone, the oil had dried within the hinges. With the first movement in years the hinges protested and fought against the pressure of John's hand.

'What's inside, John?'

'It's just a great big long room and there doesn't appear to be anything in it.' Just then there was a movement a few feet away.

'What was that, John?'

'I think it was a rat!' John exclaimed, feeling somewhat un-brave.

The rat, not knowing what was happening and not having been disturbed before, scurried past John and disappeared into the depths of the mill floor.

'You might as well come in,' Gary invited. 'But there's nothing in here.'

'There's a rat, but that's about it.'

John and Gary were right: nothing. We wandered all around that bottom floor and found nothing. Shafts of light penetrated through the broken glass in the windows that hadn't been boarded up. At the other end we saw there was a large grille. I wondered what that was for. At the side were steps leading upwards.

Ian made a discovery.

'Here's a lift. It must go up to the other floors as well as the stairs. It's a bit like the one at Browns in town – you know the one, John. The big one in the town centre. It's where your dad gets his clothes from.'

'My dad sometimes goes from the bus stands in front of that store when he's on the service to Muncaster,' I volunteered.

'Yes, but this lift seems a bit rickety,' John pointed out.

'I'm going up the stairs, Frankie.' I took the first step.

'Me too.'

Then John and Ian followed Frankie.

'You can't use the lift. It won't work, Gary. Anyway, if it did I wouldn't go on it,' John tried to advise Gary.

'Why's that then, John?' Gary asked.

'Cos it might get stuck between floors,' John finished.

The rest of the floors were like the first – nothing, just empty voids. As we went up a floor it became lighter. When we reached the top floor it was quite bright. Pigeons had made their homes up here. There were plenty of feathers and bird droppings littering the floor. We walked across it carefully. But Gary, being Gary, he had to kick the feathers. Clouds of choking dust filled the air. In the shafts of sunlight you could see the millions of tiny particles floating on the warmer air. John started to cough, and then we all started.

'Jack it in, Gary!' Ian shouted. 'What with you kicking the feathers causing the dust to rise, and all the other bits of rubbish on the floor, it's becoming a bit foggy, so pack it in. This dust is a health hazard. You don't know what we're breathing in!'

As we reached the far end of the top floor Frankie spoke: 'These are the gates of another lift that'll go down.'

'Well, if there's only four floors and we are on the fourth floor, I suspect it will go down,' Ian laughed.

'OK, clever clogs, but see over there? There's steps going up, so where do they lead to? Heaven?'

'Don't be silly.'

'You started it!'

'I don't know, but let's have a look,' Ian ventured.

The steps led up to a door.

'Will it open?' John asked.

'Give us a chance. I can see daylight around the top and down the side where the knob should be. Give it a push. It seems to be stuck.' The door didn't budge. 'Give it another push.' Ian was determined.

'I'm pushing. Gary, you give it a push.'

Slowly but surely, groaning and creaking, the door began to open.

'This hasn't been opened for many years, probably not since the place shut down,' Gary puffed. Then the door stopped struggling. Its powers to stop people from trespassing had given way. Now we were standing on the mill roof. Ian, of course, had a forte for standing on roofs!

'What do you think this door's made of?' I wondered.

'I'd say steel,' Gary spoke up. 'It would have to be strong to stop the mill workers from escaping.'

'Why would you want to escape and find yourself up here? Then what? Jump off?' I contemplated.

'I bet not many walk away after jumping from the fourth floor onto cobbles,' Gary mused as he looked over the edge.

'You know, Gary, sometimes I worry about you.'

'Only sometimes?' Frankie muttered.

'They could land a helicopter on here, they could,' Gary commented.

'But when it was built, like I said before, cars and aeroplanes were years away. Trains were the modern mode of transport. Horse and cart, walking or bikes. Don't go too close to the edge, Gary. You might bounce if you fall off! And as we aren't supposed to be here in the first place, we don't want to attract attention to ourselves, do we?' I went to pull Gary back.

'Chris, what's that down there?'

'Where are you pointing to?'

'Over there.'

'Where's over there?'

'You'll have to come a bit closer to see where I'm pointing.'

'OK, but I'm not coming to the edge like you.'

'What, are you scared of heights?' Gary gave me a broad grin.

'Yes,' I confirmed.

'That down there, what is it?' Gary still wanted to know.

I crept as close as I dared to the edge.

'Oh, that,' I said, then moved back. 'They must have delivered coal by rail – that's the old railway line. It must join up with that bit that the old coach is stood on. We'll go home that way, then if it does we can come that way to here. Better than going down Maude Lane and people wondering what we are up to. Tell you what,' I went on, 'while we're up here let's have our butties, or in Frankie's case, not.'

'Don't be like that, Chris. It's not her fault the big fish got her sandwich. Here, Frankie, have one of mine.' John was all heart.

'What you got, John?'

'Spam.'

'And what?'

'Just Spam and a Kit-Kat.'

'I like them,' interrupted Ian.

'What, Spam sandwiches?'

'No, Kit-Kats.'

'What you got, then, Ian?'

'Jam and bread.'

'What jam?'

'Strawberry.'

'What else?'

'Nothing.'

Frankie completed the round.

'What you got, Gary, or what did you nick?'

'Well, Mum made me a corned beef sandwich and I managed to prise *this* from the shop.'

'What's this?'

'A big bag of crisps. We can all share them.' Gary, generous to a fault.

'What's on your sandwiches, Chris?' asked Gary.

'Same as yours, only Mum put some mustard on – or should I say she put the mustard on first then put a very thin slice of corned dog on. Mum has another trick – she gets the bread, puts the marge on then goes over it again to scrape it off. What's left on the bread after that stays on, but most of it comes off and goes back in the carton.' I sighed as I turned my corndog around. 'Mum says you don't need a lot of marge on the bread. When she makes my sandwiches there's more bread than butter. Anyway, pass them crisps over, Gary. What you got to drink, then?'

'Water.'

'Couldn't you get anything else, Gary?'

'I tried, but after lifting the crisps I had nowhere else to put anything.'

'Couldn't you bring something from home, like we all do?' Frankie chastised Gary.

We sat there on top of the flat mill roof, hungrily eating our sandwiches. Most of the orange pop went first.

'I can't eat any more. Anybody want another butty?' I'd eaten my fill.

'Go on, then.' Frankie got in first.

'It's got mustard on,' I warned.

'Well, I don't like mustard but because I'm hungry I'll eat it.'

'You've no need. I can give to the birds.' I pulled the sarnie back.

'What, them dirty things down there? No, I'll eat this mustard-laden sandwich.' Frankie snatched it and bit deep. 'I can't taste the corn-dog, Chris.'

'No, you won't. I ate the corn-dog. It's just a mustard sandwich.'

A laugh went up. Frankie threw the mustard bread to the birds.

'See, they won't eat it.'

'What do you expect? They don't like mustard either!' I howled. Laughter mingled with birdsong.

'Right then, let's go,' I said.

'No, I don't want to yet.' Frankie and John spoke up in unison.

'So what do you want to do up here?'

'Well, it's about lunchtime and yes, I know we've just had it. And it's hot, so let's just have a lie around in the sun for a bit,' Frankie tried to persuade us.

'I want to go,' Gary and Ian agreed.

'So do I,' I echoed. 'Let's have a vote on it. OK, who wants to stay? And who wants to go?' Straight away two hands went up for staying, then three hands went up for going. 'That's it, then, we go.'

'All right,' Gary called, coming back from the other end of the roof. 'There's a lot of steps leading down over there, but not from up here. They're from the next floor down.'

'That's the fire escape,' John said.

'Why not from here? What would you do if you came up here? You can't go anywhere.' Gary tried logical thought.

'You would head for the nearest exit and that would be the fire escape. Down there as fast as you could, but don't forget other people would be joining you as you went from floor to floor to get out of the burning building.' John's words painted a vivid picture.

We were soon heading towards the point through which we entered the mill, the large green-coloured door. By this time we had all got used to the little light that there was. Ian saw something and called out,

'What's through that door there?' He turned away from the exit and pointed.

Gary was there like a shot.

'This is easy to open. Look at that. I just had to twist the knob.' With no pushing, the door opened silently to reveal a corridor.

'What's that on the wall over there, then?' Ian asked.

'That's where the workers would clock on,' I explained.

'Clock on?' There was a long rack on one side of the clock and another on the other side. 'What does it do?'

Looking over the rack, I finally found a small piece of card. It had the name E. Brightside running along the top of it.

'This must have belonged to someone who worked here. Anyway, this is what happens. You take the card, put it in the slot underneath the clock and push that lever there.' As the lever went down, the machine rang.

Frankie, John and Ian stood back in amazement. Gary's mouth dropped.

'Do that again, Chris!' It rang again.

'Can I try it?' Frankie pushed forward.

In turn we all tried it, and each time 'dong' it went and stamped the card.

'Then what, Chris?'

'Then you put the card into these pigeonholes.'

'Then what, Chris?'

'Then you go to work. So, when you start work you clock on and when you leave work you clock off.' I had all the answers.

'They did that every day?' Gary asked.

'Yes,' I replied. 'Then at the end of the week, somebody from the office collected all the cards and checked them. If you were late on any day, your pay was deducted.'

'Deducted?' Gary quizzed.

'You lost money,' I explained.

'What happened if you clocked on early? Did you get any extra?'

'No, you'd just be a silly fool. Have a bit longer in bed.'

John had a go.

'You'd be all right then, Chris.'

Ian was straight in.

'Why?'

'Well, Frankie is always telling us your mother has trouble getting you up in the morning!' Ian gave me a gentle nudge.

'You're a real fountain of knowledge, aren't you, Chris? Where do you get all this information from?' John tried subtle sarcasm.

'It's Ted Harker. He's always telling Joan things, and the trouble is I'm nearly always in when he calls. Then him and Joan go into the front parlour.'

'What for, Chris?' John piped up.

'You know what for.'

'No, I don't,' giggled Frankie.

'Well, think about it.' Gary joined in. 'They're not playing cards.'

Then John asked: 'Frankie, what do *you* think they're up to?'

'Just work it out, John. Everybody else has,' Frankie sighed.

'Oh, yes, I get it.' John had a light-bulb moment.

'Finally,' I remarked, keen to end this. 'You're such a plonker at times, John!'

'There's another door here. Where does this go? It won't open,' Gary remarked. 'It just won't open.' He was pushing with all his might.

'It never will like that. Try pulling it to one side. It's a sliding door, not a push or pull door opened by twisting the knob,' John observed. He's a bright lad.

He took action.

'If I get hold of the handle and put my foot up against that metal plate there, it might be a bit stiff but it will probably roll open. OK, Gary?'

Ian strutted over to the struggling lads.

'If you take the catch off, it might roll a bit easier!'

'I never saw that there,' admitted John.

'Well, it's a good job I did.' Ian took the catch off. The door slid back with ease. It opened into another, very short corridor. At the end stood one large door with light shining all round it.

Gary was first to reach it, but…

'This door won't open. It just won't open.'

John once again knew why.

'Instead of pushing it, try pulling the door towards you.'

Gary pulled. The door opened.

'See what I mean, Gary? Some doors open outwards and some doors open inwards. You just have to work it out.' John enjoyed practising his wit but it was wasted on Gary.

'Well, it is rather dark in here.'

'Yes, but now it's open.' The light shone into the dark nooks and crannies of what was the entrance to the mill for the workers and staff.

'Do you think the mill owner would come in this way?' Frankie wondered out loud.

I answered: 'I don't know. He probably didn't want to mingle with his workforce, not like it is these days. If we go back inside, back through the sliding door and carry on, let's see where that goes.' At the end of the corridor there was another door. 'In its day as a working mill, this door would be used by the mill owner. Lovely oak.' It still had most of its splendour. The doorknob was tarnished, but still holding its quality. The door itself was highly polished wood.

'This door would have been polished every day, the knob too. This door has probably seen other mill owners, cloth buyers from other manufacturing mills, everybody of importance who came to the mill came through this door,' I expounded as the tour guide!

Instead of a stone floor like the rest of the mill, this floor had a linoleum floor covering, now cracked and worn, bits broken off. Over the years water leaks and dirt had been caught in the corners of the doorway. To the right was a staircase, I would say a rise of about twenty steps, leading to another short corridor. At the end of this there was another door, not quite as grand as the front door but still with some splendour. The brass fittings were mostly tarnished by age and neglect but in its day a knock would have been needed to gain entrance to the room beyond.

We climbed the staircase and walked down the corridor to the door at the end.

'Who's going in first?' I asked Ian. 'You or me?'

'Do you think there will be anybody in there?' Ian hesitated.

'What are you expecting? Somebody to say, "Do come in, have a cup of tea and here are some biscuits"?' Gary mocked.

'Like I said before, I worry about you sometimes,' I repeated.

Frankie butted in: 'I worry about him *all* the time! What with you a fountain of knowledge, Gary a tea leaf and John — well, John's a ponce.'

'Where does that leave me and Frankie?' questioned Ian.

'Well, she's a girl.'

'Then where does that leave me?' Ian didn't want to be left out of the reckoning.

'I'll think of something,' I finished, leaving the character assassination open.

'Do you think we should knock?'

'Shut it, Gary.'

The door opened with ease, as though someone had gone through it before us. In front of us stood a great big table, must have been ten feet long and about four feet wide, still looking like a bit of polish would bring the glowing colours out of the wood. These windows weren't boarded up. Sun streamed through, lighting up the whole room. The walls were a creamy brown. Where a picture had hung now only a lighter patch remained in its place. Between the top of the walls and the ceiling there was a fancy pattern, mostly gathering dust, but we were still able to pick out some of the pattern. Surprisingly, five chairs stood around the table: one at the head, two on each side. The one at the head was a plush-seated large, moth-eaten brown chair.

'I'm sitting here,' I remarked, and pulled out the head chair.

'OK. We'll sit here, then.' They sat. 'Well, I am the leader of the gang, the fountain of all knowledge!'

'Don't get too big-headed, Chris! You know it's not you,' Frankie remarked. 'But we could have this place as our gang's headquarters.'

'That's a good idea,' John agreed. 'We can all meet up here and plan what we are going to do. We don't plan anything, we just say what we are going to do and do it.'

Ian took up the reins at this point.

'What do we want with headquarters? There's only five of us and we all go to the same school. I'll tell you, we'll come here when we have nothing else to do. What time is it, Chris?'

'Hang on, my watch has just dropped on the floor,' I said. 'It's four fifteen. We'd better be making tracks.'

'Are we going up the old railway, then?' Gary asked.

'Yes, Gary, and don't be telling everybody where you've been today, otherwise we won't be allowed to come back here. It will be out of bounds. So not a word, OK?'

I exerted my authority and we made our way home.

Chapter 5

Over the next few weeks, reports in the local paper gave the information that our old mill – Mars Mill, to be precise – was going to be pulled down to make way for houses and a petrol station. Gary, being Gary, and not thinking – well, not putting the grey matter in gear before his mouth – blurted out: 'I wouldn't like to live down there. The cars that go down Maude Lane, they won't have any springs left by the time they reach the bottom!'

'Don't you think they'll make a new road when they build the houses?' I asked.

'Never thought of that, Chris. It's a good job you're here to think things out. I must admit I go in with all guns blazing sometimes.'

'I know you do, Gary.'

John turned to me.

'What are we going to do about the old mill then, Chris?'

'I don't know. Ask your dad, John.'

'What can my dad do?'

'He can buy it for us,' quipped Gary.

'Don't be stupid, Gary,' John retorted.

'What are we going to do with the mill? You don't half talk some twaddle sometimes, but I think we'll go down again just for one final look around. See if there's any more places we didn't explore.'

'I know of one,' Frankie volunteered.

'What's that, Frankie?' Ian asked.

'The old engine house. We never went in there. I bet that's quite interesting.'

'Probably not to you, Frankie,' I answered, 'but to me, John and Ian. Gary might be interested, but his first instinct would be working out how much it would make as scrap iron.'

'Is it made out of iron, then?' asked John.

'Oh, yes. Everything would be cast iron and then machined so that it would all fit together properly. No gaps, like you doing your woodwork at school. I've seen some of your cobbled-together joints, John.' I laid it on thick. John said nothing.

Frankie spoke to break the silence.

'I like doing a bit of woodwork.'

'Yes, we know you do. In fact you are better than most in the class,' I complimented her.

'Yes,' Ian said, 'but your dad, Jim—'

Ian was cut short.

'Mr McKay to you, if you see him!'

'Sorry, Frankie, Mr McKay. He has his own woodworking joinery shop, so I suppose while he's making things you'll be there taking it all in.'

'Well, I am sometimes. But I want to work in a bank, so I've been using all the measurements he has for some of his jobs to add up and take away,' Frankie enlightened him.

'All very well, Frankie, but two and a half inches – what's that in money?'

'Two pounds and ten pence!' Frankie answered calmly.

I could see the puzzled look on Gary's face.

'What's up, Gary?'

'I don't understand what Frankie is going on about.' Gary was easily confused.

'Don't worry. She's in her own world when it comes to figures, and you're in yours when it comes to scrap metal.'

John rejoined the conversation.

'So what are we going to do about the old Mars Mill? Are we going to have a look round, for old times' sake? What do you all think? Another four weeks and we'll be leaving school, all going our own separate ways. Ian, have you been to see the careers bloke again? What have you decided to do?'

Gary spoke just before Ian could.

'I'm going working with my dad.'

'Yes,' I interrupted, 'we all know what you are going to do. What were you going to say, Ian?'

'Mum wants me to go and work on the railway, so I've applied for a job at the signal box just outside the station. I didn't want to go to the engine sheds. They're too dirty. Mum says I'll go nice and clean and come home the same. But I think they work some sort of shift. What does that mean, Chris?'

'Dad works shifts down at the bus garage. Mum never knows when he's coming or going but she says the money is good. Mum saves up so we can go on holiday.'

'What you going to do, John? Frankie asked. 'You said you wanted to go and work with your dad, but the careers bloke wasn't convinced.'

'Mum wants me to go work at Windle and Son like your Ted, but I don't want to do that so I've applied to work in the parks department on the council. At least I'll be outside and not stuck indoors. I hate being in the classroom. And when the time is right, I'll go and work with my dad. You'll see.'

***

The gang were gathered together.

'So it's now Tuesday. Saturday we'll have a last good look around the old mill. I expect they'll pull it down. I don't suppose it will take them long. The old buildings are already falling down in places. I wonder what they are going to do with the mill lodge and all them fish? What did you say, Frankie?' I cupped my ear with my hand.

'My dad, he's into fishing. He and some of his mates want to buy the old mill lodge and keep it as a private fishing club. Three or four of his fishing pals were discussing it in the shop when I called the other night on the way back from school. They've asked the owners of the lodge if they would let them buy it. They are waiting for a reply.' The lads were hanging onto every word.

'Saturday morning, then, we all meet where and what time?' I asked.

'Time: nine o'clock.'

'Where?'

'Outside the corner shop.'

'But don't go in, Gary. I don't want to turn up and find out you've legged it because you've been in and pinched something!'

'I don't do that. You know I don't.' Gary was indignant.

'So what do *you* call it? Borrowing? Eating with intent not to pay? We all agree that's what you do.'

'Well, I've never been caught yet.'

'One day you will be.'

'No, I won't. Anyway in six weeks *I'll* be getting paid.' Gary was on the defensive.

'You hope. I've heard about your dad.' John gave his input.

'What have you heard?'

'He's tight.'

'No, he isn't.'

Ian jumped in.

'What about those tins of paint and the damp wallpaper? You're the only person I know that's got a pink- and lime-green-painted bedroom, and Thomas the Tank Engine, Star Wars and flowery wallpaper in their bedroom.' These remarks from Ian cut Gary to the bone!

'How do you know that?'

'Because you told us all, about four years ago. Your dad had found the paint and decided that was the right time to decorate your bedroom. Then a few days later, while he was out collecting, an old lady down Assam Street gave him a few rolls of wallpaper, damp, out of her shed. He told you it was presoaked. All he had to do was put a bit of paste on and it would stick to the walls. You told us that it was like tissue paper. And then you had run out of wallpaper and you said you had one wall that was *Thomas the Tank Engine*, a part wall that was *Star Wars* then a bit of a flowery pattern, and I think you said your dad had managed to put a piece of *Star Wars* on upside down.' Ian's memory recall amazed us all. You could have heard a pin drop!

'Well, I'm the only one who'll see it, aren't I?'

'Yes, of course you are.'

***

The following week started much the same as all the other weeks. It was four weeks before we all left school for good, five days before we went down to the old mill for one last explore, then no doubt they'd pull it down. One hundred years of spinning cotton. Dad always said cotton was the 'last king'. Of what? I would ask.

'Cotton brought wealth to the mill owners and a pittance to the mill workers and prosperity to the town.'

'Who's king now, Dad?'

'Not the mills. They've all gone. There's only Eagle Mill. I take a busload up or bring them back at night. What do they do? Make plastic handbags and things!'

Mum chipped in,

'The handbags are rubbish, just plain rubbish.'

'Still, Chris, you'll be all right going to work for Farrell Bridge Engineering. I can't see them going bust. I was only talking to one of the chaps that's going to be training you. He was saying their order books are full for the next five years. So take in what they tell you, don't do anything stupid.'

'Me, Dad? I don't do *anything* stupid!'

'You know what I mean, and you should have a job for life.' Dad was having a man-to-man talk with me.

'They tell us at school there isn't such a thing as a job for life.'

'That's telling you, Wilf.' Mum spoke with a smile on her face. 'Come on, Chris, it's time you were off to school. You don't want to be late. At least you don't have to go and see if Mr Wilks wants anything. I'm looking after the shop. He's gone to see his sister in Southport for a couple of weeks. Mondays is always a quiet day.'

***

Mrs Hogan came into the shop later in the afternoon.

'Hello, Mrs Hogan. What can I get you?' Mum asked.

'Some candles, please.'

'What do you want candles for?'

'Had a note through the letterbox this morning. They're going to cut the leccy off tonight for twenty-four hours, so I'll have to have a lit candle. We won't be able to go upstairs in the dark.'

'Are you all right for cooking?'

'Yes, we are on gas,' Mrs Hogan explained. 'Cooking on gas.'

Mum asked: 'Is Ian ready to leave school?'

'I think he's been ready for the past six months. Have you heard about that lad they call Roger? He made a mess of his entrance exam to go into the police. They say his father tried to help. He's decided to go into the Army: boy soldier. He's going down south somewhere.'

'Do you think your Ian will like his job?'

'Don't know. He hasn't said much about it, but I think once he gets into the swing of things he'll start to enjoy it.'

'Well, I hope so, Mrs Hogan.'

'What about your Chris, Mrs Hart?' Was Mrs Hogan after some gossip?

'He did quite well in his entrance exam for Farrell. He's talked about nothing else since. He went down the other night to see what he was going to be doing. One of the engineers who was standing outside asked him what he was doing hanging around. Chris told him and, so Chris says, he was inside in a flash and the man was showing him around. Chris got quite a buzz from that. So now he can't wait to leave school.'

'I think Frances McKay has done all right. She's off to the bank in town. She's had a really good report from school. You know she failed her eleven-plus – well, since then she has taught herself maths. You would have thought she would have gone into teaching.'

'We'll have to see what happens in the future. Chris has got a crush on Frances.'

'You don't say!'

'Well, they're always hanging out together. He calls for her every day, then they go off to school.'

Just then Gary came in. The doorbell jangled.

'What can I get you?' Mum asked politely.

'Me dad wants a pint of Mr Blue.'

'Yes, I can do that. Have you got something to put it in?'

'I've got this pop bottle.' Gary held up his container.

'You should have a proper can, you know.'

'A can's metal and metal is scrap!' His dad's business came first with Gary.

'I'll put it in the bottle this time, but in future you will have to bring a can,' Mum said firmly.

'Mr Wilks always puts it in the bottle,' Gary assured her.

Mum went into the back and she could be heard pouring the Blue into the bottle.

'What are you going to do when you leave, then?' Mrs Hogan asked Gary.

'I'm going to work with me dad on the rag-and-bone.'

Mrs Hogan turned to Mum.

'Nothing will be safe when them two are wandering about.

'That will be one and six, please, Gary.'

'I've only got one and three.'

'Well, you can't have it, then.'

'But Mr Wilks always lets me take it. He says he can't put it back in the drum. I'll see Chris in the morning. I'll give it him then,' Gary pleaded in his most pathetic voice.

Mrs Hart relented.

'OK, Gary, but don't forget.'

He did. He always forgets.

You know, for all the twopences and threepences he's let people off, Mr Wilks could have gone to Spain for a holiday and not to his sister in Southport, but I know he likes to go and see his sister. He hasn't been the same since Madge died. It was such a shock, not only to Mr Wilks but to us as well. She never complained about anything. We didn't even know she was poorly. I don't think Mr Wilks did, either.

Mum continued talking with Mrs Hogan.

'Just before he went away to his sister's Mr Wilks was talking about selling up and calling it a day, going to live over near his sister. I mentioned that to Wilf the other night.'

'Why don't you buy it and run it like Mr Wilks?' Mrs Hogan suggested.

'I don't think there's enough work here for the both of us, but at least we talked about it.'

'Yes, well, now that Chris will be working all day you won't have him to look after and Joan is out working. By the way, how's she getting on? She used to call on her way home from school.'

'That'll be about three years ago. She's been left school just about three years now.'

'Doesn't time fly? I can remember her in her school uniform when she first started at school.' Both ladies pondered the thought. 'Is she still at that salon in town?'

'Yes. The Silver Salon, that's what they call it. She's a stylist now. I'd like her to do my hair at home but she says she never has time any more.'

'That's children for you. I expect when Ian leaves school all his time will be taken up chasing girls,' Mrs Hogan said, laughing. The two ladies were enjoying their banter.

'Hasn't he got a girlfriend at school?'

'I don't know. If he has, he's keeping it quiet.'

'Chris has never mentioned anybody, but I'll ask him.' A chance for more future gossip.

'Mind you, Ian always asks me if I want anything from the shops. He's good like that. If I want anything doing he will always try and do it for me. I just wish I could get away, take him on a proper holiday, at least once.' Visible teardrops welled up in Mrs Hogan's eyes.

There was a pregnant pause. Mum attempted to lighten the conversation: 'Did I mention it before? Joan and Ted, that's Joan's boyfriend, they're planning on getting married in December, just before Christmas.'

'Well I never!' came back a surprised reply. 'And there's me telling you about how I remember her with her school skirt and blazer calling to see if I wanted anything. Well I never!' Mrs Hogan managed a broad smile as she quietly thought about buying a new hat.

Mum volunteered: 'Ted's round every night.'

'What's his surname?'

'Harker.'

'Didn't they live over here?'

'Yes, down Greenwood Road. One of them houses down near the railway bridge. Then they came into all that money that his parents left them.' Both ladies nodded and gave a 'hm'. Mum continued: 'So they had to move to somewhere better.'

'To where?'

'To the other side of town. Our Joan started to go out with Ted just before they moved, and she's kept on seeing him. Now they are getting married.'

'Where are they going to live, then?'

Mum explained: 'Well, you won't believe it, but Ted's parents have let them have the money to buy the house next door to what his parents had on Greenwood Road. It's a small world, don't you think?'

Mrs Hogan dug deeper: 'Where does Ted work, then?'

'He's down at Windle and Son, that place just behind the council offices.'

'So what's he doing there?'

'He works in the office.'

'Office boy, then.'

'No, that's what he did when he started. Wilf always said "office skivvy", but Ted's moved up. He works with an older lady. They do the wages. He goes down to the bank in town every Friday morning around ten o'clock with old Mr Windle. He's ninety, if he's a day! Windle parks outside, Ted goes into the bank, gets the wages, back to the car then back to the office to make the wages up.'

Mrs Hogan questioned this set-up: 'You would think with all that money the bank would deliver it. What does Ted think?'

'He's been asking old Mr Windle to have it delivered, but he says they've always done it this way so that's the way he has to do it.'

'Bit risky, don't you think?'

'Yes, I do. Ted goes round the factory at lunchtime and hands out the wage packets.'

'There won't be any risk there, then.'

'No.'

All this gave Mrs Hogan plenty of food for thought: 'Anyway, Ann, won't keep you,' and she made to leave the shop.

'See you, Mrs Hogan.'

As Mrs Hogan was closing the door, Ian appeared.

'Can I carry it for you, Mum?' he offered.

'It's only a couple of candles. They're turning the leccy off, so we'll need some candles to see where we are going.'

Together they walked away down the street: 'What's for tea, then, Mum?'

'What do you want?'

'What have we? Corn-dog? With pickle on?'

'Yes, if you want that. What have you been doing at school today, Ian?'

'Not a lot. Had to go and see the careers bloke.'

'Go on, then. What did he say?' Mrs Hogan needed details.

'Told me I had got the job on the railway, at the junction signal box just outside the station. My hours would be seven o'clock in the morning 'til one forty-five. That's one week. The other week two p.m. 'til nine thirty at night.'

'How are you going to get there early in the mornings?'

'Chris told me I could have his bike. That's what I'm going round there for tonight.'

'What about your own bike?'

'That wreck? It's not fit to go to the other side of town on!'

'Well, repair it then, Ian.'

'I'm still going round to Chris's tonight and I might come back with a bike.'

'What does Mrs Hart think about it? Anyway, have your tea before you go out. At least I'll know where you are tonight. Be home by nine-thirty at the very latest. You're still at school. You haven't left. Ten o'clock at the latest or I'll be on the phone, and you don't want me to be seen checking up on you, do you?'

'OK, Mum,' Ian conceded as he departed through the door.

A few minutes later Ian was round at my front door.

'You must be psychic,' Ian said.

'Why?' I asked.

'As I got to your door you opened it.'

'No, Ian, I saw you walk past the window. You better come in.'

Ian entered and closed the door behind him.

'Where's your mum?'

'She's in the kitchen. Why, what do you want her for?' I was naturally curious.

'I want to ask her about your bike. I can't just take it.'

'No, I'm giving it to you.'

'Still, I want to ask if I can have it.'

Just then Mum walked through the door.

'Now, Ian, what d'you want to ask me?'

'Chris says I can have his bike to go to work on when I leave school.'

'Did he?' Mum turned to me. 'And how are you going to get to work, then?'

'I can walk it. It's only about half a mile away. Ian has to go to the other end of town, Mum, and there's no buses at that time of morning.'

'Why, what time do you have to start, Ian?'

'Six o'clock,' Ian informed her.

'Yes, you're right, there aren't any buses then. But I thought you already had a bike.'

'I do, but it's clapped-out.'

I butted in: 'It's not fit to repair, and he would be better off on mine. At least it's roadworthy.'

'Yes, your dad made sure of that a few weeks ago when he had to use it to go to the garage to pick his car up. Well, if Chris doesn't mind then it's OK with me, but mind you look after it and keep it in good nick, Ian Hogan. We're just going to have our tea. Chris has volunteered to go to the chippy.' Mum got her purse.

'Which one shall I go to?' I asked.

'Go to Joe's. He seems to have the best fish at the moment. Ian, do you want to have some tea?'

'OK.' Ian was starving.

'Well, here's some more money, then. Chris, get what Ian wants and don't be long. We all want to eat. Don't forget anything.'

'I'll only be two ticks,' I shouted as I dived through the door.

I placed the order with 'Mrs Joe' (I didn't know her real name). A few people at the back of the shop were talking.

'I hear the old Mars Mill is up for sale. Good for redevelopment,' one said.

Another said: 'You could get quite a few houses on there.'

Another said: 'I heard it has been sold. They are going to put houses on it. But the old engine house – someone wants to keep it going as a museum.'

I finally got my order and took the family meal home. I started telling my mum what I'd overheard in the chippy.

'That's common knowledge. If you'd read the paper, you would have seen what it said.'

'I don't read the papers – well, I do for the footie to see what's happening, but everything else is for the old folk.'

'I'm not old!' Joan said abruptly. 'Come on, eat your tea.'

Mum spoke up: 'It's been in the local paper a few weeks now, people suggesting what they would like to see happen to the old mill site once it's been taken down.'

'You mean they are going to pull it all down?' Ian asked.

'Yes. Some big company has bought it. They are going to redevelop the site.'

'What's Mr Hart going to do? They wanted the mill lodge for a fishing club, so Chris was saying.'

'He's been in touch with the people who have bought the mill. Providing they put a fence round the lodge then Dad and his cronies can use it for fishing.'

'So Dad's off to price up fencing for it – and not the fencing you are thinking of, if at all,' came my reply. Ian looked on, puzzled.

Later on, Ian and me disappeared upstairs as Ted came knocking at the front door.

'See who that is, Joan,' Mum said.

'I know who it is, Mum.'

Ted and Joan disappeared into the front room for some quiet time, or so they thought. I burst in on them: 'What's on the telly, then?'

'Go away.'

'No.'

'Go away. We have things to discuss.'

'What things?' I demanded.

'Things you know nothing about.'

'Well, I won't if you don't tell me, will I?'

'Well, I'm not, so buzz off!'

'No, I want to watch the telly.'

'You can't.' Joan was annoyed now.

'Mum, they won't let me and Ian watch the telly,' I shouted across the house.

'What do you want to watch, Chris?'

'I want to watch what's on the telly,' I bellowed.

'But you don't know what you want to watch, so I suggest you leave Joan and Ted alone.'

'But Mum—no, but mum-' spoken in the voice of a sulky child trying to get his own way, but knowing he won't.

I looked at Ian.

'We'll go over and see Frankie, see what she's doing.'

As they were going out through the door I turned to Ian.

'What did I tell you? About what they were doing? *Kissing*, and Ted was doing the other until we arrived on the scene.'

'We are like a deterrent,' Ian surmised.

'I wouldn't go that far, Ian, but we certainly stopped Ted in his tracks! A few minutes later and God only knows what he would have been doing!' I gloated.

It was a short stay over at Frankie's. No sooner had we got through the front door than we were on our way out. Frankie told us that her dad had asked her to help him with his bills and, as she was going to work in the bank, it would help her with her adding up, as he put it.

'I'll call for you as normal in the morning,' I said to her as we went out the door.

'OK.'

'Let's go back to mine,' I suggested to Ian.

'OK,' Ian replied.

As we went in, we could hear the television was on and someone was talking about the weather.

'Let's see what they are saying. It's rain for tomorrow,' Mum said.

Ian expanded that to: 'Wall-to-wall rain. Didn't expect that, Mrs Hart. We have had about four weeks of warm, sunny days.'

'What do you expect? It's summer,' I said.

'Less of that, Chris,' Mum said.

Ian sat glued to the telly, not saying a word.

'What are you thinking, Ian?' Joan asked him.

'Another couple of weeks and I'll be working. Schooldays over.'

'Better make as much of it as you can,' Ted advised.

'What shall we do at the weekend, Chris?' Ian asked.

'I don't know, but we'll sort something out tomorrow when we see Gary and Frankie. We'll have to do something, even if we only go down to the old mill.'

Ted said to us both: 'You want to be careful if you go down there. I've heard they are starting to pull the place down.'

Ian was a little surprised: 'What, so soon?'

'It was sold about a month ago, you know, and I expect they want it down so they can build houses on it, or whatever they are going to do with the land.' Ted picked up the local free paper to read.

Chapter 6

I woke around seven o'clock on Friday morning. Looking through the window, the weatherman was right – wall-to-wall rain, heavy rain. But it was summer so it should have been hot!

'So how long is it going to rain, Mum?'

'I don't know. You saw the weather forecast last night, just like I did.'

'Has Joan gone to work?'

'Yes, she went with Ted.'

'Boy, he must have come over early for her.'

'He stayed over last night,' Mum said. 'They are nearly married.'

'Has Dad gone as well?'

'You're asking a lot of questions this morning, Chris. It's not like you. You're usually late and I have to make you sit down and eat something, even if it's only cornflakes. So why all the questions?'

'I don't know, Mum. It must be because I don't have to go round to Mr Wilks. I'm always under pressure.'

'No, Chris, it's because you are always getting up late. Still, when you leave school you will have to be up early.'

'Why?'

'Because you will have to leave to be in work for seven thirty.' I looked at her. 'You know I'm right, so enjoy this last six weeks – because when you leave school, that's when your life begins. You're still in your childhood – a big child, but you're still classed as one.'

'But, Mum, I'm a teenager.'

'But you're still classed as a minor. And isn't it time you were off to school? Frankie will be waiting.' Frankie was always waiting.

No sooner had I opened my front door than Frankie was doing the same with hers. 'Hi, Frankie,' I shouted.

'Hi, Chris,' she replied.

I crossed the road and we set off walking to school. Ian met us on the corner and as we approached the shop Gary, being his usual self, was waiting for us to appear.

Frankie spoke to Ian and me: 'I wonder if Gary's been in the shop for his usual takeout.'

'Or borrowed it, as Gary would say, for his dinner,' I added.

Gary never had school dinners: not that they were bad, more indifferent. Ian said the cooks didn't have much imagination. Not when it came to throwing it together, Gary often added. Gary never had any money to spare. That's why he had got so used to borrowing from the corner shop. He came very close to getting caught a few times, but he always seemed to be one step ahead of the shopkeeper.

'I wouldn't have thought so. He's hanging around the outside of the shop. If he'd been in he wouldn't be there,' Frankie observed.

'You're right,' I agreed.

'What's up, Gary, lost your bottle?' Ian shouted as we approached.

'What do you mean?' Gary questioned.

'It doesn't matter,' I shouted back.

'I've just *got* to tell you,' Gary whispered.

'What are you whispering for, Gary?'

'I don't want anybody to overhear our conversation.'

'What conversation is that, Gary?' I asked.

'But there's only us four here. There isn't anybody else in the street. So what's so important that you have to whisper?' demanded Ian.

'Last night when I got home from school after helping Dad unload the truck…'

'Yes, we all know what you do when you get home,' Ian mumbled.

Gary continued: 'Dad said he would like to have a wander down to the old mill—'

'Yes, we know, to see what he could pick up in scrap.' Ian interrupted the flow again.

Back to Gary: 'As Dad puts it, "A bit of free enterprise goes a long way." We were on the ground floor and walking towards the doors and we heard voices coming from the loading bay. We managed to get behind the doors. They were open slightly, so we could hear what they were talking about.' Gary went on to describe hearing men talking about what sounded like a robbery but no specific day or time or place. We were intrigued, to say the least, but sceptical.

I was unsure how to handle this immense news but I wanted to take charge, and quickly.

'Let's face it, Gary, if you and your dad are telling the truth and you heard three blokes discussing a *robbery*, but you don't know where or when it's going to happen, what can we do about it?'

Ian spoke up: 'Gary?'

'What?'

'Gary, why didn't you stay until they'd gone? We would have something to tell the police.'

'We couldn't.'

'What do you mean you couldn't?'

'Well, there was one of the blokes a bit taller than the other two. From what me and my dad could see, he had like a knitted hat or something, but his hair was real ginger. He kept waving something around in his hand. I thought it was a small piece of wood, but then there was a loud crack and something hit the big metal door we were hiding behind.' Gary was in full flow and unstoppable.

'The other two who were with him shouted, "Put the bloody thing down before someone gets hit!" It slammed into the door then ricocheted off. And, would you believe it, it hit one of the lights in the loading bay ceiling. All three blokes started laughing. The one with the ginger hair spoke: "I had you worried there." Had *them* worried? Dad said, "Let's go. I think we have heard enough."'

Ian was still critical.

'You might have heard enough, but really you didn't. If you had got there a bit sooner, or left a bit later, you might have found out where and when the robbery is going to take place. But as it is, there's nothing. One was brandishing a gun then fired it, you said.'

Gary told more.

'They had a sawn-off shotgun on the bonnet of one of the cars!'

Now I started to get more involved.

'But if we go to the police and tell them all of what you've told us, Gary, are they going to believe us? Or are they going to think we are schoolkids with vivid imaginations? What do you think, Frankie, Ian? Have you got any ideas?'

'I can see where you're coming from, Chris.' Frankie offered her support.

I continued: 'The thing is, we know there's going to be a robbery because Gary and his dad heard them planning it in the old mill.'

'There's no point, Chris. The police just wouldn't believe us,' Frankie declared.

'I think you're right, Frankie. We'll just sit on it. But I think if they were planning it from the old mill, they might go back there when they've pulled it off.'

'What do you mean?' Gary asked me.

'Have I got to explain everything, Gary? When they've done the robbery, they'll have to go somewhere to share out what they've stolen. They won't just do the robbery, go round the corner, pull up and share it out. They'll have somewhere earmarked to share out their ill-gotten gains, and that place could be where you and your dad were last night, in the old mill!' I took a deep breath. 'So tonight we'll all meet at the old mill.'

'Where?' asked Ian.

'In the weighbridge office. From there we can watch to see if anything happens. What about seven o'clock? You never know. They might turn up.'

Frankie was working it out.

'Have you ever thought the robbery might be today, this morning, while we are at school?'

'It might be, Frankie, but we can't really bunk off school thinking there might be a robbery.'

Ian voiced his thoughts: 'It might not be in this town.'

Me again: 'Oh, I think it will be. You're not going to plan a robbery here then travel twenty miles and go do it in another town. No, I think they are planning to do it round here. Where and when we just don't know. Right, Gary, Frankie, Ian, we best get to school or we'll be late – and with only six weeks to go before we leave for good, I don't want to give us all a bad name by arriving after the school bell has rung. Let's go!'

We reached the school.

'See you at break, Frankie.' We went through the school gates as the bell started to ring.

'That was a close-run thing, Chris,' Ian panted.

'Yep,' I replied.

Break came and went. So did dinner. I was out first, followed by Frankie and Ian. 'Where's Gary?'

Ian knew.

'He's having to have a word with the teacher.'

'What about, Ian?'

'Something he said to Miss White.' Just then Gary appeared.

'Got sorted, Gary?' Ian shouted.

'Yep.'

'What was it about?'

'She said I called her names.'

'Like what?'

'Mint balls!' Gary punched the air as a loud, resounding cheer went up. They needed that!

***

'See you at the old weighbridge around seven, Gary,' I reminded him as Gary left us at the corner shop.

'Yep,' Gary replied.

'You're not saying a lot today,' Frankie noted.

'Nope.'

'See you, then.' Frankie arrived at her front door.

'See you tonight, Frankie,' I confirmed. 'Me and Ian will give you a knock at 6.45. Are you having your tea with us, Ian?' I asked. 'I'll get Mum to ring your mum to let her know where you are.'

'OK.'

Later that evening me, Frankie, Gary, Ian and John met up at the weighbridge office.

'Right, what's the plan of action?' Gary asked me.

'We'll go into the loading bay and see if we can find anything. You never know if they've left some scraps of paper.'

'Did you say scrap?' Gary's ears pricked up.

'Not that sort of scrap. I meant they might have written something down on paper then thrown it away,' I continued.

Ian joined in: 'If you mention anything about scrap, Gary only sees pounds, shillings and pence.'

'Just keep those thoughts to yourself, Gary,' Frankie said.

I took the lead again.

'When we get inside the loading bay, get your eyes used to the murky light then we'll have a look round.'

'Why don't we open one of the big doors?' Ian thought aloud.

'Because we don't want anyone to know we are here looking around.'

'Got ya,' came four whispered answers.

'Found anything yet?'

'No, but there are quite a few tyre marks on the floor.'

'One of the cars must have an oil leak.'

'Why?'

'Because here, look, it's oil.'

'Yer, but that might have been from one of the lorries that delivered here.'

'I don't think so.'

'Why?'

'Well, if it was from a lorry it must have been here recently.'

'Why?'

'Because in time the oil would have soaked into the concrete floor, so I think it will have come from one of the cars that was here the other night.'

'What sort of cars were they, Gary?' I asked.

'One was a reddy-coloured Jag. It was gleaming, wire-spoked wheels, and laid across its bonnet was, as my dad said, a sawn-off shotgun! The car was well polished. A stream of light caught the bonnet and part of the roof and the car just sparkled.'

'What about the other?'

'That appeared to be black. Dad said it was just like an old police car. I think they were Wolseleys, but I don't know. Anyway, that was black. It didn't seem to soak up any sunlight. The one who fired the gun, he got out of the black car. Dad said he was a right cocky git! The two who got out of the Jag were a bit well-spoken. Dad said he thought they were the masterminds. The other guy in the black car, he just stood around.' Gary gave us plenty of detail to mull over, and this time we were glad to listen to him.

'Did you see the number plates of both cars?'

'No, we were looking at the cars about three-quarters side view, and it was quite dark except for the shafts of light coming in. Then the tall bloke fired the pistol and the bullet ricocheted off the steel door. It hit the light fitting and, as they say, that was that. I could see that Dad was a bit shaken and it was then that he said we should leave.' Gary brought his description to an end.

'Chris.'

'What, Frankie?'

'Look at this. What do you think?'

'That's a set of number plates.'

'What do you think they're off, Chris?'

'Probably one of the cars – but which one, I don't know. I suspect the one that looked like a police car. You better leave them where you found them. They might come back for these. What you found, Gary?'

'This, Chris.'

'That's the spent cartridge case from the gun you said he fired. Well, I think it is. You found anything, Ian?'

'Nothing yet. There's no scraps of paper lying around, just tyre marks and that oil spill you found earlier.' Ian shuffled around, still looking for evidence.

'Gary!'

'What?'

'There's a car coming.'

'Right, let's get behind the door into the factory, quick.'

We just managed to get behind it as two men came through the doorway.

'I thought you shut this the other night,' one man said.

'I did,' answered the second man.

'You thought you did, but you couldn't have. Anyway, where did you put the shotgun?'

'It's over there.'

'Where?'

'Under the loading bay, behind the sacks and tins.'

'Well, you'd better get it. And what's these?'

'The number plates.'

'I thought you said you'd got rid of them!'

'I did.'

'Yes, but it's not good enough. You should have thrown them in the canal or something like that, not just stuffed them under these sacks. If this robbery is going to work, and work it will, you'll have to start getting your act together. Now get rid of them tonight, Brian. Tonight, and don't forget!'

'OK, Reg.'

Me, Frankie, Ian, John and Gary sat motionless on the floor behind the big steel door.

'Right, Brian, you have the gun and cartridges. I've got the masks in the motor.'

'OK, Reg.'

'You know the drill. We do the job, come back here, fire the car then get in the other car with Bert and Jim and make our getaway. We'll split the cash and we go our separate ways. Not long now, Brian.'

'Not long, Reg.'

'This time, Brian, shut the door. Make sure nobody gets in.'

'OK, Reg.' And with that the big door slammed shut. I slid open the factory door.

'What do you think about that, then?' asked Gary.

'We're still no wiser,' Ian answered.

'It's a bank job.' I went into Sherlock mode. 'They've two cars. One appears to be a Jag. The other we are not quite sure of, but it's got new number plates. They appear to have a pistol and a sawn-off shotgun. We know all that, plus we think the original number plates for the car are going in the canal. But we don't know where or when the robbery is going to take place.'

Frankie got involved.

'Do you think we should go to the police? We know what is going to happen – the trouble is we don't know when or where. But you never know if the police might have other information that we haven't got. What do you think, John? You're always thinking but saying nothing.'

John spoke up.

'We can always give it a whirl. You never know, they might just listen – and besides, if we go to the police and ask for Roger's dad … he's a detective, isn't he?'

'I don't know,' said Frankie and she turned to Gary. 'You should know, Gary.'

'Why me?'

'Your dad's always talking to the police about something or other. And with your dad always on the fiddle, John, you should know what he is.' Frankie didn't pull her punches.

'Sorry, no can tell.' John was miffed.

'Or won't tell, John!'

'Tomorrow morning, let's all meet up and go down the nick,' John suggested bravely.

Frankie looked at Gary, then at John, Ian and me.

'You're right in what you're thinking. Gary's down the nick already,' quipped Frankie.

'No, I'm not,' Gary protested.

'Well, when we meet up make sure you are clean and tidy, Gary. We don't want to give them the wrong impression. Right, where are we meeting?' I scanned the gang.

Ian put in: 'What about the corner shop where Gary always manages to get something for his school lunch? What about you, John?'

'I'll ask my dad if he'll run me over.'

Ian laughed.

'You don't want to ask him that! Knowing your dad, he probably *would* run you over!'

'All right, I'll ask him if he will *bring* me over.'

'Just say you are meeting Chris and Frankie at the corner of Maude Lane, where the shop is. Gary will no doubt be around, probably in the shop having a chat and no doubt going to "borrow" something for his lunch.'

Strange, but when we all went out on a Friday night or on a Saturday during the day, Gary never pinched anything. Only when he was off to school. It became a challenge, the daily challenge to get something for nothing for lunch. Didn't matter what, but it had to be food.

Chapter 7

'By gum, you're up early for a Saturday morning. What's up, can't you sleep?' my mum expressed her surprise.

'Yes, I can but I'm meeting John and Gary at Maude Street at nine o'clock. Ian should be round any time, then we are calling for Frankie.'

'So, what are you up to today, seeing as you've already made plans?'

'We are meeting Roger outside the cop shop.'

'That's a strange place to meet,' Mum quizzed.

'Roger's dad works there and he said he would ask him to drop him outside.'

Just then there was a loud knock at the front door and Ian walked in.

'Are you ready, then?'

'No,' Mum said. 'And you're not going out without having something to eat. There's a bacon butty. Do you want one, Ian?'

'I wouldn't mind, please.'

'Here you are. You can have mine. I'll do myself another one later.' Ian hesitated. 'No, take it, a growing lad like you. Yes, take it.'

'Thanks, Mrs Hart,' Ian replied politely.

'Are you ready, Ian? Frankie will be waiting.' I wanted to go.

'If you put your skates on, Dad's on the nine thirty into town. He'll probably let you all ride free, but mind, you'll have to be quick.' Mum ushered us out.

Gary and John were waiting at Maude Street corner shop.

'Right, let's go,' I said. 'Dad's on the nine thirty to town, so if we hurry we should catch it.'

'Where's Frankie?'

'Oh, she's at the bus stop, waiting for us to turn up. She'll keep Dad there 'til we do.'

'I'll race you,' John shouted to Ian.

'No, I'm not running. I've just had a bacon sandwich at Chris's.'

'Anyway, I can't see Gary running more than about ten feet. He's no good at the cross-country.'

'Not like you, then, Ian: built for speed.'

'Yes, but Gary's built for comfort.'

Gary asked: 'What do you mean?'

'You'll find out when you get married,' I replied. 'Come on, then, or we'll miss the bus and will have to pay on the next one into town.'

As luck would have it, as we arrived at the bus stop Dad's bus was rolling to a halt. Ian said: 'He's got one of those new ones.'

'One-man operated things,' I replied. 'He doesn't like them. He was telling Mum the other night they've to take the money, watch what the passengers are up to and drive the damned things. They had a union meeting the other night about pay and conditions while working on these new buses.'

'What do you mean?'

'They want more money for what the job entails.'

With that, the bus set off with a jolt.

'Hey, Dad,' I shouted, 'there's no one on the bus, only us.'

'Yer, well, when I got to Brick Road turnaround the other one was just leaving, so he will have picked up all my passengers.

You lot will be the only ones 'til the next stop, or it might only be you to the bus station. Anyway, where are you going and what are you getting up to today?'

'Can you drop us all at the cop shop, Dad?'

'What have you done? Or are you taking Gary in for questioning?'

'I haven't done anything wrong, Mr Hart!' Gary insisted.

'So why the police station, then?'

'We're meeting Roger. He's getting a lift into town with his dad, and as he works at the police station we said we'd meet him there.'

Just then Dad applied the brakes on the bus and we rolled to a halt.

'Here you are, Mr Hart. I've found this on the floor.'

'What is it?'

'Half a crown.'

'You have it, Frankie.'

'No, we haven't paid. Mind you, we don't when you're on the bus, so take it. You're always good to us, Mr Hart.'

'Thanks, Frankie,' Dad said cheerfully as Frankie got off the bus with the rest of us. As he drove away he thought,

She's a really good kid. I hope our Chris meets someone like her. She would be all right for Chris to settle down with. I'll mention it to Annie when I get home today, see what she thinks.

Little did he know, but Frankie and me were already becoming an item. Dad, as always, never saw any signs! But my mum had. Little things that I said and did. I was always there to look after and protect Frankie. Mum knew something was starting to happen between us. Dad, on the other hand, came home from work, had a wash and a cup of tea. He would say,

'I'll just have five minutes with the paper,' and as soon as he picked it up, he would be out like a light.

***

'Hi, Roger,' John shouted out. 'Been here long?'

'About ten minutes.'

'We came down in our own personal bus.'

'You mean there wasn't anybody else on it?'

'Well, you could say that.'

'You lot must be costing the bus company big bucks.'

'It's only a fifteen-minute ride into town. Well, it's not really town – he still has a couple of stops to make before he gets to the bus station.'

'I take it the old man – sorry, your dad – is in work today.'

'But not for long. He's taking Mum shopping. They said they were going to have a look at a new bed.'

'What, just a look, not buying it?' Gary questioned me.

'You know what I mean, Gary.' He always tries to come out with something witty.

Ian tutted: 'I know, Chris. We better get in the cop shop before *he* goes and has a look at a new bed. Who do we ask for at the desk?'

'I'll do the talking,' Roger said.

John remarked: 'Over and out.'

'There's always one,' Ian joked.

Roger pushed open the big brown doors that said *Police Public Entrance* and we all barged in. One door would have been sufficient but no, we had to make a grand entrance. The doors, as we passed through, were left swinging vacantly in space behind us. As we approached the desk a voice boomed out: 'What can I do for you?'

'Where's that coming from? There's nobody about.' We all turned to look in different directions, a bit like meerkats! Then a face and a body started to appear from under the counter until the whole person stood upright. We all stood in awe of this *very* tall policeman.

Gary said quietly: 'Cor, how tall is he?'

The policeman must have heard Gary. He said: 'I'm six feet nine, and that's without my boots and helmet on!' We all stood mesmerised, staring at the great height of this man.

'Can I help you?' he spoke again.

'Er, er … Can I see my dad?' Roger said.

'Can you speak up, son?'

Roger raised his voice: 'Can I see my dad, please?'

'And who might your dad be?' the very tall policeman demanded.

'Er, Detective Sergeant Kidd.'

'Just one moment … I'll see if he's in today.' The intercom crackled: 'Would DS Kidd please come to the public entrance? Someone wants to speak to him.' Once again the intercom crackled.

Just then the desk phone rang.

'Desk PC, can I help you? Yes, there's a young person here to see you.' He looked down at Roger. 'Your name, please? He calls himself Roger Kidd. His friends are with him, all five of them.' He put the phone down carefully. 'He says I have to tell you he'll be down in a mo.'

As the policeman spoke, the door at the side of the desk swung open. DS Kidd was a small but well-proportioned man in his late forties, with receding brownish-coloured hair but with a bit of white at the sides. That was probably because of the workload he had. DS Kidd had started with the police when he came out of the forces. In actual fact he had been a military policeman, so to transfer into the local police force was quite easy. As he was now a detective, the uniform had gone years ago. Now he wore a very smart suit. You would have thought that he was going out on the town. But as it turned out later, talking to Roger, DS Kidd had dressed for taking Roger's mum out. I think he said they were going to the pictures to see *Whistle Down the Wind*, then he planned to take her for a meal.

'Why all this?' I remember remarking to Roger.

'It's Mum's birthday today. He always treats her on her birthday,' Roger informed me.

When it's my mum's birthday Dad buys a big bunch of flowers and he always manages to find the ones she likes, along with a big box of chocolates, Dad's favourites. Mum always says the same thing each year: 'These flowers are my favourites. I'll put them in a vase. Chris, put them in the front window. Now where's that box of chocolates? There's too many there for me. Wilf, can you eat a few?' By the time Mum gets round to eating a few more herself, most have gone, and most are in Dad! Usually by the end of the night all but one or two hard centres are left.

DS Kidd stood amongst us.

'What can I do for you? Roger mentioned that you were all coming to see me this morning. What's young Gary been up to?'

'I've done nothing wrong. Everybody thinks I've been up to no good,' Gary said indignantly.

'So what is it?' DS Kidd asked.

I spoke up: 'Could we go somewhere we can talk in private, please?'

The detective paused for thought: 'Well, let's see. Right you lot, follow me. We'll see if there's an interview room available.'

One room was being used and the other had boxes and boxes of files in it.

'We are having a bit of a change around, and boxes turn up in the strangest of places. Tell you what: Trevor's not in today, so we'll use his office.'

Detective Inspector Trevor Marshall was boss over DS Kidd. He had a very smart but, I would say, work-like office. Not like Roger's dad's, with papers, empty coffee cups, pencils and pens all over the desktops.

'How do you work with all that on your desk, Dad?' Roger asked him.

'I know where everything is, son. Don't touch a thing!' But we were now in Trevor Marshall's office. 'That goes for you all,' DS Kidd said. 'Don't touch anything in here.'

Through the office there was an open door into a small room.

'Here we are. Right, sit where you can. Frankie, Ian and John, go and get yourselves a chair, and when you come back and get comfy we'll start.'

I asked: 'Can I have a drink?'

'Can I have one, please?' asked John.

'OK, before you start telling me what you want to tell me, does anybody else want a drink?' In the end everybody wanted one. 'It will have to be orange juice.'

'OK.' DS Kidd rang to the kitchen. A few minutes later a young lady appeared with six glasses of orange juice and a mug of coffee for him. John said to Ian: 'That was Ena Trotter. She was in the next year up. You will know her. She was always a bit, well, scruffy. Never seemed to care about her appearance.'

'Well,' Ian replied, 'she has changed. She looks as fit as a butcher's dog. Are you thinking what I'm thinking?'

John agreed.

'Yep, but it's no good. She has a ring on her finger. I bet you any money she's going out with one of this lot.'

'Right, now that you have had a drink and something to eat, who's the spokesman? Better still, what's this all about?'

We sat there looking at each other again.

'I better speak for us all,' I said. 'Well, it's like this…' and I started to tell the story about the old mill.

'Just a minute,' DS Kidd cut in. 'The old mill is out of bounds to all. You know that it's been derelict for a few years and now they are going to pull it down because it's unsafe.'

'Yeah, but Dad says it's only the mill chimney that's unsafe. Dad and a few of his mates are buying the old mill lodge so they can use it and are hoping to form a fishing club.'

'Carry on.'

'Well, Gary and his dad…'

'You mean Singleton and Son Scrap?'

Gary sat there silently but grinned when DS Kidd mentioned Singleton and Son Scrap. 'Nothing too big or too small.' You could see the sentence going through his mind.

'Gary,' DS Kidd said. Gary came out of his daydream with a jolt. 'You and your father went down to the mill?'

'Yes, the one down Maude Lane.'

'Yes, I know the one you're on about. What was your plan, or should I say why did you want to go to the old mill?' DS Kidd grilled Gary.

'Dad wanted to see if there was any scrap metal lying around.'

'Oh, I see. You were going for a look around and then no doubt you, or your father, would go back the day after and just pick it up.'

Shock and horror crept across Gary's face as he realised what he had just said.

'We'll let that slide,' DS Kidd said. 'You were in the old mill. Where?'

'Behind the sliding door that leads from the loading bay into the factory.'

'Then what?'

'We had walked all round, been on all the floors and were making our way back out when, as we were about to slide the door open, we heard voices. The sliding door was open about two inches. We both froze. Dad whispered, "Don't say anything. Just listen." We were there about twenty, twenty-five minutes. We only left when one of the men fired a gun!'

DS Kidd sat up.

'You did say fired a gun?'

'Yes, the bullet hit just above the steel door where we were, then shattered one of the light fittings.'

'Right, hold it there,' DS Kidd said. 'Just a minute.' The intercom crackled. 'Is PC Duggins still in the canteen? If he is, can you tell him to come to interview room three? I want a word with him. Thanks.'

A few minutes later there was a knock at the door. Duggins pushed the door open. You wouldn't have got a feather between him and the door frame. He was enormous! Fat and big, with a round, chubby face.

'I see you have had an egg sandwich, then,' DS Kidd chided. You could see most of the egg down the constable's slightly holey jumper and bits of yellow yolk at the corners of his mouth. Whereas the PC on the front desk was very tall and slim, PC Duggins was the complete opposite. Short, fat, overweight, much more plump. He was in his late forties; he had a son who was going to the grammar school on the other side of town. We played them at football and rugby. It was always them and us, with us being the better side.

'I see you have been filling your face again,' DS Kidd spoke.

'Why, can you tell?'

'Well, sort of. You have canteen medals down your jumper and there's bits of egg at the corners of your mouth. Anyway, you and your sidekick Montrose take the car and go and collect Singleton senior.'

'What if he won't come?'

'Just tell him we have his son in here and he is helping us with our enquiries.'

'What if he isn't there?'

'Where?'

'At home?'

'Just go, Duggins.'

'He won't be home,' Gary said.

'Where will he be, then?' asked Duggins.

'I think he said he was going to pick some scrap up from Joe Faulkner's place on Lizard Street. Property repairs.'

DS Kidd spoke again: 'Anyway, Duggins, try Lizard Street first. You can't miss his truck. It's green and has plenty of rust.'

'No, it's not!' Gary protested.

'Why, what colour is it now?'

'We got a new truck the other week. It's red and has a sign above the front windows. It says *Singleton and Son Scrap Merchant*.'

'Well, now you know what you're looking for: a red truck and Mr Singleton, who should be in the vicinity of it. Now go, Duggins. Go!' DS Kidd waved a hand towards the door and Duggins left.

'Now Gary, where were we? You said you were hiding behind the steel door leading from the warehouse loading bay into the factory. Tell me in your own words what you saw.'

Gary took a gulp of air and began.

'As we were peering through the door, light was coming through the big doors. We could make out two cars. One was a red-coloured Jag. Dad said it was a Jag. It had wire wheels.'

'What about the other one?'

'That was black, or appeared to be black when we all went back last night.'

'You went *back*!'

'Well, we had to see what we could find.'

'And what did you find?'

'This.' I took the empty gun cartridge out of his pocket and laid it on the desk.

'You realise what I have to do now?' DS Kidd rested his chin on his hand.

'No, what?'

'Take all your fingerprints.'

'Why?'

'Well, you all might have touched this and anything else. It's only to eliminate you lot from everything you have touched.'

'We all put our fingers in the pool of oil that was on the loading bay floor,' Ian pointed out.

Half an hour later me, John, Gary, Frankie and Ian had had our fingerprints taken. Roger hadn't. He had not been anywhere near the old mill the other night.

'Right, where were we? Did you see anything else?'

Gary continued.

'They had a roll of paper laid out on the bonnet of the Jag and were discussing something, but I couldn't tell what they were saying. They rolled up the paper and threw it on the back seat of the Jag.'

'Anything else?'

I told some more.

'Yep, last night when we had a look around the old mill Frankie found a pair of number plates.'

'Where are they now?'

'I don't know. We heard a car coming so we went and hid behind the same steel door that Gary and his dad hid behind.'

Now Ian took up the reins: 'The car pulled up and two men got out. One was smoking, the one with the ginger hair. He flicked his cigarette into the warehouse. You could see the lit end gradually fade out. The other one said, "Where did you put the number plates? You were told to chuck them in the canal, so go and get them and get rid. And get the shotgun."' Ian went on: 'Both the gun and the number plates were hidden under old sacking under the loading bay.'

Frankie spoke for the first time: 'I found the number plates, and if we hadn't been disturbed I would have no doubt found the shotgun.' The story was unfolding.

'I mentioned before that a gun had been fired,' Gary said.

'You said it was a shotgun. Did it have a long barrel?' asked DS Kidd.

'No, Dad said it was a sawn-off shotgun.'

At that moment PC Duggins appeared at the door.

'We managed to track down Singleton's scrap wagon. You were right. He wasn't at home. Gary, that's a fiery dog you have there! It had Montrose at bay. He just couldn't get past it. He wasn't at Faulkner's place, either. He was parked up at the butty truck on Glen Road.'

'So what took you so long to bring him in? Don't tell me you had a butty yourselves?'

'Couldn't resist.'

'I'll be having words with you later, Duggins. Now, can you show Mr Singleton into interview room number one? I'll be along to see him shortly.'

'We told him he could park his truck round the back with the police cars. You don't mind, do you?'

'You know, Duggins, when I send you and Montrose out on a job it's like the Keystone Cops going out. It's a good job it's not a cattle wagon parked in the back. There would be some complaints.'

Gary's dad was shown in.

'Morning, Mr Singleton,' DS Kidd said. 'As you are aware, we have your son with the rest of his gang members. They are all helping us with our enquiries, so we would like you to clarify what they've said.'

'But you wouldn't have any enquiries if me and Gary hadn't gone into the mill the other day.'

'That might be so, but as they've come forward with information regarding a possible robbery…'

Gary's dad interrupted: 'I think it's more than likely there is going to be a robbery. You wouldn't have two cars and four men stood around in a dimly lit warehouse discussing the time of day, would you? And besides, one had a gun, which he fired. At what I don't know, but it went off with a hell of a bang.'

'Right then, Singleton…'

'It's *Mr* Singleton to you.'

'All right, then, Mr Singleton. What can you tell us about what you saw and heard? In your own words.'

Mr Singleton proceeded to tell DS Kidd what had happened on the evening they had decided to have a look around the old mill and the reasons as to why they made the visit. The only thing he couldn't do was tell DS Kidd when and where the robbery was going to take place. All he could say was that, in his opinion, he expected it to be sooner rather than later, and that was because one of the robbers got too cocky and blurted out something he shouldn't have.

'Can I go now?' Gary's dad asked.

'I think so. You've told us exactly what your son and his mates have. PC Duggins will escort you to the main entrance, and thanks once again for your help.'

As Mr Singleton walked out through the main entrance Gary, Frankie, Ian, John and me followed.

'Anybody want a lift back home, other than Gary?'

'No thanks,' we all replied together.

'Gary, get in the truck. I want a word with you!'

'But Dad…'

'Get in the truck!'

'See you later,' John shouted, then: 'What are you lot going to do now?'

'We …' I said, 'we'll have a wander round town then see if we can get a lift back home on Dad's bus. He's working all day today, so it should be a free ride.'

With that, Mr Singleton started the new truck up, with clouds of black smoke belching out.

'I thought Gary said they had a new truck.'

'Well, I expect it was new to them. The person who sold it to them probably thought it was going for scrap!' Just then the truck passed them, turned onto the main road and roared off into the distance.

'Come on, let's go into town. Have you got any money, John?'

'Why, Chris?'

'I just fancy a Mars bar. Don't you?'

'You and food,' John replied.

Chapter 8

Saturday night was slightly different to all the other Saturday nights. We'd just had tea when there was a loud thud, thud, thud at the front door.

'Who can that be?' Mum wondered. 'Better go see, Lenny.'

Dad opened the front door, to be confronted by a uniformed policeman and a man in plain clothes.

'Can we come in? We would like a word with your son, Chris.' We later found out that the man in plain clothes was Detective Inspector Trevor Marshall.

'Right, son,' DI Marshall said. 'I want you to have a look at these faces, or as we call them, mug shots. See if you recognise any of them.'

I started looking at the pictures of faces very slowly. DI Marshall, in the meantime, was asking Dad if he'd seen anything different over the last few days. Dad said he hadn't noticed anything untoward.

'Have you found a face you recognise?'

'No, I'm sorry, I haven't.'

'Have you remembered anything else that you didn't mention this morning down the station?'

'What station was that?' Mum asked me.

'The police station,' I answered.

'And what were you doing down there?'

'Well, er…' Just as I started to tell her, the DI spoke.

'He was down the police station with the rest of his gang.'

'Don't tell me you're in trouble!'

'No, Mum.'

'Far from it,' DI Marshall said. 'They and Mr Singleton – you know Singleton's Scrap? Well, Mr Singleton and his son Gary were down the old mill the other night…'

'No doubt seeing what they could pinch,' Mum remarked.

'Well, at this moment in time we are not too bothered.'

'So you are turning a blind eye to Mr Singleton's activities?'

'For the moment, yes, because he and his son witnessed four men planning a robbery. Unfortunately we don't know where and when this crime will take place. But on the day that your son Chris and the rest of the so-called gang were in the old mill warehouse, a black car pulled up and two men got out and went into the warehouse. Chris and his mates had to hide so they wouldn't be detected. They overheard the men talking about the old number plates and how to dispose of them and then one said to the other, "Where's the shotgun?" One of the blokes walked over to the loading bay and pulled away some sacking to remove a shotgun, which will no doubt be used in the robbery they are planning.'

DI Marshall paused for all this to sink in, then said: 'So you can see why at this moment we are not really interested in Mr Singleton's plans. But he has been warned about it, take my word. But, at the moment, what your son Chris and the other gang members have told us is very interesting.'

'Who else have you shown the mug shots to?' I wanted to know.

'We have seen Ian Hogan, Frances McKay…'

'Frankie to us.'

'You and John. We are now off to see Mr Singleton and his son Gary to see if they recognise anyone in the mug shots. Thanks for your time, Chris and Mr and Mrs Hart.' The two officers turned to leave: 'We'll see ourselves out. Thanks once again for all your help. If you think of anything, would you let me know soonest?' And then they were gone.

'So go on, Chris, tell me what you saw. You know, Lenny, I just couldn't understand why Chris had to be up and out so early this morning. I usually have to drag him out of bed on a Saturday morning, and on Sundays.'

'Not any more.'

'What's that, Chris?'

'I've turned over a new leaf.'

'I don't believe it,' Mum remarked.

'I have, Mum. From now on I'm going to be out and about early doors.'

'Seeing is believing!'

'Anyway, in a few weeks I'll be working.'

'Yes,' Dad said, 'then you will have to be up early.'

Just then there was another thud, thud at the front door. This time I went and answered it.

'Come in, come in.'

'Who is it?' asked Mum.

'It's only Ian and Frankie.'

'I was crossing the road just as Ian was coming down,' Frankie said. 'I see the police have called.'

'Yep.'

'What did you think of the mug shots?'

'Well, there were some I wouldn't want to meet in the dark,' said Ian.

'There were some I wouldn't want to meet night or day,' Frankie said.

'I think you're both right.' I smiled.

'Do you two want a drink of something?' asked Mum.

'Glass of orange wouldn't go amiss, Mrs Hart,' Ian asked.

'Do you want an orange as well, Frankie?'

'Yeah that will be fine.'

'Ian, have you had any tea?'

'Just a butty.'

'Would you like something else?'

'What have you got?'

I piped up: 'Mum will make you anything you want. You know she has a soft spot for you!'

'Where are the police going next?' Frankie asked me.

'Well, they've been here, they've been to yours and Ian's. I think they said they've been to John's place. Roger's not involved, only his father, so they must be leaving the best 'til last – the Singletons! God help them if they can get past the dog.'

Frankie sighed: 'No doubt we'll get the line-by-line account on Monday morning on the way to school.'

***

Nothing was heard from Gary. Me, Mum and Dad took the dog for a walk on that Sunday. We went passed Singleton's Scrap but there was nobody about. Only their dog was barking as we passed the gates into the scrapyard. We didn't see Frankie or Ian, but that wasn't unusual. Sunday was always a quiet day.

Monday morning came, wet and horrid. I went round to see if Mr Wilks wanted anything but no, as expected. The same answer as always. Back home I shouted: 'Nothing, Mum. He says he will see you later.' I grabbed a jam sandwich: 'I'm off to school. See you at teatime.'

'OK,' Mum shouted back, and I was straight out of the door just as Frankie was leaving.

'Come on, Chris,' she shouted.

'We won't be late, will we?'

'No, but we want to know how the police went on at Gary's on Saturday night, don't we?'

'It's not that we won't be told. Gary won't be able to shut up about it all day and a few days more. Each story will have a different end or beginning.'

We met Ian at the end of the road. Dad's bus went flying by with a toot-toot and a wave.

'He must be a bit late, going at that speed,' Ian observed.

I corrected him: 'No, when he gets to the bus station and when all the passengers are off, he'll park up and go for his break. Sooner there, longer for a break.'

We met Gary at the shop. His pockets were bulging with stuff he had lifted.

Don't Mr and Mrs Cherry suspect anything? I thought. They mustn't have. They were always having loads of kids and adults in. If stuff went missing on a regular basis, they were probably unaware about Gary. Let's face it: he'd been doing this regularly for a few years. I suspected that when Gary left school and started working with his father, the shop's profits would start to rise.

'Hi, Gary. What have you been up to since you left the police station with your dad in your new-but-old truck?'

'It's not old,' Gary disputed.

'Well, it's rusty.'

'Yeah, but it's newer than the other truck.'

'The old truck was near on clapped-out when you got it!' I sniggered.

'Yep, but this truck is newer than that one.'

'Well, it would be, wouldn't it?'

Ian butted in: 'Chris, drop it. You and Gary are going round in circles. Just agree to disagree. You're trying to make a point, but Gary can't see it. Anyway, Gary, what have you been up to?' He knew full well that DI Marshall and a PC had called on them on Saturday night.

Gary was desperate to tell all.

'You're not going to believe it but we had a visit from the police, about half past seven. The dog started barking and Dad went out to see what all the noise was about. A man on the other side of the gate was saying: "This is the police. Can you open the gate? We would like to talk to you, Mr Singleton, and to your son." Dad said: "Just hang on a minute, I'll fasten the dog up," which he did, and let them in.'

He went on to describe exactly what happened.

'DI Marshall talked to Dad first. He said: "Mr Singleton, you made a statement earlier today regarding what you and your son saw the other night down at the old mill."

'"Yer?"

'"We want to make sure about one or two things you saw and heard, and I've brought along a book of faces. We call them criminal mug shots. Have a look through them, please, while I have a word with your son."

'Dad shouted me from the next room: "This policeman wants to have a chat with you about what we both saw the other night." I didn't want to talk to them, but Dad insisted.

'"Right, Gary," the policeman says. "I want to hear in your own words what you saw in the old mill warehouse the other night. Just take your time. You have nothing to be frightened of."

'It must have been a good hour later that DI Marshall reappeared from the back room. "Have you had a good look at the mug shots, Mr Singleton?"

'"Yes, I have, and I've picked two out that look like them."

'"Oh, that's good. Now, Mr Singleton, if you could go into the room that Gary is in and show me the two pictures you've chosen I'll let your son Gary have a look and see if he can pick the same two out."

'They moved into the other room and browsed through the mug shots again with me. "Right, Mr Singleton, as I said before, I want to go over a few things that you said while making your statement this morning." Forty minutes later, or thereabouts, they had finished.

'Mum knocked at the door. "I've made you all a cup of coffee, and there's loads of biscuits. Help yourselves. You must be parched, with all that talking. Did you manage to pick anyone out from the photos, Gary?"

'"Just this one, that's all. I'm quite sure that's the only one that really sticks out."

'Mum sat in an armchair, listening, watching. DI Marshall spit biscuit crumbs as he spoke. "Well, Mr Singleton, the two mugs you managed to pick out were actually the two police officers that came to pick you up this morning. The one Gary picked out I believe is still in The Scrubs, but I'll have to check that out when we get back to the station."

'Twenty or so minutes later they left. As the yard gates shut behind them I let the dog out from its kennel. One minute he was there, the next he was barking his head off at the gates. "Good night, Mr Marshall," Dad said between the barks. No reply came back, just the doors on the police car slamming shut.

'Dad asked me what I made of it all. "I don't know, Dad," I said. "But I can't see them two blokes you identified being crooks, can you?"

'"As they are two coppers … no, not really. But that's the two I picked out." So that's what happened on Saturday night, Chris.' Gary's story was told, for now.

'They came round to ours,' I said. 'In fact they went to John's place then Ian's, Frankie's and ours.'

Ian added his bit: 'Yeah, and at each house they had a cup of tea or coffee. They must have been bursting when they left your place, Gary!'

'They didn't want to use the loo at ours, so they must have been already.'

'You mean they didn't want to use *your* loo?'

'What do you mean by that?'

'Nothing, Gary.'

'We have a really clean loo!' Gary defended.

Ian continued: 'Yes, you might have, but it's *outside*!'

'So?'

'Well, most houses these days have the loo *in* the house.'

'Yeah, but it's outside and if we're working outside it's handy.'

'But if you're inside and you want to use it and it's raining, you have to make a dash for it.'

'But it keeps us fit.' Gary could give as good as he got every time.

Frankie had heard enough: 'Just drop it, Ian. We'd better get a move on or we'll all be late for school.'

'We could do a bunk. Let's face it, we are only sitting around most of the day,' Gary enthused.

'You might be, Gary, but some of us are still trying to cram as much in as possible. Hey, John, have you been to see that bloke Hinchcliffe about what you want to do when you leave?' Frankie turned her attention to her next victim.

'You mean the careers officer? I have to see him tomorrow.'

'What are you going to tell him?'

'The same as I said before. I want to go and work with my dad.'

'But he said that was a no-brainer.'

'Well, that was then. He might have changed his mind.'

'So you have nothing else in mind job-wise?'

'I could be a brain surgeon!'

'Don't you need one first?'

'What, Frankie?'

'*A brain!*'

'Oh, ha ha, very funny.' John saw the funny side of that one.

'Come on then,' Frankie led. 'We're going to be late. See you all at break.'

'OK, Frankie.'

John, Ian, Gary and me just managed to get into class as the bell went. 'That was a close-run thing, Ian.'

'You're telling me.'

The day finished and nothing much had happened. Gary as usual got a telling-off for throwing chewing gum. I don't suppose it was the throwing, but where it landed – just at the side of Mr Hodges on the blackboard as he was writing out a question. But that was Gary. Nothing seemed to deter him.

Gary left us at the corner shop on our return home from school. As the three of us walked home, Ian said: 'It was strange that Gary's dad picked out the two policemen from the mug shots.'

'You know why, Ian?' I answered.

'No,' said Ian.

'They are the two who went to bring him in for questioning. While you are being told what's happening, you're subconsciously looking at their faces. So as Gary's dad looked through the book with their mug shots, he would pick them out straight away.'

'I never thought of that,' Ian conceded.

'Well, that's the only thing I can think of,' I said.

'You don't think they are part of the gang of robbers, do you?' Frankie asked.

I replied: 'I wouldn't have thought so, but you never know. Anyway, nothing has happened so far. And don't worry, when something does happen we'll hear about it. Even if it happens in school time, the news will fly round the classrooms. You know what Gary would be saying now?'

'What?' Ian asked.

'Are we having a day off for the robbery?'

***

Nothing noteworthy happened for the rest of that week. We all met up on Tuesday night and went down to the old mill. Nothing was happening there either, except a crane and a bulldozer had arrived.

'I expect they'll be wanting to pull it down shortly,' I commented.

'Then what?'

'Well, Dad approached the firm that has bought it to ask if his fishing friends can buy or lease the mill lodge so they can have fishing matches on the lake. Dad said if they get the chance of buying it or leasing it, they'll have to put a fence around it to stop people, or should I say kids, from falling in. What's up, Ian?' I asked.

'If they are going to use this place as a hideaway, they are going to have to do the robbery soon or there'll be no hideaway for them. See that big ball of metal on the end of that steel rope on the crane? Once that starts swinging, it won't take long for it to demolish the old mill,' Ian contemplated.

Suddenly a police car roared into the mill yard and stopped in a cloud of dust. The officer driving wound down his window.

'What are you lot doing here? You know you're trespassing!'

'But, but—' Ian was going to say something.

'Never mind,' I said briskly. 'Let's go, then we won't get into trouble.'

As we walked away Frankie spoke, then Gary said the same thing.

'Those two policemen are the same ones Dad picked out on Saturday night. Don't you think it's strange?'

'Well, they are the police and they do strange things,' Frankie said.

'Shall we go up the old railway line?' Gary asked.

'No, we better stick to the road.' Just as I said that the police car sped up the dusty road, leaving behind a cloud of dust.

Gary was home first as he lived closest to the mill, then me and Frankie. Ian was the last as he lived in the next street down. Mum was at home when I walked in.

'Where have you been tonight?' she asked.

'Down at the old mill. They've got a big crane there and it's got this massive steel ball hanging down from the jib. And there's a bulldozer. So it won't take them long once they start to pull it down.'

At that moment Joan walked in, with Ted following behind.

'You'll be like that for the rest of your life,' I kidded him.

'What do you mean, Chris?'

'Always one step behind our Joan.'

'Oh, go on, then. You're taking the micky again.'

Joan turned and looked. Ted knew by her look that I was right: she would become 'number one lady'.

'I hear you've been interviewed by the police,' Joan said to me.

'Yeah, but me, Frankie, Ian and John went in on our own. We didn't have to go.'

'What about Gary? Did he go or was he pushed?'

'We all decided to go when Gary told us what he and his dad saw the other night. The night after that we all saw two men turn up in a car, by which time we'd managed to hide where Gary and his dad hid the night before.'

'So go on, Chris. Tell us what happened.' Ted was hungry for details.

'Have I got to?'

'Well, if you don't we'll never know – or we'll hear it from someone else and it will be a completely different story. So go on, Chris, tell us.'

'All right, then,' I started.

Ted interrupted.

'Once upon a time…'

'It's not a nursery rhyme!' I barked.

'Come on, Chris.' Joan looked daggers at Ted for making that remark.

Nearly an hour later they had heard both accounts: my version of events, plus what Gary had told us had happened the night before. As I finished giving the blow-by-blow story I mentioned what had happened a few hours earlier, about the two policemen who had gone to the old mill and told us that we were trespassing. I told them about Gary's remark that these were the two faces his dad had recognised from the book of mug shots, as DI Marshall called it.

Ted said they would put the odd familiar face in just to see if people who were looking at them weren't simply looking and picking anybody out at random.

Chapter 9

The rest of the week passed much the same as it always did: bed, school, home for tea and mucking about. I didn't go near the old mill. Mum had heard they were pulling it down and Dad had warned me: 'Don't go down there. It's dangerous. And tell the rest of them: don't be heroes and land yourselves in hot water.' Strange way to put it, but I knew what he meant.

Ted stayed over at ours a couple of nights.

'Where's Ted sleeping, Mum?'

'Never you mind.'

'But I only asked.'

'He slept on the couch last night.'

I knew he hadn't. I could hear Ted and Joan whispering. They're only in the next bedroom along the landing.

'I bet it was uncomfortable on that, Mum.'

'What, Chris?'

'The couch!'

'Well, he said he had a bit of an achy back this morning.'

'I bet he did,' I mumbled to myself under my breath.

'What did you say?' My mum's got the ears of a bat.

'Nothing, Mum. Have I to go round and ask if Mr Wilks wants anything?'

'Yes, you would be a love if you could.' Love must be in the air. It's a long time since she has said anything like that to me!

'I'll nip round now, Mum.'

'Ask him if he wants anything from town. I'm going down this morning. Tell him you will drop it off for him when you come home from school like you always do. You know what to do, Chris.'

Just then Dad walked in.

'Where you off, Chris?'

'Round to Mr Wilks to ask if he wants anything from town. Mum's going down town by taxi.'

Dad smiled: 'It's a big blue-and-white taxi, don't you mean?' He meant his bus, of course.

'Must go, Dad.'

'See you, son.'

I didn't see Dad again that day. Sometimes I would see him at lunchtime or when I was walking home from school with Frankie and Ian. We usually left Gary at the corner shop. He never went into the shop at night, though I suppose he went if his mum wanted something later when he got home. He was always coming out of or going into the shop when we met him going to school in the morning.

Dad had had a letter asking him and his fishing friends if they would get in touch with Filby Developments about their proposal to buy or lease the old mill lodge. This made Dad smile even more.

'What's the letter about, Lenny?' Mum asked.

'It's about the old mill lodge. They want to meet and discuss our plans.'

'When are you meeting them?'

'It doesn't say – just gives a telephone number to ring, and soonest. I'll have to have a chat with the other members.'

'I didn't know there were other members.'

'You know: Bert, Big Mal and Geoff. And I sometimes see Mark. We all go fishing together sometimes.'

'You spend most of your day working.'

'Yes, driving that big blue-and-white taxi. You know why I'm working all those hours, Annie – to pay for the wedding. But don't worry, when they're both off our hands—'

Mum stopped him mid sentence: 'That's not a very nice thing to say, Lenny.'

'Well, you know what I mean. Then I'll be able to spend a bit more time…' He stopped and you could see what he was thinking. 'I'll be able to spend more time with you and Chris and do a little more fishing.'

'You haven't mentioned the dog.'

'You know he likes to go fishing with me.'

Mum had her own thoughts about fishing.

'He thinks he's going for a walk and where does he finish up? Sat on a grassy bank watching grown men holding a stick and dangling a bit of string, or something of the sort, in the water. No wonder the poor old dog goes to sleep!'

Just then I came in to tell Mum that Mr Wilks only wanted a lettuce and a couple of tomatoes.

'Are you going to school now?' Mum asked.

'Yes, I'm going with Frankie and Ian.'

'Annie, I'll be on the 10.15 into town,' Dad shouted through.

'OK, Lenny, see you then. Have a good day, love,' came Mum's reply as he walked out through the door. The bus company he worked for was losing a few pounds each week but saving Dad a few pounds by not charging the family to go into town. Because Mum had worked for the same bus company a few years ago – she was one of the first lady clippies – she had a lot of friends that still worked on the buses. They were nearly all drivers now, and Mum could get anywhere without paying.

Thursday of that week. Got up. Raining. It rained all day. Ted had stayed every night since the weekend. Usually when we had our tea at night it was me and Mum at the table. Joan didn't get in until around 6.30 and Dad was always working. But this Thursday was different. Dad had worked an early shift and wasn't required in the afternoon. Ted had finished early, and so had Joan. They were off to see the vicar. So on this Thursday we all sat down for tea at the same time, as a family.

'What's up, Ted?' I asked.

'What do you mean, Chris?'

'Have your mum and dad moved abroad, emigrated?'

'No, why?'

'Well, you're always here!'

'It's love. We're in love,' Joan asserted with a big smile. 'You'll be the same one day.'

'I don't think so,' I replied brusquely. 'You mean like Mum and Dad?'

'Well, yes and no,' Joan said.

'So how many kinds of love are there, Mum? Joan says there's many kinds of love and you and Dad have a different kind of love to them.'

'My love for your dad is much deeper, and no doubt he would say the same about me. Ours is a more meaningful love.' Mum gave Dad an affectionate look.

'You've lost me now, Mum.' I was baffled.

'Don't worry, son. One day you will find the same sort of love that Joan and Ted have!' Mum assured me.

Ted joined in: 'What about Frankie? What about her? You love her, don't you Chris?'

'No!'

'Then why are you going red? Your whole face has gone red!' Ted pressed his point.

'Mum.'

'What, Chris?'

'Can I have some more gravy, please?' I desperately tried to change the subject.

'Are we right?' Ted wasn't letting go.

'No, I don't love Frankie!'

'OK, Chris, we'd better leave it at that. Now eat your tea.' Mum had the last word.

Dad made conversation: 'Saw old man Singleton today. We had a bit of a chat. He'd come up to those old houses by the terminus. He was telling me that he had recognised two blokes out of the mug shot book, but it turned out one was still in prison, or so that inspector bloke said. The other one was that Duggins. He's a policeman, so I don't know what to think. Singleton said he'd been over the other side of town early morning and there was a lot of police walking about.' Dad paused to drink his cuppa. Then he said that while he had been in the bus station he'd seen two or three police cars around and he thought that was a bit odd, but other than that, there was nothing unusual. In fact, he thought the roads were very quiet for a Thursday morning and market day. Well, it had rained for most of the day.

'What time are you two off to see the vicar?' Dad asked Joan.

'About 6.30.'

'OK. The police seem to think something was going to happen but I haven't heard anything. Have you, Annie?'

'No, I haven't. Nothing's been on the radio, either.'

Joan remarked: 'Nothing has been said at the salon.'

'Nobody came in and said there's been a robbery at…' Dad asked Ted.

'I wouldn't know,' Ted replied. 'Old man Windle won't let us have the radio on in the office. He says it's a distraction.'

'I don't know why you work there,' Dad remarked.

'It's a job,' said Ted.

'But I think with your brains you could get a better job somewhere else. That place, Windle and Son, it's a dump. I think the windows and doors were last painted with a job lot of paint from the war.'

'Which war was that, Dad?' I asked.

'The Crimean War.'

'When was that, Dad?'

'When was what?'

'The Crimean War?'

'Sometime in the 1890s, I think. Anyway, you should know. You're the one at school.'

'Yes, but we're doing modern history, not that ancient stuff you did when you were there,' I scoffed.

Dad went on: 'Why don't you try that new engineering company that's starting up on Reads Road? I would think they'll need office staff. It can't be any worse than Windle. From the road it looks like a good place to work, I pick up one or two from there at night. I'll ask them if there are any vacancies for office staff. You never know. I'll see what I can do. At least you will come home as clean as you went. Not like now: go clean, come home grubby.'

Ted took the huff: 'Do I look grubby, Joan?'

'Sometimes you do!'

'What about now?'

'I think you should go and put a clean jumper or shirt on,' Joan suggested. Ted wears the jumpers, Joan wears the trousers!

I saw an opening: 'So, Ted, I take it you've moved in here, then?'

'No, not really.' Ted looked to Joan for support.

I was relentless: 'Well, how *would* you put it, then? You sleep here, you eat here and no doubt Mum washes your clothes here.'

'Now that's enough!' Mum barked. 'Ted's here for the time being. He is family – well, almost!'

'What are you doing tonight, Chris?' Dad tried to lighten things up. 'Staying home, going to watch a bit of telly?'

'What's on, Dad?'

'Football.'

'I won't, then. I think I'll just nip over the road and see Frankie.'

'What, your girlfriend?'

'No, she's not. I just want to see her about something.'

'What something? You were going to watch telly 'til you found out it was football.' Dad smiled at Mum.

Tea finished and me, Joan and Ted left the table. Mum and Dad stayed put and talked on.

'I told you a few days ago that Chris thought a lot about Frankie.'

'I knew months ago, Lenny, but you being a man it takes ages to sink in. Every time you mention Frankie he either goes red like tonight at tea, or he doesn't want to talk about her. You mark my words, Lenny.'

'I would have thought that Ian was more interested in Frankie than our Chris.'

'No, he likes that girl up near the terminus. Sandra Williams, I think that's what they call her.' Mum crunched a ginger nut.

Dad relaxed into his chair: 'How do you find all these things out, Annie?'

'Well, Ian's mum mentioned her a few weeks ago and when Ian's not round here or out with Chris and Frankie, he's seeing Sandra. In fact, Sandra went round to Ian's mum's house this last weekend.'

'Wow, what else do you know?'

'That would be telling.' Mum poured Dad a cuppa. 'All right, then. There's more but you mustn't say anything. You know Chris likes Frankie? Well, I was talking to Frankie's mother the other day in Old Man Wilks' shop. She'd come in for some candles and torch batteries, and she was saying Frankie says, "Chris does this, Chris does the other." It's all Chris, Chris, Chris. Then she said she had been in Frankie's bedroom and noticed a letter written to Chris starting *My darling Chris*… But don't you breathe a word or I'll be in trouble and so will you be. OK, Lenny?'

'OK, Annie, my lips are sealed.' Dad chortled softly.

'I hope so, for your sake.'

I came back into the room.

'I'm going over to Frankie's,' I told Mum and Dad.

'How long are you going to be?'

'Don't know, but not too long. OK, Mum?' And with that the front door slammed shut and I was gone.

Dad turned to Mum: 'I'll look out for that Sandra Williams. What's she look like?'

'Blonde, I think. A real looker. Quite small, a bit smaller than Ian, and slim. We'll hope it starts to blossom. Ian's a good kid. Mrs Hogan's done him proud, and being a single parent hasn't been easy. Still, we've played our part.'

'I'll see if I can spot her,' Dad mused.

'But don't do like you always do and give her a free lift. Make her pay. She's not part of our family or Ian's yet. No wonder the bus company isn't making any money, the way you and your cronies are doling out free rides. One of these days you'll be getting a visit from the inspector.'

'Yes, I know, Annie, but he's in our pockets. You know what I mean.'

'Yes, but all the same, be careful.'

'OK, Annie, I get the message.' Dad kissed Mum's cheek.

Next day, Friday, came with the usual sort of moan and groan, and to cap it all it was, or looked like it was, going to be a nice bright day. By the time I got up Ted had gone to work.

Friday was always an early start for Ted. He had to be in early as he had to get everything ready for payday before he took a trip into town with old man Windle in his shiny black Rolls-Royce. It was a joy to ride in, and Ted said it made him feel like royalty as he sat in the back.

There was just me and my big sister Joan for breakfast. Joan said: 'I don't want anything this morning, Mum, but I'll have a cup of tea. I can get something at the cafe. You know the one, the Golden Spoon, next door to the salon.'

'Are you sure?' Mum replied.

'I wouldn't get anything from there,' I said.

'Who's asking you?' Joan rounded on me.

'Well, John's dad calls it "Greasy Lil's". It's grotty in there. We were in there the other Saturday after we left the cop shop. The police dropped us in town and we decided to go in there for a coffee. We sat down and John put his hand on the table and it stuck to it. Just so greasy, you could tell it hadn't been wiped. We left. It's real crappy. Mum, you should make Joan have her breakfast or something before she goes out to work.'

'Oh shut up, Chris! Just shut up.' Joan was unsure.

'Anyway, hadn't you better get a move on? You're going to be late for work.'

'I'm fine. It's only five minutes to the road, then I'll get the bus. I have plenty of time.'

'I don't think you have.'

'And what makes you think that?'

'Well, if you look at your watch it says eight o'clock when in fact it's 8.20 by the clock on the wall!'

Joan looked aghast: 'Gosh, you're right, Chris. I'd better get my skates on. See you tonight about 6.30.'

Mum came in with some food: 'Where's she gone?'

'Gone to work, Mum.'

'She was in a rush! Why?'

'Because her watch had stopped. Joan was under the impression that it was only eight o'clock but it was 8:20.'

'OK, what time are you going?' Mum asked me.

'Why? Do you want me to go round to Old Man Wilks?'

'Don't call him old.'

'Well, he is, isn't he?'

'He's not that old.'

'He sure looks it!'

'No, I don't want you to go round there. I just wanted to know when you are going to school.'

'In the next ten minutes, Mum.' I turned to leave the room.

'Thank God. A bit of peace.'

'What, Mum?'

'I said a bit of peace. Nice and quiet for a change.'

Chapter 10

Friday morning dawned. Ted, as usual, had to be in work an hour early as this was payday for the workers. He could have got everything ready the night before but no – the person doing the wages had to start work an hour early. That's the way it had been done for years and years, so Ted just did the same.

Mr Windle would come into work and sit behind his highly polished huge brown desk at one minute to nine, never late. That was his motto: always be early, never late. But this morning *was* different. He was late!

Ted asked,

'Where's Mr Windle?'

Nobody knew or was prepared to say. It got to 9.30 then 9.45. Where was he? Still no sign.

'Perhaps he's broken down,' someone guessed.

'No, that can't be,' Ted answered.

'Why not?' Mrs Weston, one of the pay clerks, asked.

'That car he drives has never broken down,' Ted assured her.

'Well, there's always a first time.'

Mr Windle's car was a shiny black 1931 Rolls-Royce with a massive long bonnet and huge headlights that were more like searchlights, only they didn't move.

'Well, if he doesn't come soon I won't be able to go to the bank. And if I can't get there, I hate to think what will happen on the factory floor!' Ted complained.

Just then the car rolled to a halt outside the entrance to the offices where Ted was waiting.

'Sorry I'm late, lad. Had to take the wife to the salon. You know, the one where your young lady works. She's off out tomorrow with some of her friends, and you know what women are. Well, you will when you get married. *Are* you getting married, lad?'

'Yes, Mr Windle.'

'That's good. So are you ready to go, lad?'

'Yes, Mr Windle.'

'We'd better be off. Can't keep them down at the bank waiting.'

Ted sat on the back seat of the car. This was a car of sheer splendour. Ted started to think out loud.

'You know, Mr Windle, I would love to be driven away from the church in a car like this. It's so majestic, and I think Joan would like it as well. What a way to start married life! What a way to go on your honeymoon!'

'So this is the car you would like for your wedding car?'

The Rolls-Royce glided out towards the main road, the tyres crunching over the gravel before they made contact with the newly laid tarmac. Nothing further was said about the wedding or the car.

Mr Windle wasn't a slow driver, more a case of 'Let's get there and get back', but he was not mad either. Each week they went down the same roads. Ted's thoughts went to Joan. Would he see her today? They always went past the Silver Salon where Joan worked. Sometimes he would catch a glimpse of her, though most times he didn't if Mr Windle was going too fast.

'There seems to be a lot of traffic on the road, lad.'

They ground to a halt opposite the salon. Joan was there. Ted could see her. She turned her head. A smile appeared, then a wave. Ted raised his hand. Just as Mr Windle set off again, a police car whizzed past in the opposite direction, blue light flashing.

'I hope it's nothing serious, lad.'

Ted didn't hear him. He was still in another world, Joan's world. Seeing her in the window, a slight glance and a wave – that had made his day. He could now cope with anything the day threw at him. A broad smile crept over his face.

'We are almost there, lad. Are you ready?'

'I am,' Ted replied. 'The briefcase is attached to my wrist, as always.'

'Sorry we're a bit late, but you'll find out when you're married. Most times there's no reason.'

'I don't know how you do it, Mr Windle. I've been coming with you to the bank for nearly two years and you always manage to park right in front. How do you manage it?'

'Pure luck.' The car pulled silently to a halt. 'Right, off you go, lad,' Mr Windle instructed.

Ted left the car and walked to the bank's big brown doors. Once inside, he made his apologies for being late. The money was passed over, put in the briefcase and the briefcase was locked and safely secured to Ted's wrist.

As always, Ted went in through the bank's front doors but came out through the side door, the tradesman's entrance. It was always done this way. Why should today be any different? But just as the door was being unlocked there were two loud explosions!

'What was that?' the bank teller asked.

Ted replied: 'It's a car backfiring. We hear it most days. Somebody living near to Mr Windle's factory has an old car and it's always backfiring. I'd explain what causes it but I was late coming to the bank. Some other time maybe.' But, as it happened, it wasn't a car backfiring.

Mr Windle sat in his car waiting for Ted to re-emerge from the bank. He was twiddling with the knobs of his radio, as he always did. Having missed the ten o'clock news because they were late, he was trying to find the Home Service. He didn't like Tony Blackburn or Diddy David Hamilton. They played loud music, too loud. His wife had had the car the night before. He mimed what she was saying to him silently in his mind:

'You don't half listen to some rubbish.'

'What do you mean?'

'All you want to do is listen to the Home Service. Brighten up. You're becoming an old fart.'

He could hear himself saying,

'No, I'm not!'

Mr Windle only realised what was happening when he heard the first of the two bangs and steam started to rise from his car radiator. Suddenly his car door was wrenched open.

'Get out and get in the back, now!'

'What?'

'I said get out and get in the back now, old man.'

'I'm not old.'

'Into the back of the car now.' Another shot rang out, this time into the front tyre, and peppered the wheel trim with shot. The tyre hissed loudly as it slowly went down.

Mr Windle glanced at a car that had pulled across the front of his. It was a police car and the person behind the wheel was, he thought, a policeman with a face mask on. The man who was now bundling him into the back of his Rolls also appeared to be a policeman with a face mask on! No, it couldn't be the police. That was his last thought as he was pushed into the back of the car. He was knocked on the back of his head then he rolled off the back seat, out cold.

Ted had gone through the side door of the bank and had heard the door close and lock behind him when the gunman appeared. He had reloaded the shotgun in the short distance between Mr Windle's car and Ted. On seeing the policeman, Ted asked him what the problem was.

In reply he heard: '*Give us the money.*'

'Why?' Ted asked without thinking.

'Just give us the money and you won't get hurt.'

'You're not going to hurt me. You're a policeman.' Then the penny dropped. Ted could see the beads of sweat forming around the edges of the face mask. By this time another shot had been let off. Pigeons had taken off again from the surrounding buildings and most of them were circling quite high in the blue sky. Thud, thud and splat! The splat was from a pigeon that didn't quite make it, and it hit Ted right on the top of his head. On the way down his face it left two streaks of blood, so it appeared that Ted had been shot. Dead and bleeding, the pigeon fell to the ground.

'You can't have the money. The briefcase is attached to my wrist. The key is in Mr Windle's pocket,' Ted blurted out nervously.

'*Which one?*' demanded the policeman as he dragged Ted towards Mr Windle's car.

'I don't know. He changes it every week,' Ted whimpered, struggling to stay on his feet.

'Never mind. Get in the back of the car!'

'Which one?'

'The bloody black one. You can see the other car can't move!' shouted the angry policeman.

At this time people would normally have been going about their own business, but the street was noiseless. You could have heard a pin drop. On the other side of the road the door of the black car opened. Ted entered; he didn't see anything else because he too was hit from behind. He slumped on the back seat.

Two men got into the front seats of the car.

'OK, let's go. Couldn't get the briefcase. It's attached to his wrist. That's why he's coming along with us.'

'What are we going to do?'

'Just put the siren on and get us out of here.'

Within a few minutes they were out of town, heading for the car changeover. As the police car sped out of town with the blues and twos going, word started to spread that there had been a robbery at the bank in Leech Road. By lunchtime the whole school was talking about it.

My dad became aware that something had happened as he turned the corner into Leech Road. He had noticed a police car indicating to pull away from the bank. Thinking nothing of it, he flashed the bus lights, allowing the police car to go. As he passed Mr Windle's car he noticed that it had a flat tyre and there seemed to be a lot of water in the road, but he was unable to see anyone in the Rolls-Royce and thought that Mr Windle had gone into the bank. Also, it seemed strange for a Friday that Leech Road was very quiet. Normally on a Friday there were a lot of people out shopping.

As Dad pulled up at the bus stop, passengers started to leave the bus. He glanced in his rear-view mirror and saw two police cars arriving behind him. Then an ambulance drove into view. Being quite a nosy sort of person, as the last of his passengers got off the bus Dad decided he would go and find out what had happened. By this time there was quite a large police presence. He heard a few bystanders talking: 'There's been a robbery,' 'Some young lad has been shot,' and 'That's what the ambulance was doing here.'

A thought went through his mind that this was the bank that Ted collected the wages from. He asked around: 'Anybody seen the man who's the driver of that car there?'

Nobody spoke. Dad went over to the car and had a look in the front. Nothing. Wait a minute! He could hear a groaning sound coming from the back. As he opened the back door of the car, Mr Windle's foot dropped out.

'Over here, mate! This man requires medical attention!'

'Who is he?' asked the nearest policeman as he dashed to help.

'It's Mr Windle. He owns that factory just out of town – Windle and Son.'

'Where's Ted Harker?' Dad asked Mr Windle. Nothing. 'Where's Ted Harker?' Dad tried to get a response.

'I don't know, but I think he went with the robbers,' Mr Windle said in a weak voice.

The policeman asked,

'What do you mean, went with the robbers?'

'Well, he had a briefcase that had the money in but it was attached to his wrist by a metal cord, so he couldn't take it off and give them the money. He had to go with them.'

'He'll be OK,' the policeman tried to reassure Dad.

'I hope you're right,' said Dad and went back to the two policemen, who were looking at something on the ground. Lenny looked down and saw spots of blood.

'What do you think?' one policeman said to the other.

'Looks like someone has been shot.'

Dad said: 'Or it could be those pigeons over there. They seem to have quite a lot of blood leaking from their bodies.'

A policeman looked hard at Dad.

'And who are you, then?' he demanded.

'Well, I'm the bus driver that let the first police car go.'

'What do you mean, let the first police car go?' So Dad explained what he saw and what he did. 'Did you get the number of this car?' the policeman asked.

'Well, no – but hang on. You know how many police cars you have. You should be able to work it out from the description. It was a police car!' Under his breath Dad said: 'No wonder they are called plods. This pair are as thick as two short planks.'

'Anyway, I have to go. I have a bus and passengers to take to the other side of town. If you need to speak to me again, get in touch with the bus company. No doubt you have their telephone number.' Dad started to walk away.

One policeman asked: 'What is the number, then?'

'Sorry, I must dash.' Dad was away to his bus. The bus filled up with passengers and they left the scene. Most of the passengers were talking about what had happened at the bank.

The only person who wasn't talking about anything to anybody was Ted Harker. He was lying face down on the back seat of the car he had been thrown into. Now he was coming round, he didn't say anything but started listening carefully.

The radio crackled into life.

'Duggins, where are you? And who have you got with you?' a voice broadcast.

'Montrose,' PC Duggins replied.

'Where are you?'

'Down near the old mill, Sarge.'

'What the hell are you doing down there?' The voice got angry.

'Some horses have got out of their field. We are trying—'

Duggins was interrupted.

'You *are* trying! Now get your butt and Montrose back into town. Better still, get to the bank and report to DS Kidd. He'll tell you what he wants doing – and don't stop along the way for a butty.'

'What about the horses, Sarge?'

'I'll get in touch with the owner. Now get a move on.'

'Sarge, what's happened at the bank?'

'There's been a robbery and whoever did it has taken a hostage. Now get moving.'

'OK, Sarge.' The radio went dead.

PC Montrose spoke to Duggins: 'As if you didn't know what happened at the bank this morning! We both know we robbed it.'

'Yes, *we* know that, but you have to make out you didn't know, stupid!'

'So what are we going to do with our friend in the back?' They both turned around and looked at Ted, who still appeared to be out cold.

Ted had been listening to the conversation between these two and the sergeant, thinking that no one would suspect two policemen of robbing a bank. Mind you, they did have what appeared to be an old police car and they were wearing face masks to protect their identity. Then the penny really did drop with an almighty thud.

'I'm their problem now. They thought I would just hand over the money but I couldn't because it was attached to me, to my wrist. Shit!' That was the only word that sprang to mind.

At the same time, shit came out of Duggins' mouth: 'Go on then, clever clogs. What are we going to do with him and where are the other two? You know, our partners in crime.'

Just then a burgundy Jaguar car came over the brow of the hill and flashed its lights once. Duggins did the same. The Jag rolled slowly to a stop.

'Sorry, lads, it took a bit longer this morning. Problem in the town. One copper we spoke to said there had been a robbery at the bank and they had taken a hostage.'

They all laughed, except Ted. He had just realised that Duggins had come round to speak to me about what we had seen in the old mill.

'You're right. We had to take a hostage.'

'Why?'

'He had the briefcase fastened to his wrist. That's the one thing we didn't plan for. Anyway, he's in the back of the car, still out cold.' That's what they thought.

Ted thought,

'I'd better stay that way so they don't think I've overheard anything.'

'The sarge wants us back in town. Pronto!'

'Right, get him out of the car and dump him in the back of ours. We'll sort him out.'

'What you going to do with him?'

'First things first, get something to cover his eyes. Don't worry, we'll get the briefcase. Didn't he have any keys with him?'

'No, the old man in the car had them but it was too late to ask him for them.'

'Why?'

'Cos he was hit over the head and bundled into the back of his car.'

Ted was dragged out of the back of the car, blindfolded and dumped into the Jag.

'Right, we'd better be off. Wipe that bit of blood away, otherwise we'll have some explaining to do.'

Duggins and Montrose drove back into town. Roadblocks were being set up. They arrived back at the bank and reported to DS Kidd.

'You've arrived! I hear you have been on a round-up. Let's see if you can round up the ones who did the bank job, then!'

***

Dad arrived back in town with another load of passengers. As got off the bus, another driver was waiting to take over. 'You've been relieved,' he told Dad.

'Why?'

'Well, word has got around that the person they've taken hostage is none other than Ted Harker. You know – your Ted, the one that's going out with your Joan. The boss has sent me down to relieve you. Go and collect Joan. She will be in a bit of a state. Take her home.'

Dad stood for a second.

'Ann, my Annie … if she hasn't heard it on the radio yet, she soon will. It's the talk of the town. OK, I'll go. Thanks, Bert.'

'No doubt you will be in touch with the boss. He just said, "Tell him to go".'

'What shall I do with the takings from today?'

'Put them in the green bag and I'll hand it over when I get in.'

'OK, Bert, see you later.'

Dad arrived at the Silver Salon. Joan was in a bit of a state.

'Come on, Joan, love, don't worry,' he said.

'But they've got Ted!' Joan was shaking.

Dad put his arms around her.

'I'm sure Ted will be all right. He has his head screwed on, and he won't do anything daft. You'll see. He'll be home in no time. Come on, Joan, you know I'm right.'

'But are you, Dad?' Joan was inconsolable.

'There's a taxi outside, Mr Hart,' a voice said.

'Thanks.'

The salon owner spoke softly.

'I hope everything goes all right.'

Dad said,

'There's a lot of police around. There are roadblocks everywhere. I can't see them getting too far, can you?'

'I hope for everyone's sake they catch them soon. You don't know what the world's coming to, do you?' She held the door open for Dad and Joan as they walked to the taxi. Dad didn't reply.

He spent the journey home trying to comfort Joan. Mum heard a car pull up outside. Before the car doors slammed shut, she was waiting by the open front door. Joan rushed into Mum's arms and burst into tears.

'Come on, love,' Dad heard Mum say. With that, they all went into the house.

'Have you heard what has happened?' Dad asked Mum.

'Yes, it's been on the radio all morning. They say Mr Windle is in a bad way: head injuries and shock. Shock can do more damage than anything else. Ted was talked about as the one that has been taken hostage.'

Mum sat down with and comforted Joan as best she could.

By the time lunch came around in school, everybody was talking about the bank robbery.

'They say one was shot dead. The guy with the money, he was dragged kicking and screaming to the getaway car.' There was a real buzz in the schoolyard as well as in the classroom.

'Sir, sir, what's happening now at the bank?' one lad asked his teacher.

A message came from the headmaster: would Chris Hart go to see the headmaster right away?

I knocked once at the headmaster's door.

'Come,' came the reply. I walked in wondering if I had done something wrong, but I knew I hadn't.

'Sit down, Chris. I just want to have a word with you.' The headmaster told me what had happened at the bank that morning, not the confused statements that were circulating around school. No murderers, just the plain truth. Then he told me that the police were coming to talk to me. I was suspicious and asked why. The head didn't have an explanation.

'But what do the police want to see me for?' I questioned again.

'They want to have a chat with you, then they'll take you home. I believe your dad took Joan home this morning,' was all that the head could say.

The police arrived shortly after the headmaster finished telling me what had happened.

'Right, Christopher, I just want you to help us with a few questions,' the policeman said firmly.

'You should be talking to Mr Singleton and his son, Gary. They saw everything the night before. We went back into the old mill for, as we thought, a look round. Then they came back.'

'You said they took the old car number plates away. Did any of them say what they were going to do with those?'

'Chuck them in the canal. I think that's what one of them said.'

'Anything else?'

'They rummaged under the loading bay and one of them pulled out some old sacking. There was, or it looked like, a shotgun, but one with a very short barrel.'

'Sawn-off shotgun,' the police officer replied.

I described the scene.

'The man with the gun pointed it towards us but he couldn't see us, and then we heard a click. The other man said, "Put it away," then he pointed it towards a skylight and just fired the thing with a tremendous bang. Pigeons scattered. A couple plummeted to the ground, with lots of feathers spiralling down behind them. One of the birds was fluttering its wing. The man who fired the gun walked over to it and kicked it away into some old tins.'

'Is there anything else you think might help us with our search for these robbers, Christopher?'

'I don't think so, but you should have a word with Mr Singleton. He might be able to help you.'

The police concluded their interview with me, for now.

'Right son, we'll take you home. Your dad told us what school you went to and we said we would escort you back.'

'Am I going home in one of your new police cars?'

'No, just an old police car.'

The policeman and I walked out to the police car that was waiting for us. I turned to the policeman and said that the car used by the two men I saw on the night after Gary and Mr Singleton was just like the police car parked there.

'Are you sure?'

'Yes,' I said. 'Just like that one: a Wolseley 6.40. If you go round to see Mr Singleton he will tell you what type of car it was. I know when I saw it it was black like that one, but it didn't have any signs on to say it was a police car. It was just plain black.'

'Did you see the number plates that they were going to get rid of?' the policeman asked.

'No, but Frankie did. She found them hidden under some rags and things.'

'Frankie will be Miss Frances June McKay?'

'Yeah, she lives right opposite us. You can't miss her – she has red hair.'

'I think we'd better have another chat with her when we drop you at home.'

We got into the car and set off with a roar out of the school gates. I felt quite important being driven home in a police car! The sirens were turned on for a while so we could cut through the traffic. They soon got me home.

The policeman went over to Frankie's and asked about the number plates but Frankie couldn't remember what the numbers or letters were.

I found out the day after that they had called on Ian and John. They couldn't give the police any more information. Mr Singleton was able to confirm that it was a Wolseley but what type he wasn't sure. Gary, as usual, just stood holding the dog and looking thick. Well, he couldn't *look* thick – he *was* thick!

By the end of the day Mr Windle was in hospital, nursing a big lump on his head and cuts and bruises. Those were caused by falling off the rear passenger seat and not being able to get up. Ted was still missing and nobody knew where he was. Hopefully he was still alive – everybody hoped he was. The bank had lost some of its money and the robbers had got clean away. By nightfall the roadblocks were being dismantled and traffic started to move a bit quicker. Joan was at home, sobbing her heart out. Mum kept trying to console her but to no avail.

I said,

'Will I be going to school tomorrow?'

'No, I don't think so, not until we find out what's happening,' answered my dad.

'But I'm supposed to be playing for school against Wingates. It was put to Saturday a few weeks ago. I told you at the time.'

'I don't think you will be playing so you can forget it, OK?'

'OK!'

The only things we knew for certain were that Ted had gone missing, taken hostage, and the robbers were driving a black car like a police car but without police markings on it. But they must have put the siren on and police signs for the robbery. Plus, the driver was wearing a policeman's uniform, just like the robber, but they both were wearing face masks. It couldn't have been one of the police's real cars as they were all out on patrol.

The kids and Mr Singleton mentioned a red-coloured Jag, but not one red Jag had been seen by any of the police at the roadblocks.

'So, DS Kidd, where will your enquiries go from here?' DI Marshall asked as he walked into DS Kidd's office.

'I don't know. I just don't know where to start. We have nothing really to go on except this so-called police car. I've been round all the car dealers in the area. Nobody has had one for sale for ages and some have never sold one at all. The ones that have have all been legal and above board. What do you think, inspector?'

'Have you rung round all the other police forces to ask if they've sold their old cars on?'

'Yes, I've spoken to every police force in the UK. Nothing doing,' DS Kidd lamented.

'Anything on the sawn-off shotgun?'

'We did find some cartridges, locally bought, but weeks ago.'

'Did the old man, Mr Windle, see anything?'

'He just said the police car flashed past him going the other way.'

'About what time?'

'Just after ten, near the Silver Salon. Then within about ten minutes they pulled in front of him at the bank. They blasted his radiator and front tyre, then hit him. He didn't see anything else.' DS Kidd shook his head, mopped his brow and sighed.

Chapter 11

Detective Inspector Marshall brought his fist firmly onto the desktop … thud! Everything rose up and crashed back down. Pens, paperclips, even two old dog-ends, stubbed out in an old bottle lid deputising as an ashtray.

'What have we got so far? Nothing but one person missing and one old guy in hospital. It's not good enough. I want these robbers. They're on our patch. They must be somewhere out there!' Little did he know that one of the crooks was standing just behind him: the one who took Ted hostage, the one who fired the shotgun. Yes, Duggins.

'What do you want?' demanded DI Marshall.

'I've made you a mug of tea, sir.'

'Right, thanks,' Marshall replied.

'I expect I'll have a new partner tomorrow,' Duggins quizzed.

'What makes you think that, Duggins?'

'Well, Montrose is off on his holidays.'

'When did he decide that?' asked a surprised inspector.

'Weeks ago, sir.'

'I don't think he is. All police leave has been cancelled!'

'But—'

'There's no buts. While this lot are out there no policeman is going anywhere – Blackpool or Benidorm. Got it? And while you're here, Duggins, you can tell Montrose I want to see him in my office right away, and I mean right away! Got it?'

'Yes, sir,' Duggins replied, standing at attention.

Montrose was waiting, nursing a mug of coffee.

'Are you ready, Duggins?'

'Yer, but you aren't.'

'What do you mean by that?'

'The boss…'

'Who?'

'DI Marshall wants to see you in his office right now, and don't be late.'

'What's it about, then?'

'Can't say. He just wants to see you right away.'

Montrose hurried out. A few minutes later he was back, firing on all cylinders.

'The bastard! He's cancelled my leave. Damn. But we're flying out to Spain first thing in the morning. What am I going to tell the wife?'

'Tell them nothing. Go on bloody holiday. You deserve it, man. Just go sick with something.'

'What about today's little escapade?' Montrose was seething.

'Don't worry. We'll just carry on working to the plan. I'll see you later, then you'll know what happens. You have your story, you're on holiday. They won't suspect a thing.'

'OK, see you about eight o'clock.' Montrose calmed a little.

They met up at eight o'clock and walked down to the old mill, as arranged. It was still quite light. There were no horses in the field next to the mill, which was strange. There were always horses in there. It never dawned on them that there hadn't been any horses there for a few weeks. The owner of the field had sold it to the people who were going to build houses on the mill site.

They were lucky that the mill was still standing when they had started to plan the robbery. Then they started to pull it down. Plans got altered. The bank robbery was brought forward. Then demolition work stopped due to asbestos being found in the pipework that needed specialists to clear it away. So then the robbers got some leeway. Now they had done the job.

'All we have to do is split the money,' Duggins told Montrose. 'You're on holiday. I'll be working with my ear to the ground, so to speak. Then when the dust settles and they can't get any further with their enquiries, I'll be able to go away and soak up a bit of sun myself.'

'You're forgetting one thing.'

'What's that, Montrose?'

'The hostage. What are we going to do with him? Answer me that! And what are you carrying by your side?'

'It's the gun.'

'I thought you got rid of it this morning.'

'No.'

'Why not?'

'I didn't have time.'

'So where has it been all day?'

'Under my seat.'

'What, in the car?'

'Yep.' Duggins was smug.

'Are you mad, or what?'

'When we went in for lunch I carried it in. You saw me go to my locker.'

'Yes, but I didn't know what you were doing.'

'I put it in the locker. Then tonight, while you were seeing the boss, I went and got it.'

'And nobody saw you?'

'Well, yes.'

'Who then?'

'That scatty new WPC, Christine Thingy.' Duggins shrugged.

'You mean Christine Thompson?' Montrose gasped.

'But she didn't have a clue. I don't know how she got into the police. She's all over the place.'

'Well, you'd better hope you're right. And what are you going to do with the other problem?'

'What, that young lad? Blow him away! Headline in the local paper – *Hostage Found Dumped In A Ditch Dead.*' Duggins was blasé. Montrose was scared.

'The police'll start to look in every nook and cranny, as you well know, being one! So am I! They'll go through everything, leave no stone unturned. So think very carefully before you do something you will regret … we'll *all* regret, right? Think on, Duggins!'

'OK, you made your point. What are we going to do with him? Have you never thought the other two might have already got rid of him?'

'We can only wait and see.' By this time they were quite close to the old mill gates.

'Can you see the car?'

'No. I wonder where they are.'

'We did arrange 8.30, the old mill yard.'

'Well, yes. Do you think they are out getting rid of the body?'

'In your dreams, but I hope they haven't done anything stupid. Don't forget, the one with the Jag has just come out of prison.'

'Yeah, but what had he done time for?'

'I heard it was armed robbery down in the Smoke. They got quite a lot of money, but someone in the gang grassed him up to the police.'

'Yes, our lot. Who's the other bloke?'

'Oh, you don't want to tangle with him. He knifed someone during a robbery. They eventually died. He got eight years in nick.'

'So they are the two professionals and we are the two mugs who do all the hard work.'

'It wasn't hard, was it? We'd gone over and over it. It went like clockwork.'

'Yes, until you couldn't get the money – sorry, you did get the money and you also got a hostage!'

'Just give it a rest, Montrose.'

'How much money do you think we got?'

'About fifty thousand pounds.'

'Never!'

'Well, work it out. Windle employs about fifty men on the shop floor, then there's three or four drivers making deliveries, plus all the office staff – and it's coming up to the annual holidays. There's weekly pay and holiday pay. Yes, I think there will be around fifty thousand pounds we've netted.'

Just then there was a whistle. They both glanced to their right. Words rang out: 'Over here, come on.' Within seconds the four robbers were together in the old loading bay.

***

By the time the school bell rang for home time, stories of the robbery were rife. Schoolchildren told what had happened in many different ways, from Ted being killed at the scene to him giving away the bag of money. Ted Harker had been a pupil at the school up to about four years previously. Good results had got him a job at Windle and Son. The son might have still been around but for a motorcycle accident about two years ago. He was motorbike daft, but it was the speed that killed him. Rain or shine, he would turn up to work on his bike, but going home at night was a different kettle of fish.

He lived about four miles from work, just past where his father Mr Windle lived. Mr Windle left work first, his son a few minutes later. He just had to catch his dad up and overtake him before he reached home. On the night of the accident it had been raining most of the day. Mr Windle and his son had just received a big order from the Middle East and had been working out production plans. Both left late. In fact Ted, who usually worked on, left before them. The next morning there was deathly silence in the office. Nobody spoke.

'What's wrong, then?' Ted enquired.

'Haven't you heard, Ted?'

'Heard what?'

'Mr Windle's son was killed yesterday!'

'What? When?'

'Last night, going home from work. You know he always went flat out trying to beat his father home. He got to that bad left-hander by the railway bridge, lost control going too fast and went straight across the road. And, would you believe it, he crashed into the front of Big Harry's wagon coming the other way! The road was closed for about four hours, they say. He was killed outright!'

'You mean *our* Big Harry?'

'Yer, he's just got a new Leyland Hippo!'

'I can't see Mr Windle being in today. He and Mrs Windle will be very upset at losing a son like that.'

Just then the door opened and in stepped Mr Windle! Everybody's jaw dropped.

'Sorry to hear about your son,' they chorused.

'Thank you all, but work must go on.' Mr Windle went and sat quietly at his desk as usual.

Two years later, the same sort of thing was happening again, only this time Mr Windle was in hospital and Ted Harker had vanished off the face of the earth.

Big Harry didn't go into work the day after the crash. He took a few days off: doctor's orders. He still works for Mr Windle and yes, he is still driving his Leyland Hippo.

***

Frankie, Ian and Gary had heard on the grapevine that the police had taken me home earlier in the afternoon. Frankie walked home with Ian and Gary. They said their goodbyes to Gary at the corner shop.

'Tell you what, Gary, if we're going out later we'll call for you,' Frankie said.

'OK, Frankie,' replied Gary.

'I think I'll call on Chris when I get home. What do you think, Ian?'

'That sounds fine. I was going to call but I don't think I will.'

'Anyway, if you're going out later give us a call,' Frankie invited

'We haven't got a phone. It's been cut off,' admitted Ian.

'Haven't you?'

'No.'

'Then come round to ours about seven.'

'OK,' Ian replied.

Frankie called at my house.

'How are things?' she asked with genuine concern.

'Not too good. Joan's upset. It's on the radio all the time. We've found out it's going to be on the telly at six. Mum's upset because Joan's upset; Dad's upset because Mum's upset. The dog's upset.'

'Why is the dog upset?'

'Well, nobody will feed him!' I smiled at Frankie.

'Are you coming out later, Chris?'

'Dad,' I called out.

'What?'

'Can I go out later, just for an hour or so, round to Frankie's?'

Mum shouted back: 'Don't go wandering off.'

'We might go down to Gary's.'

'OK but don't be late. We don't want you to go missing.'

'As if. See you at seven, Frankie.'

'Ian said he would come round and I said to Gary we might call for him as well. OK. See you at seven, Chris. Where are we going? Have you any ideas?'

'What about the old mill? It's just about flat, but Dad says they can't do any more as there's something called asbestos and they need special people to remove it. They won't be able to get rid of it for a couple of weeks so I think the old loading bay is still there. That asbestos is in the boiler house and I think Dad said it's wrapped around the pipes to keep the heat in. Well, something like that.'

Ian duly arrived at seven o'clock and banged on our door.

'Mum sends her regards.'

'Mum,' I shouted through.

'What?' Mum replied.

'Ian's mum sends her regards and she is sorry for what happened to Ted.'

'Tell Ian to tell his mum thanks when he sees her later on.'

'Did you hear that, Ian?'

'Yep.'

'And don't be out too long tonight. It's been a long day for everyone. And don't forget.' Mum laid down the law.

'OK,' I replied.

'Come on, let's go for Frankie. Then we'd better call for Gary. If we don't, you know what he's like – he'll be moaning on Monday.'

'Shall we go down the old mill?' asked Ian.

'Might as well. I don't know of anywhere else to go. Dad was saying that the bloke who bought the old mill is going to build houses on it and he's keen on fishing. So Dad, along with his mates, has invited this bloke to be president of the fishing club. That way the bloke, whatever he's called, will fence off the mill lodge and landscape it.'

'Why fence it off?' Gary asked. By this time we had called for him and he had, as usual, started asking silly questions.

'Why do you think, Gary?'

'Don't know.'

'To stop young children from falling in.'

'But there's no *sharks* in there, so they won't get eaten!'

Frankie slapped Gary on his shoulder: 'Are you for real, Gary?'

'What do you mean?' Gary looked surprised.

'The fence is to stop young kids from getting anywhere near the side of the lodge and to stop them from falling into the water and drowning,' Frankie said sternly.

Gary still looked vacant then he uttered a reply: 'They should learn to swim!'

You could see in Frankie's eyes that she was starting to get mad. She didn't suffer fools gladly, certainly not this particular fool!

'Just leave it, Frankie. You're wasting your time,' Ian told her.

'I know, but how thick can you be? He just can't see it.'

By this time we were getting close to the old mill.

'There's not much left now, is there?' Ian stated. Standing right in front of us was a pile of bricks – some whole, others broken up. Window frames were broken and glass scattered all over.

'Be careful where you tread,' I warned.

Gary blurted out another question: 'Why?'

'What do you mean, why?'

'Well, Gary, you don't want to cut your feet.'

'But I have boots on.'

'All right, you have boots on. Just be careful and watch out for nails.'

Before Gary could ask another 'why' question, Ian joined in: 'Because you might get one through the sole or heel of your boot,' he emphasised strongly. That kind of shut Gary up for a while.

We walked through where the gateway used to be. On one side the wall was attached to the big stone pillar where, at one time, hung one half of a pair of huge iron gates. The other pillar was lying on its side looking like a fallen statue, and this was where the gatehouse with the weighbridge once stood. The weighbridge platform was still there, but the gatehouse was mostly just a pile of bricks. The gatehouse door hung from a door frame that was supported by half a wall and part of a window frame with little glass in it. The loading bay appeared to be intact but the huge roller door, once dark green in colour, was now out of its runner. On one side, and about six feet from the ground as you looked in, it appeared to be very dark and dank. The boiler house, like Dad had said, was still standing. Most of the windows were broken. It looked like someone had tried to wrench the door from its hinges but had failed, leaving the door half-on, half-off.

Me, Ian, Frankie and Gary entered the boiler house. The two massive boilers had their fire doors open, just waiting to be lit. The brass pipes and valves, once polished so you could see your face in them, had now turned to a dull hue.

'What do you think will happen to all this?' Frankie pondered.

'I heard they are hoping to preserve it. That's why they are having these people in to remove the lagging and replace it with new material. No doubt they'll overhaul the big beam engine, get that up and running.' I gave my thoughts.

'What's the point?' As expected, Gary had to ask the question.

I tried once again to educate Gary.

'Well, Gary, it's like this. This was one of the very last working mills in the area to be driven by a coal-fired beam engine. So, as it's being demolished, quite a number of townspeople have put up a petition to save it and make it into a working museum. Are you with me so far, Gary?' Still the vacant look. 'And just think, one day you might bring your son or daughter to see it working!'

'I'm not getting married – and if I do, we are *not* having kids!'

'You never know, Gary. Things might change for you in a few years' time.'

'Dad always said he never wanted kids,' Gary said.

'And then you turned up,' Ian tutted, then under his breath said he wished Gary's dad had drowned Gary at birth. Me and Frankie looked at Ian and agreed. Gary, in the meantime, stood poking at the bricks.

'What are you looking for?' asked Frankie.

'Scrap!'

'Is that all you can think about?'

'Yep, every minute of the day, and probably during the night as well, Frankie.'

By now we'd been in the old mill about half an hour. We were about to leave the boiler house when we heard something approaching.

'Better stay here and stay low. We don't want to be seen. The police are always coming down here,' Gary said.

'How do you know that, Gary?' Frankie asked him.

'Because they go past our place and they go shooting past when I've been out with the dog at night. Some nights I've had to step right back into the hedge. I know it's a rough old road, but that doesn't stop them from flying up and down.'

'What do you think they hope to find?'

'I don't know but it's not scrap metal.'

'Why's that, Gary?'

'Because me and me Dad have got it all – well, most of it.'

'Have you had permission to take it, then?'

'Yep. Dad went to see the bloke that's running the show and asked him if we could take all the scrap metal,' Gary informed us.

I sensed a joke and said: 'Yes, just like that TV ad: "The Man from Del Monte, he says yes."'

'I don't think that's the name of the firm that's doing the demolition,' Gary answered.

'Forget it, Gary,' Ian said. 'They are called Jones Brothers.'

'Who are called Jones Brothers?'

'The firm that's pulling down the old mill.'

'Not Del Monte?'

'Just let it drop.'

'Let what drop?'

'Forget I ever said anything about Del Monte!' I insisted.

Just then the red-coloured Jag entered the mill yard about twenty feet from the door to the boiler house, just where me, Ian, Frankie and Gary had entered less than forty minutes earlier. The Jag rolled to a stop in a cloud of brick dust and general road dust.

'What are we going to do now, Chris?' Frankie muttered.

'We'll just have to sit tight and hope they go away in a few minutes.'

The bloke driving the car looked around then set off very slowly and drove into the old loading bay, getting the car out of sight.

'What we going to do, Chris?'

'Like I said, we'll have to stay here 'til they go. If we try to go out through the door we came in they'll surely see us, and heaven knows what will happen then.' I was trying to keep the situation under control. 'There was a door at the end of where the cylinder is and that leads into the warehouse. We are better off going near to that door. If I remember, when we were looking round months ago I noticed it on the warehouse side. There were piles of old pallets, so you couldn't get through. So if we go to where the door is, we might be able to open it slightly and listen to what they are saying.'

As luck would have it, it was quite dark and the door was open about a foot. What stopped it from opening further were the piles of pallets. As we looked through the gaps in the pallets, we could make out two figures – the two who had arrived in the car. The taller one was smoking. You could smell the cigar and, as he drew air through it, a red glow appeared at the end.

'What time did you say we should meet here, Jim?' asked the man with the cigar.

'Eight o'clock.'

'Another twenty minutes to wait, then.'

'No point in standing around out here. Come on, we might as well wait in the car.'

'But I'm smoking.'

'Well, sit in the car and have the window open slightly.'

'No, I'll have another couple of drags then I'll put it out.'

The cigar was stubbed out and the men got into the car.

'What are you doing?'

'Putting a bit of music on.'

'Well, don't put it on loud. We don't want to draw attention to ourselves.'

'But if anyone sees the car in here with the radio on they'll think we are a courting couple, especially if the windows get a bit steamed up. Nobody will take any notice.'

Me, Frankie, Ian and Gary were listening to all this.

'What do you think? Make a run for it while they are in the car?' Ian suggested.

'No, we better hadn't. It appears that they are going to meet somebody at eight o'clock. We can't very well go – and besides, these two blokes are in the robbery or something to do with the robbery. It's the same car we saw the other week and Gary says they are the same two blokes he and his dad saw the other night.' I was thinking clearly. 'They might know what happened to Ted. You know Ted? Him that's going out with our Joan!'

'All right, Chris, don't get upset,' Frankie whispered. 'So we are better off sitting tight and we might find something out, perhaps more than the police. I see they aren't down here.'

'Well, they won't be, will they? They'll be running around town like headless chickens,' Ian said.

***

DS Kidd had hurriedly organised a meeting to discuss what they had found out and where they were going next. Nowhere! All their searching had got them nowhere.

Meanwhile, PC Duggins and PC Montrose were wandering down the road leading towards the old mill. Duggins, being the cocky plonker of a PC that he was, had the shotgun and was waving it about. It was in an old sack so you couldn't tell what it was. Every now and again he took aim at dandelions and tried to knock the heads off. Once or twice he succeeded, but more often than not he missed.

The swinging of the shotgun got the better of Montrose.

'For God's sake, Duggins, just walk sensible with the shotgun down by your side. Anybody would think you were Audie bloody Murphy.'

'Who?'

'You heard me.'

'Oh, all right, then.'

By this time they were nearly at the mill yard.

'Can't see the car, can you?'

'Well, it's not going to be stuck in the yard, standing out like a sore thumb, is it?'

'No, I see your point.'

'This point?' Duggins swung the shotgun towards Montrose for effect.

'No, not the bloody gun again. Why didn't you get rid of it when you were told? Do the job, and then get rid.'

'While I have it they won't find it and won't be able to trace where it is at the moment! Got it, numpty?'

Chapter 12

'Can you see the car?' Duggins asked Montrose.

'No, but they should be here.'

'What time did they say?'

'Eight.'

'Are you sure, Montrose?'

'Yes. They said eight, and don't be late.'

'Well, you know what Jim and Bert are like. We'd better go into the loading bay.' Duggins led as the pair walked into the loading bay and saw the Jaguar with their co-conspirators standing in the shadows behind the vehicle.

'Have you been seen?' Jim asked when they all met.

'No, there's nobody around,' Duggins answered.

How wrong could they be? Since the Jag had arrived they had been watched. Firstly as the car drove into the mill yard, then as they drove it into the loading bay. Every move they made, everything they talked about, four young people were watching and listening. Of the three windows in the boiler house one had more broken window than glass. The other two had several panes cracked but no real damage. Me and Frankie were at one window, Ian and Gary at another.

'Keep your heads down,' I whispered.

'What did Chris say?' Gary asked Frankie.

I whispered again: 'Keep your head down. You don't want anybody to see us, do you? OK, Gary? And you, Ian, you keep a watch just in case someone else turns up and let us know. Me and Frankie will see if we can hear what they are talking about.'

***

'So what have you got there, then?' Albert asked Duggins.

'Got where?'

'Don't try and be clever. That long thing by your side.'

'Oh, that's the shotgun.'

'What have you brought it with you for? And why didn't you get rid of it when we were discussing it? Do the robbery, dispose of the shotgun. Even you, being a police officer, must realise that keeping hold of a firearm is going to get you in all sorts of trouble! Now I suggest that when you leave here you get rid of the bloody thing. Got it?'

'OK, Bert. What did you do with the lad?'

'Who?'

'That young lad you dumped on us this morning. He had the money bag but it was on a chain attached to his wrist.'

'Oh, him. We used some bolt croppers to remove the briefcase.'

'What did you do with the lad?' Duggins persisted.

'We won't have any more trouble from him,' Bert said.

'Why, what have you done with him?'

'He's been silenced once and for all!'

Frankie pulled at my sleeve: 'What does he mean?'

'I think he may have been killed.'

'What, *dead*?' Frankie almost screamed.

'Yes, dead!'

'*Oh my God!*' Frankie exclaimed.

Just then Montrose spoke: 'You mean you've bumped him off?'

154

'Well, not quite, but you won't be seeing him for a while.'

'Why, where is he?'

'That I can't tell you – and anyway, Montrose, you're going on holiday tomorrow so you don't have to know.' Bert turned away.

'So how much money did we rob?' asked Montrose.

'What do you mean, Montrose?' asked Jim.

'I was the one who stopped the old man from going anywhere.' Montrose held firm.

'Yes, you blew a hole in his radiator and front tyre, then knocked him on the back of the head. Then, because you couldn't get the money off the lad, you fired a shot into the air and killed a few pigeons.'

Montrose came back with a flippant: 'Well, there are too many flying about.'

I said quietly to Frankie: 'There are two less pigeons now.'

She smiled at me: 'It's not all bad. We thought Ted had been bumped off, like Montrose said, but it appears that he's alive somewhere. We'll have to find him.'

I reassured her: 'We will, but not right now. We have to keep listening and see what we can find out.'

Jim said: 'Yes, Montrose and Duggins, you dumped a young lad on us. I just hope he doesn't recognise you two.'

Duggins felt threatened: 'Why should he? We are traffic police!'

'Well, God help the rest of the force.'

'We are a force to be reckoned with, so the boss says.'

Jim turned to his mate: 'What do you think, Bert?' Nothing came back from Albert, just a smile. Jim continued: 'Go on, then. Tell Duggins where the young lad is.'

'I will, when we have finished sharing out,' Albert replied.

'So how much did we get?' Duggins asked.

'Just short of thirty thousand pounds,' Bert informed them.

'That's not bad for a few hours' work. Is that each?' quipped Montrose.

'No, numpty, that's what we robbed. Me and you get about seven and a half thousand pounds each,' answered Duggins.

'That's not much,' Montrose moaned.

'What do you mean, that's not much? Only a few moments ago you said it's not bad for a few hours' work!'

I turned to Frankie.

'Seven and a half thousand pounds and they're starting to fall out already. I wouldn't mind seven and a half thousand in the bank.'

'One day, maybe,' Frankie said.

Montrose and Duggins were handed their shares of the proceeds of the robbery.

'What about you two, then?' asked Duggins.

'Well, here's mine.' Jim showed them a couple of bundles of notes. 'And Albert got the same.'

'Wasn't there any loose change?' quizzed Montrose.

'Yes, a bit.'

'So what have you done with that?'

'We stuffed it in the lad's pockets. Is that all right? You see, he now becomes a criminal.'

'How do you make that out?'

'He's accepted the money, knowing it was stolen.'

'And what did he say when you gave him the money?'

'Nothing!'

'What? Nothing?'

'Well, he couldn't.'

'Why not?' Montrose and Jim were at loggerheads.

'He was blindfolded and gagged *and* he was out with the fairies. Does that answer your questions? Now you'd better make tracks, Montrose. You'd better not go together so you go, Montrose – and by the way, have a good holiday but make sure you don't spend any of the money.'

'Why?'

'The serial numbers. They'll know where it has come from by the serial numbers.'

Bert turned and spoke to Duggins: 'Is it part of your training that you have to appear *thick*?'

Duggins only grunted.

'Right, Duggins, you would be better walking up the old railway line. At least you will be on your own. And get rid of the shotgun.'

'Where can I get rid of it?'

'I don't know. Use your imagination. No doubt you will think of something.'

'You were going to tell us where you had put the young lad,' Duggins reiterated.

Albert said: 'You know when you walk up the old line there's a small cabin. I think they called them platelayers' huts.'

'Well, well, so he's in there?'

'No.'

'So where is he, then?'

'Go just a bit further up the line and there's an old railway coach. It's been there years. He's tied up in there. I should get him released in a couple of days. But that's where he is. Mind you, you'll have to look in and make sure he's OK.'

Jim spoke to the two policemen: 'We'll give it a few minutes and we'll go, so all I can say is thanks. But you don't know me or Albert and you have never seen us before. We'll do likewise. Got it, Duggins?'

'Yes, got it, Jim.' Duggins strolled out of the loading bay and up the old railway line. A few seconds after he had passed the boiler house a shot rang out, shattering two panes of glass right above where Ian and Gary were standing! Neither of them uttered a sound as shards of glass rained down on them. With a thud, the body of a pigeon hit the ground right beside Gary. He jumped.

'What was that, Gary?' Ian spoke quietly.

'A bloody pigeon, a bloody dead one.'

Five minutes later the Jaguar drove out from inside the loading bay, smoothly and quietly until it got through the mill yard. Then it sped up the rough road, clouds of dust following in its wake.

I shouted to Ian and Gary: 'Are you all right?'

'Yep,' came their reply. 'The glass that fell just missed us both but the pigeon wasn't so lucky. It must have been close to the window and got the full blast. Anyway, it won't be flying no more. So what do you think?'

I quickly summed up: 'We have found out that Ted's OK. It appears that he's in the old railway carriage. You know, the one that one that Dad always talks about. They got about seven and a half thousand pounds each and apparently Ted had his pockets stuffed with all the loose change. Montrose is going on holiday tomorrow but we didn't hear where he is going. The two blokes with the Jag – one's called Jim, the other's called Bert – and, of course, Duggins was the one who fired the gun.'

Gary said: 'You know the other week when we were interviewed, you know when the inspector called at night? I had to go outside while they interviewed my dad and I'm sure the one called Montrose was the police driver.'

'Didn't you see him?' I asked.

'No, just the inspector. He came in and talked to me.'

'What about you, Ian? Did you see the police driver?'

'No, the car was parked at the top of the street. You know what our street is like, Chris: all cars, all day and all night.'

I looked at Frankie: 'What about you, Frankie?'

'I didn't see anything. Dad went to the door to let him in and when he had finished Dad walked with him to the door and let him out.'

'So what are we going to do?' asked Ian.

I said: 'I better go home. Mum told me not to be out too long and it's nearly nine o'clock now. I think we'd better all meet up tomorrow morning and go back down to the police station and tell them what we know. We aren't going to prove anything tonight.'

Frankie was concerned: 'What about Ted? We can't leave him there.'

'We have to, don't you see? If we release him before Duggins goes to see if he's OK tomorrow, Duggins will start thinking there's something fishy going on. No, Ted will have to stay where he is for now.'

'Are you going to mention this to anyone at home? Joan, maybe?' Frankie asked me.

'No, I'm not going to say a word. What about you lot? Gary, I mean you!'

'No, Chris, I won't say a word. What time are we going to meet up – half seven?'

'What, Gary? Half seven? Can you get up for that time?' Ian wondered.

'Yes, I can, but can you lot?'

'I can,' Frankie said.

'And I can,' Ian added.

'And I suppose I'll have to,' I muttered. 'Where are we meeting?'

'The usual place. The corner shop.'

Gary nodded.

'OK, but don't do any borrowing of food,' Frankie told Gary.

'Why?'

'We are off to the police station. We don't want you to be cautioned before we go and see about what we have heard tonight, OK? I'll be there at half seven.'

We all agreed as we went home.

***

'My, you're up early, Chris. What's the idea?' Dad asked.

'We are off to see our team play Albert Street School. It should be a good game. Not working today, Dad?'

'No, son, it's my day off. Or it would have been if it wasn't for this mess with the robbery and Ted.'

'Is Joan still in bed?'

'Yes. Mum's been with her all night.'

'I heard Mum whispering so as not to wake anybody during the night. Only I have been awake most of the night.'

'So have I, son. So have I.'

'So how has Joan taken it about Ted?' I sat opposite my dad.

'Terrible, just terrible. Let's hope Ted's OK and they find him pretty soon.'

'Oh, I think they will, Dad.'

'I hope so.'

'Have you heard how Mr Windle is?'

'Not since yesterday afternoon.'

'What did you hear?'

'He was still out with the fairies but making progress. Anyway, Chris, you want to know a lot today. Why?'

'You know I'm off to the footy. Whoever I see there will want to find out the latest news so I might as well give them the true facts instead of a load of make-believe.'

'Good thinking, son.'

'Right, Dad, must be off.'

'Catch you later, son. Hope it's a good game. I expect your school will beat them.'

As I walked through the door, I had a wry smile on my face. I had no intention of going to watch the school footy. We were all going to the cop shop to trade some facts and see if we could get Ted freed.

Frankie came out just as I was halfway across the road.

'Come on, Chris, I can see Ian. He's waving.' We walked side by side and caught up with Ian. We arrived at the corner shop as Gary came through the door, beaming.

'Come on. Let's go, gang,' Gary enthused.

'What's the rush?' asked Frankie.

'Here you are.' Gary produced three Mars bars and two bags of crisps. Old habits die hard, you know.

'What did we tell you last night on our way home? One day, Gary, you're going to get caught.'

'It was a piece of cake. Old man Cherry hadn't got a clue. I even offered him money. He took it then gave me change – more than what I gave him in the first place! Plonker.'

Frankie was annoyed with him: 'There's no need to be like that, Gary. One day he will wise up to your scams.'

'Come on, then. Let's get the bus into town.' I went in front.

'Will it be a free ride?' Gary asked.

'I don't think so. Dad's not working today, he's at home. Rest day.' I didn't tell Gary the real reason.

'Oh, well, we might be lucky.'

We weren't. It was one of the new clippies. I paid the fare for all of us. Gary wasn't going to spend his ill-gotten gains on bus fares if he could get someone else to pay for him.

The bus stopped right outside the police station. We managed to cross the road together as the traffic was very light. This time Gary pushed open both doors at the police station.

'Why didn't you just open one door, Gary? You always have to make a grand entrance. Same in school: double doors in the corridor … he has to push them both.'

'It's more impressive. Both doors swing open, everybody on the other side looks straight away.' Gary smiled and walked in.

All four of us stood in the foyer then headed for the reception desk.

'There's nobody about.' Frankie spoke, but not quickly enough. Gary managed to get to the desk first and raised his left hand. He brought it down swiftly onto the bell, which rang out with an ear-piercing clatter as a head appeared from below the desk.

Chapter 13

I spoke up first: 'We would like to see DS Kidd, please!'

'You mean Detective Sergeant Kidd,' came the reply. 'And what's it about, may I ask?' The desk PC looked down at us. 'Well, never mind. He won't see you. He's got too much to do. It's this robbery yesterday in town!'

'Just ask him if he'll see us for five minutes.'

The officer picked up the telephone and dialled a couple of numbers.

'I have four young people here. They want to see you.' It was a conversation but it appeared to be one-way.

I turned to the others: 'There's only one way they are going to solve this crime, and that's by listening to us. This lot are running round in circles, don't know which way to turn next.'

Ian remarked: '*The Muppet Show.*'

Frankie nodded her head and Gary, as usual, just stood and stared straight ahead.

'Sorry, he's too busy. I told you he wouldn't see you.'

'OK, have it your way!'

'What do you mean by that?' demanded the desk officer.

'If you want to…' As I uttered those words, Inspector Marshall walked through the door.

'What are these four young people wanting?' he asked the desk PC.

Before the man could answer, I spoke up: 'We think we could help you with your enquiries about the robbery yesterday in town. And if you remember, sir, you came to see us all regarding what we had seen and heard down at the old mill, the one they are demolishing.'

'Oh, yes,' the inspector recalled. 'Constable, get DS Kidd to come to my office right now. Now, you lot, follow me. And after you have got hold of DS Kidd can you arrange some coffee and cakes for these young people and me?'

'Yes, sir,' the constable said obediently.

'What are you lot waiting for?' the inspector rounded us up. 'Come on. I expect this is going to be a very interesting meeting.'

We all marched away. It was like follow-my-leader as we tramped down a dimly lit corridor to DI Marshall's office.

'Right, where are you all going to sit? I fear this is going to be a rather long meeting! Just a minute,' he said as the intercom crackled into life when he pressed the button. 'Is DS Kidd still there?'

'Yes, sir.'

'Can you ask him to bring a couple of chairs with him? We haven't enough chairs to sit on in here.' Within seconds a very slim PC arrived, armed with three chairs.

'Where would you like them put, sir?'

'Just plonk them there. We'll sort them out. Where's my coffee and the drinks and cakes for these four?'

'I'll get on it straight away, sir.' As the PC went out through the door DS Kidd came in.

'Right, Kidd, you sit there, and you four sit over there,' DI Marshall instructed. I moved my chair so I could sit closer to Frankie. Ian sat on the other side of her while Gary, for some unknown reason, sat close to the door.

'Are we ready to start?' asked DS Kidd.

'Not quite yet. I've ordered my coffee and a tea for you and they are bringing up some orange juice and cakes for our four guests.'

The door opened and a female PC entered carrying a tray full of drinks and cake. Unfortunately she didn't see Gary's leg sticking straight out and Gary, being Gary, didn't bother to retract it in time. She stumbled, the tray carried on as normal, and the WPC lost her balance and let it go. It seemed to travel in an arc in a forward direction. The WPC crashed to the ground just as the tray smashed into the front of the inspector's desk. Luckily the orange juice went straight up as it hit the front of the desk. As it returned to the carpet it missed everyone except DS Kidd! He was splashed not only with orange juice but with hot tea and coffee. Cake tumbled off the tray and landed on the floor.

'So sorry, sir. I'll need to go and get some more.' The WPC was shaken by the ordeal. By this time Gary, who had caused the incident in the first place, had drawn back his leg to a more respectable sitting position.

'Sorry, sir,' the young red-faced WPC said again.

'I think you should be! And look where you're going when entering a room in future.' The DI was not amused.

'Yes, sir. Yes, sir,' she apologised. Ten minutes later there was a knock on the door.

'Come,' shouted the DI.

The WPC entered once again, still red-faced, but this time instead of cake the plate was piled high with bacon sandwiches.

'Now that's what you call—'

'Shut up, Gary.' I spoke quietly and firmly. Gary got the message.

DI Marshall began: 'Right, let's get started. You say you have information that might lead us to capture some, if not all, the bank robbers.'

I spoke out: 'I think that with our help you will capture *all* the bank robbers.'

'That's quite a bold statement, young man,' the inspector said. 'Are you taking notes of this conversation, Kidd?'

'Yes, sir.'

'Go on, then, son. Tell us what you know.'

I began to tell all: 'A couple of weeks ago, or maybe longer, we came to the police station to tell you what we had seen and heard at the old mill. Later the same day, about teatime, you called at our house. It was you personally, with a police driver.'

'That's right. I remember.'

'And you asked me further questions. In fact you called at all our homes and I believe you asked the same questions of each and every one of us.'

Gary piped up: 'You wanted to see me as well as my father. I was standing outside with our dog and your driver was sat in the police car. I recognised him as being part of the gang of robbers but you said that it was impossible. "He's a very good copper," you said. Well, I'm sorry to say that yes, he is part of the gang! Dad came to the door with you. In fact, he walked past me holding the dog, and walked a few paces more to the waiting police car. Dad also recognised the driver as being part of the gang.'

'Interesting. Kidd, find out who was my driver on that afternoon.'

The intercom crackled and DS Kidd spoke into it. The person on the other end replied: 'I'll get back to you. I'll have to look at the rosters for that day.'

DI Marshall spoke: 'Why didn't the rest of you mention my driver when I questioned you at your homes?'

'Because, sir, we hadn't been hiding in the loading bay on that night. It was only Gary and his dad.'

'So when did you realise it was my driver from that Saturday?'

'When we saw him and that other policeman with him last night. Gary pointed him out.'

'What do you mean, the other policeman?'

'When we were in the mill, a few weeks ago, we saw and heard them discussing the robbery. We didn't know at the time that they were policemen. The thin one, quite tall, somebody – I don't know who – called him "Mon".'

'Montrose!' Kidd let out.

'Montrose!' the inspector echoed. 'So what did the other one look like?'

Frankie spoke: 'Big, plump, couldn't run a mile. Couldn't run twenty feet!'

Once again DS Kidd spoke: 'Duggins … Duggins and Montrose!'

'Isn't Montrose the one who appears to be a bit scruffy, quite lean-looking, never seems to have had a shave? Eh, Kidd?'

'Yes, sir. I had a word with him about that but there has been no change. That's why I decided months ago to put him in Traffic. He's had all the training. Passed everything with flying colours. The only other officer without a mate at the time was PC Duggins.'

'Quite a mixture, don't you think?' commented the inspector.

'Yes,' DS Kidd agreed, 'the Laurel and Hardy of Traffic!' They paused to drink and eat.

DS Kidd continued: 'Duggins and Montrose were on the early shift last week. And yesterday, the day of the robbery, we were able to keep in touch with all our traffic police but when it came to Montrose and Duggins, apparently they were down at, or near, the old mill. They told control they were trying to get some horses back into a field.'

'What? I don't think so,' I spoke up. 'There haven't been any horses in those fields near the old mill in the last six months!'

'Are you sure, son?'

'I am positive. The field was rented off a bloke that lives behind you, Frankie.'

'Yes, that's right. But he sold the field to the people that are going to build houses on it.'

Just then the intercom came back to life with another crackling buzz: 'I've got the information you wanted, Inspector. Montrose was your driver. He was in, working his rest day.'

'Good. And can you tell me, Montrose and Duggins – were they or are they on early turn this week?'

'Montrose went on leave last night for a week. I believe he flew to Spain this morning with his wife.'

'What about Duggins?'

'He's in. He finishes his early turn at 14.00 today, sir.'

'Thanks.' The inspector sat back and the intercom was silent once more.

'Right, we'd better get Duggins in for a chat.'

'No, no,' me and Frankie said together. 'You can't do that.'

'Why not?'

'Because we also know where Ted Harker—'

'Ted who?'

'Ted Harker, the young man they took hostage.'

'How do you know about this Ted Harker being taken hostage?'

'Because Ted Harker is engaged to my sister Joan. They are planning to get married at the end of this year.'

The discussion continued for some time.

***

Meanwhile, the hunt progressed for the gang that had robbed the bank and taken Ted as a hostage. At the same time another hunt was taking place. The police, when they found out the name of the hostage, went quickly to inform Ted's parents. They weren't at home. The police were under the impression that they were both at work or out shopping. Further enquiries drew a blank, only for the police to discover that they had gone away on holiday just a few days earlier, leaving no forwarding address.

Later that day, Mum realised that Ted's parents were away and informed the police. But she was unable to give them any further details, only to say that they had gone away for a few days to somewhere in the south-west of England. DS Kidd passed as much information about Ted's parents as he could to the Devon and Cornwall police, hoping they would find them before it was crackled over the airwaves by the BBC.

As he was leaving the crime scene, DS Kidd noticed that the BBC was starting to interview local people. They approached DS Kidd, only to get: 'Sorry, no comment at the moment. No comment.' The local rag reporter was there. He got a 'No comment.' But no doubt Kidd was thinking that another partly made-up story would hit the streets tomorrow.

'Even if I stood and told them everything, it would still finish as a made-up story,' Kidd said to himself.

***

Down in the south-west of England, Bert and Mabel, that's Albert and Mabel Harker, were making their tea and relaxing in the holiday cottage.

'Let's just see what's on the news.'

'You and your news,' Mabel remarked.

'Well, you have to keep up with what's going on.' Bert nodded.

'We are on holiday,' Mabel gave back.

'But…' Just as Bert was going to turn the radio on there was a knock at the door.

'I wonder who that can be?' Bert questioned.

'You will only find out if you answer it.'

'Nobody knows us down here.'

'So open the door and see who it is, then.'

There was another knock, this time a bit louder.

'OK, OK, I'm coming. Hold your horses.' Albert opened the door to a very large-framed policeman.

'Sorry to trouble you, but are you Mr Albert Harker?'

'Yes, but what have I done wrong? What's the problem?'

'Can I come in, please?' the police officer asked.

'Yes, certainly.' They went inside.

'I think you had better sit down.'

Mabel and Bert sat down, perplexed. They held hands.

The officer looked at his notebook: 'You have a son, Ted Harker?'

'That's right.'

'And he works for Windle?'

'Yes, Windle and Son.'

'Well, last Friday Mr Windle drove your son to the bank.'

'Yes, he does that every Friday. They collect the pay so he can make the wages up for the workforce who are paid later that day.'

The officer went on: 'That morning there was a gang of robbers waiting. And as Ted, your son, wouldn't or couldn't give them the bag of money, they dragged him away and took him hostage.'

'Is Ted OK?' Mabel spoke in disbelief.

'I'm sorry. I don't have any more information than what I've told you.'

'We must pack, love, and get back home as soon as possible.' Mabel was hugging Albert.

'We can get you back to your home, sir. There's a police car down at the station. All I have to do is make a call. We'll transport you and arrange to have your car and belongings taken to where you live. Is that OK? Shall I make that call, sir?'

Mabel said tearfully: 'I think that's best, don't you, Albert?'

'Yes I do, dear. Just make the call, officer.'

The policeman spoke into his radio, passing the message on.

'The car will be around in about twenty minutes to pick you up. Do you want me to stay?'

'You'd better,' Alf said. 'I think we could all do with a cup of tea.'

Half an hour later, Alf and Mabel were setting off for home in a police car.

'What are the locals going to say when we get back home?' Mabel asked.

'Nothing, dear,' Alf said. Six hours later they were at home, and the car that had brought them had gone.

'I think I'll give Annie a ring to see what's happening.' Mabel was in need of information.

The phone rang at home. Dad answered.

'Hello, Wilf. It's Mabel.'

'What?'

'Yes, the police brought us back home. We have just arrived back, want to know the latest news. How's Joan?'

Dad told Mabel everything that had happened, as far as he knew.

'They were quick in finding you,' he said.

'I think with us being strangers, they put two and two together.'

'We're so glad you're home.'

'Tell Annie I'll be round first thing in the morning.'

'She should have been working in the shop, but Mr Wilks called and told her not to go in. Joan's in bits. The doctor's been and given her a sedative to calm her down and hopefully make her sleep. But you can well imagine what she's going through. Anyway, Mabel, we'll see you in the morning, first thing.'

***

After a brief lull during their meeting, Inspector Marshall spoke: 'Right, Kidd, you say that PC Duggins is in work today and his sidekick, PC Montrose, has gone on his holidays. Where to, do you know?'

'No, sir.'

'Better not ask Duggins but I want to know where he's going, pronto!' The intercom crackled into life. 'Put the desk sergeant on.'

A few seconds later a voice said: 'Can I help you, sir?'

'Did Montrose say where he was going for his holidays?'

'Only the other day he mentioned where he was going, sir. I know he was flying.'

'Flying? He must have money to burn!'

'I think he said it was Alicante.'

'Alicante… Where's that?'

'Spain, sir.'

'Did he say which airport they are going from?'

'The local one. He will be there now. I think he said they were taking off around eleven o'clock.'

'Thanks, Bob.' The intercom went dead. 'DS Kidd, I want Montrose taken off the flight and brought back here. But don't mention what for. And let's get Duggins in for a chat as well, but—'

I spoke up quickly: 'But you can't do that. Duggins is going to check on Ted when he finishes his shift this afternoon. If you bring him in for a chat, he'll figure there's something fishy going on.'

At this point Frankie and Ian looked at Gary. He looked back at them and said nothing. Inspector Marshall looked at DS Kidd as he put the phone down: 'What's up?'

'Montrose is in the air now, sir. I've told them that we want to question someone on the plane. The people at the airport say they'll divert the aircraft to another airport, giving a technical fault as the reason for landing.'

'Do we know which airport?'

'Not at the moment, sir.'

'Right. Can you get hold of some bods? I want that old railway coach watched. Let's see what happens. But make sure our lot are not seen. We don't want to give the game away – and we'd better have a couple of armed officers there as well. You never know. Duggins is always bragging about his firearms skills.'

Just then the telephone rang. DS Kidd picked it up. A few moments later the phone crashed back into its cradle.

'The plane that Montrose is on is being redirected to Bristol Airport, sir.'

'Bristol! But that's over two hundred miles away,' the inspector huffed.

'It will give us time to see what Duggins does when he gets off shift at two o'clock,' said Kidd.

'Yes, you do have a point. Is Duggins still in the building?'

'Yes, he's writing up a conviction at the moment.'

'So Montrose and Duggins actually catch crooks as well as rob people?'

'It appears so, sir.'

***

'There seems to be a problem with the aeroplane,' Montrose muttered to his wife as the plane dropped softly onto the runway. 'I wonder how long we are going to be here for.'

'I hope we aren't long. This is all part of our holiday,' she replied, as the plane rolled to an unscheduled stop.

A voice came over the radio: 'Would you all get up and leave the aircraft and make your way to the departure lounge, where drinks and food will be provided.'

Little did PC Montrose know that while they were leaving the plane, a frantic hunt for their bags was taking place in the baggage compartment.

'Found them!'

'Right. Let's have them off. These people won't be flying on this plane out of here.' The Montrose baggage was discreetly removed.

***

Back at the police station the phone spluttered into life. It managed one ring and a ping.

'Yes…? Thank you, we'll be in touch. Just a minute.' Kidd turned to Inspector Marshall. 'They want to know if you want the Montrose bag searched at Bristol.'

'If they can do it without Montrose seeing what's happening.'

'They say they'll try. They want to know what they should be looking for, sir.'

'Lots of money. Paper money!'

After Kidd hung up, the inspector said,

'Well, Kidd, while they are looking after Montrose we can see what Duggins gets up to when he finishes work. He turned to me.

'Right, young man, you say that Ted Harker is in the old railway carriage?'

'Yes, but we don't know where he is in the coach. What we heard from the man who spoke to Duggins as he was leaving was, "Make sure you check on the bloke who is in the old railway carriage when you finish work tomorrow."'

Inspector Marshall said: 'Can we get our guys in place before Duggins goes off shift, and is there any cover for them? We don't want anybody giving the game away.'

Before Kidd could answer Ian spoke up: 'The old coach is up against some buffers in a slight cutting. The top of the cutting is just above the height of the coach roof. On the opposite side there's about six coal wagons. They are pushed into the siding, waiting to be collected on Monday morning.'

'Thanks for that information, son.'

Ian coloured up slightly.

'So now that we've got the lie of the land, let's get down there. How long before Duggins goes off shift?'

'A couple of hours, sir,' DS Kidd replied.

The inspector addressed us: 'Thanks for all your help. We can now act on it and hopefully get a result.' As he was speaking the phone rang.

DS Kidd answered it.

'What? That's good news: just what we were hoping for. Thanks again. We'll make all the arrangements from this end.'

'What did they say, then?'

'Bristol have managed to search the Montrose cases and, would you believe it, he had about six grand in notes in one case, wrapped up in newspaper.' DS Kidd grinned, then continued: 'The aircraft left a few moments ago. Montrose is on the ground and his wife and son are on their way to Alicante.

'Montrose can't go. He's lost his passport, or he thinks he has. Our chaps down at Bristol have it. So, when he comes to his senses, we'll bring him and his case back up here. Let's see what he has to say about things then.'

Chapter 14

'Make sure these young people have something to eat before they leave the station,' Inspector Marshall said with a smile.

'OK, sir,' DS Kidd answered.

As we approached the canteen door, Duggins appeared. As he walked out of earshot I turned to DS Kidd: 'That man is the one who was talking to the man with the Jaguar last night!'

'Are you sure?'

'Defo!' All four of us agreed at once.

'Make yourselves at home, you lot. Have whatever you want. It's on the governor.'

We sat down and ate cottage pie, and sponge pudding and custard. Gary, being Gary, had two helpings of both. The lady behind the counter remarked: 'I would sooner keep you for a week than a fortnight!'

Gary's face was a picture.

'What do you mean?'

'It means, son, you eat like a horse. Mind you, working with your dad on the rag-and-bone round, you will need quite a lot of food to keep your strength up!'

Gary just grinned widely and ate his fill.

'Now don't forget what Inspector Marshall said. Don't go anywhere near the old railway coach today. Got it?' DS Kidd ordered.

'Yes, sir,' came a chorused reply. As we went down the steps at the front of the police station Ian spoke first: 'What are we going to do now?'

'Well, we haven't a lot of money between us so we can't go to the flicks,' Frankie noted.

'Tell you what, Frankie. We were told not to go to the railway coach but we have plenty of time, so we could see if Ted's there,' Ian suggested.

'Yes, but we can't free him. Duggins will be suspicious if Ted's not there.'

'Yes, but we can tell Ted what is happening. We have a couple of hours before Duggins goes off shift.'

'But the cutting where the coach is will be bristling with cops.'

Gary added: 'Yeah, but we know cops aren't that good. Shall we go?'

'Come on, then.'

About thirty minutes later we were at the bridge about two hundred yards from the rear of the coach.

'Now what?'

'Can you see any police?'

'No. Can you, Ian?'

'No. Can you, Gary?'

'Not a thing.'

Then Frankie said: 'Yes, there's one, and it looks like two more over there.' We all looked.

'You're right but they are on the other side of the track, too far away. Now we should be able to get down the side of the bridge. Once down there, we'll be able to walk alongside the track. There's plenty of bushes, but keep looking out for the cops. We don't want to be seen — otherwise they'll escort us away, probably back to the cop shop. Right, let's go and keep a lookout.' I led the way.

We descended down the side of the bridge and walked by the side of the track, making use of the bushes and brambles that grew there. A train rushed by. Clouds of white smoke lay in the cutting, gradually disappearing into the air. When we were almost there we heard voices, but could see no one.

Reaching the buffer stop where the coach rested, I whispered: 'Quiet, go under the coach.'

'What, Chris?'

'Go under the coach but stay within the bogie.'

We all finished up under the coach.

'Now what? It's a bit dirty under here,' Gary complained.

'When have you ever worried about a bit of dirt, Gary?'

'I was just saying…'

'And what have you got there?'

'I found it back there.' It was a lump of wood, about four feet long, narrower at one end, and the other end had nails that had been bent over.

'What are you going to do with that, Gary?'

'I don't know, but it might come in handy. You never know!'

'Did you hear that? Voices coming from the other side of the tracks.'

'I haven't heard anything over here. Have you?'

'No, they all appear to be over there where those empty coal wagons are. What are we going to do now, Chris?'

'Gary, if you go and crouch down under the coach door I'll get on your back. Ian, you climb up over us, open the door and get inside. Frankie, can you be the lookout?'

'OK, Chris,' she replied.

'If Ian manages to get in you can give us a hand up, then Gary and you, Frankie, watch both ends. Make sure nobody turns up, especially Duggins. Me and Ian will see if we can find Ted and tell him what's going to happen later on today. Got it?'

They all said 'Yes!' and, 'Let's do it!'

Gary was first out from under the railway coach's wheels. I was next, and I managed to get on Gary's back. Then Frankie stood up to keep watch.

'Right, Ian, you climb up over us and open the carriage door.'

Ian climbed up.

'OK, I'm in.'

'Get down on the floor,' I whispered, then climbed up. 'Right, we are both in. Gary, you keep watch and give the carriage side a bang if someone is coming. If you bang on the side, dive under the carriage and lie low. Got it?'

Frankie and Gary nodded and said yes quietly.

Chris said: 'Stay low, Ian, at least below window level.'

'Why?'

'So no one will see us.'

'Where do you think Ted is?'

'Don't know. Just look in each compartment.'

Six compartments: nobody, only bits of paper. One full of bird muck – the window had been left open for how long?

'He's not in this one. The only place he can be is in the guards' van.'

We opened the door slowly. The stench gripped our nostrils. In the far corner we could see what appeared to be a bundle of clothes.

'Ted, Ted, is that you?' I whispered. The bundle moved. 'Ted, is that you?'

A mumbling sound came out of the bundle of clothes.

'They have certainly tied you up tight, Ted.' Me and Ian knelt beside him. 'Right, Ted, now listen carefully. We can't set you free just now, and we have to leave your blindfold on.' Ted shook his head and tried desperately to speak. 'Shh … Quiet. Just listen. We went to the police this morning after overhearing what the robbers were talking about last night at the old mill. They told Duggins – that's the one who had the shotgun – where you were, and he's coming to check and make sure you're all right after he finishes his shift today.' I looked at my watch. 'We'd better get a move on, Ian! Anyway, Duggins should be here in about twenty minutes. We told the police everything. They're watching this coach, so you should be freed by tonight.'

Ted nodded. He couldn't do much else! By this time he had managed to sit up.

'By gum, Chris,' Ian said, 'they've put ropes everywhere. Tell you what, Ted, we'll loosen the ones round your feet and your hands. You look awful! What's happened to your clothes? It looks like you were dragged here.'

'I expect he was, along the tracks,' I said.

'And what's that smell?' Ian asked.

'He's shit himself, and peed himself as well.'

Just then there was a bang on the side of the coach. Ian, Ted and me jumped.

'We'd better be off. See you later, Ted.'

Ted mumbled a weak reply. Then there was another bang.

'We better hide in one of the compartments. In here, Ian, quick.' We both went into the same compartment. 'Pull the blinds down so whoever comes past won't suspect we're in here.'

'Leave them where they are. If it's Duggins he'll think Ted's in here and open the door.'

'What are we going to do?'

'Climb onto the luggage rack and lie still. Hopefully he won't notice us!'

'What was that?'

'I think that was a shotgun being dropped onto the carriage floor!'

With a lot of grunting and groaning, Duggins managed to climb up the side of the carriage and get through the open door.

'Did you leave it open?'

'No just on the first lock.'

Clump, clump. You could hear Duggins walking down the corridor. You could hear him open the guard's door.

'Are you in there?' A faint but audible mutter could be heard. 'You're coming with me. I have plans for you. God, what have you done? Shit yourself!' A big hand grabbed the back of Ted's shirt and he was lifted skywards. 'Right, son, if you do as you're told you won't be getting hurt. You mess me around and I'll blow your brains out. Got it?'

Ted was panic-stricken and could only mumble.

'Right, as you can't see where you're going I'm going to pull you along behind me.' Duggins tied a piece of rope around Ted's waist. 'Off we go.' Duggins pulled and Ted began to shuffle along. It wasn't long before the pair were passing the compartment where me and Ian were lying on the luggage racks. Duggins was in front. One hand was carrying his broken-open shotgun, and the other hand had the rope wrapped around it. Ted was following behind, staggering. They reached the open carriage door.

Duggins was thinking ahead. How was he going to get down and get Ted down as well? He propped the shotgun against the door. He thought: '*I could jump down, but that's a bit risky. The length of rope from me to Ted isn't that long.*' Then he said: 'Right, you, on your knees, then lie on the floor.' Ted got down on his knees with some difficulty. 'I said lie on the floor!'

By this time Duggins had unwrapped the rope from his hand.

'I'm going to jump down. Then I'll get you down, OK? I said OK?' Ted muttered a reply a second time.

Duggins must have thought he was in the paras, leaping out from the carriage door. His landing wasn't up to much. All you heard was a crunch.

'Me feckin' knees! Me feckin' hand's bleeding!'

He turned and grabbed the dangling rope. The other end was still attached to Ted's waist.

'You're coming out now.' With a couple of tugs, Ted was hanging out through the carriage door. Another tug and he was a crumpled heap on the ground.

Duggins had to pull Ted up because Ted had no way of standing. At that moment Gary came out from underneath the coach and, with the lump of wood that he had found earlier, he hit Duggins across the top of his shoulders. *Thwack!* Duggins stumbled and fell forward. Gary was instantly back under the coach.

'Where the hell did that come from?' Duggins raged as he looked around but saw no one. Gary was back out again. *Thwack!* This time he hit Duggins right behind his knees. That stopped Duggins. He had to bend down and rub his knees hard. 'By, that hurt!' This time Gary struck with venom. *Thwack!* Right on his neck.

Duggins slumped forward, banging his head on one of the axle boxes. He caught sight of Gary slipping under the carriage.

'*I'll get you. Just wait!*'

While Duggins was going down the corridor dragging Ted, me and Ian were hiding but watching. Once he'd passed, we climbed down from the safety of the luggage racks. Chris slid open the compartment door just enough to see what was happening.

'He's managed to get Ted to the open door and he's propped his shotgun up against the door frame. It looks like Duggins is going to get out first. He's taken the rope off his hand but it's still tied to Ted. Now what? He's sitting in the doorway with his legs dangling down. He's gone.'

Thud!

'Feckin' bushes, feckin' hell!'

'I think he landed in the brambles.'

'I know. He's doing a lot of swearing.'

'Right, let's go – but keep low, Ian. We can get as far as Ted.' We crawled.

'Sorry, Ted,' Ian said as he crawled over him. 'You're right, Chris. Duggins is in the brambles – he looks as if he landed face first.' Then Ian noticed Gary standing just behind Duggins with the lump of wood, poised to strike. *Thwack!* Right across Duggins' back.

'Feckin' hell!' Duggins fell forward again into the brambles.

Gary looked at Ian, put his finger to his lips and disappeared back under the carriage. In the meantime Ian had retrieved Duggins' shotgun and taken both cartridges out, then placed it back where it had been.

Finally, Duggins freed himself from the brambles but was unable to see anybody when he stood upright and looked around.

'Whoever you are,' he shouted, 'I'll kill you when I get hold of you! Come on out. I've got a gun, mate, and you're dead! Better run if you know what's good for you.'

Duggins staggered over to Ted, who was still crumpled on the ground, groaning.

'Moan, moan, that's all you do. You want to be thankful you're still alive. Now, on your feet. Up, now!' He was mad as hell.

Before Duggins could lift Ted upright … *Thwack! Thwack!* Gary once again seized the opportunity, got behind Duggins and hit him hard. He fell and again smashed his head against one of the coach axle boxes. Again Gary was gone as quick as he appeared. While this was going on, me and Ian managed to get out of the coach and dive underneath it. Duggins, meanwhile, stood up again, a little the worse for wear. Holding onto the footboard, he reached into the carriage with his other hand and grasped the shotgun stock, only for it to fall away from his hand. As he couldn't see what he was doing, and he was trying to find a foothold to see where his shotgun had fallen, his foot slipped. Once again he fell backwards, over Ted, into the brambles.

'Feckin' bushes, feckin' carnage!' Yet again he managed to free himself. This time he found a safe foothold and raised himself up so he could see where his shotgun lay. It was just within arm's length. He stretched, and with his fingertips just managed to pull the shotgun to the edge of the open door.

'Got it.' He pulled the shotgun out from the open doorway.

While Duggins was preoccupied with retrieving his firearm me, Gary and Ian managed to manhandle Ted over the railway line and under the coach, hiding him under the bogie. Frankie got to work trying to undo the knots that kept Ted secure.

'God, you *smell*, Ted,' she said, choking.

Gary spoke: 'He must have shit himself, or peed – probably both, by the smell.'

Duggins propped the shotgun against one of the coach's wheels and turned round.

'Where's the body?' He turned round twice. Ted was nowhere to be seen. Duggins scratched his head: 'Where the hell has he gone?'

He bent down and looked under the coach. Gary once again seized the moment. *Thwack!* He caught Duggins full in the face this time with the end of the lump of wood with the bent nails. My, that must have hurt him! Duggins fell back, his face covered with blood. He now knew where me, Ian and Gary were hiding. By this time Ted had got as close as possible to the side of the rail under the coach, making him invisible.

'Feckin' bastard! You wait 'til I get my gun!' Blood was running down Duggins' face. His hand as he clutched the shotgun was sticky with blood.

Gary came out from under the coach and faced Duggins: 'Come on, then!' he shouted. Dazed and swaying, Duggins pulled the shotgun to his waist and fired both barrels at Gary. *Click-click!* Nothing!

Gary came at Duggins. It looked like a duel but Duggins had the upper hand. He took a swipe at Gary and knocked the lump of wood from his hands. Another swipe with the shotgun. Gary slipped backwards and hit his head on the rail, making it bleed profusely. Gary lay there with his eyes shut!

We looked on in horror, thinking Gary was dead and we would be next. Duggins looked down at Gary and said: 'That's one feckin' less. Where's them cartridges?' He fumbled through his pockets. He found two cartridges and loaded both barrels. Still talking to himself, he said: 'Right, let's go a-hunting.' Once again he looked under the coach but was unable to see anybody. We had moved to the other end of the coach, leaving Ted – who was very hard to see in the shadows, and close up to the rail.

Duggins let off one barrel, thinking he knew where we were hiding. The blast rippled past Ted and made bits of litter and dead leaves rise and flutter back down to the ground. Duggins stood back then moved round to the end of the coach.

***

'How's things going, Kidd?'

'Not bad,' came the reply as Inspector Marshall crouched at the side of DS Kidd. 'Just one thing, sir.'

'What's that?'

'You have a look through the glasses at the railway coach, just above the rails.'

'My God! That's the young people we saw this morning.'

'Yes, sir, but there was four up until about fifteen minutes ago. Now there's only three.'

'What's happened?'

'We don't know, but there was a shot fired and we haven't seen him since.'

'So what you're really saying—'

'Yes, sir. I have asked for a police marksman. He's on his way. Should be here any time. The steam trains don't help.' Another one raced by, blanketing everything with clouds of smoke that seems to take forever to clear.

'Leave that to me. I'll speak to the stationmaster, see what we can arrange. What's happening with Montrose?'

'He's travelling up as we speak, sir, in the back of a police van. What he doesn't know is that we have his suitcase in the front with the driver. If anything, it will give him time to think about what he has, or hasn't, done. The one thing he won't find out about is what's happening here. Do you want me to interview him when he arrives at the station?'

'No, do it tomorrow. Let him stew in a cell overnight! What's happening now?'

DS Kidd looked through the binoculars.

'It appears as though Duggins is on the move, sir. He's moving to the far end of the coach.'

Just then: 'Sir, I'm the marksman you have asked for.'

'Right, can you get yourself into a position a bit further down the hedge, about where that tree is? We may not need you, but make sure you have a clear view of the rear of the railway carriage.'

'Right, sir. Give me about five minutes. I'll signal you when I'm ready.'

Duggins moved to the rear of the coach. He bent down, hoping to see something in the dull light then caught sight of Ted's foot.

'That's where you're hiding! Not for much longer.' He grabbed Ted's foot and started to pull. 'You're coming with me, sunshine. Like I said before, I have plans for you.'

A megaphone crackled into life as DS Kidd spoke: 'Throw your shotgun out and put your hands on top of your head!' This voice came as a shock to PC Duggins. He dropped Ted's foot and stood bolt upright, startled like a deer in the headlights of a car.

'*What?*' he screamed.

'Throw your shotgun away from you and put your hands on top of your head, then walk towards us,' the megaphone instructed.

PC Duggins shouted back: 'My snout told me where the hostage was and I've rescued him!'

'Just do as I say,' the reply came.

Duggins raised the shotgun to waist height and fired just as a goods train started to pass. The shotgun pellets struck the engine, the tender and one or two wagons: *ping, ting, twang, clatter.* It did the engine no harm, but the driver and the fireman had to duck to keep out of the way of the shot.

The train passed. Smoke lingered longer this time. As it cleared, PC Duggins was standing holding the shotgun ready to fire.

'This is the last warning, Duggins. Throw the shotgun away and stand with your hands on the top of your head…'

DS Kidd was unable to finish the sentence before Duggins fired again. This time there was return fire from the police marksman. His bullet struck the corner edge of the coach and whizzed inches above Duggins' head. Enraged by this, Duggins fired another shot – this time into the grass bank below where the marksman was lying.

The police marksman ducked as stones flew and grass, twigs and leaves filled the air. This time the marksman took careful aim. His intention was to bring Duggins down, to stop this maniac causing more harm. He took aim and fired. The gun cracked as the bullet left the barrel and ripped through the air, hitting Duggins. The bullet struck, but not where expected – not on his shoulder, thus disabling him. Duggins moved slightly a fraction of a second before the shot was fired. The bullet struck home, clean through his windpipe, flicking his head backwards.

His hand reaching up to his throat, Duggins dropped his shotgun. Blood started to spurt out. Nothing much at first, then more started to run between his fingers. It ran down his pristine white shirt. A look of horror passed over Duggins' face. His eyes started to glaze, his mouth began to move. He spoke but nothing came out. He tried to walk – stagger, more like – but dropped to his knees onto the gravel. His face had gone from bloody-red to grey. Now it was turning white. He tried again to speak, but only spluttered blood out of his mouth. Then he fell forward, his face smashing into the gravel.

As this was happening the police officers were darting about all over the place. Me, Ian and Frankie emerged from under the coach to be met by DS Kidd.

'Where's the other one?'

'Gary's round the other side. We think he's dead! Duggins hit him hard with the shotgun and he fell and struck his head on the rail. Can you go and look, sir?' I asked.

Me and Ian dragged Ted out from underneath the bogie. Finally a police officer cut the ropes from Ted's hands, legs and feet.

Ted was able to speak for the first time in two days: 'Oh, thank God for that,' he said to Frankie. 'I can breathe.' He took several deep breaths. 'Frankie, how's Gary?'

'I don't know. DS Kidd has gone to see how he is. I think he's dead.'

'Don't say that! He gave Duggins, him over there under the blanket, a right pasting whenever he got the chance.'

'How do you know that?' Frankie asked, amazed.

'There were tiny gaps in the bandage that covered my eyes, so I could just see bits if it was close up. I only saw a bit but that last time it was like a duel. I saw it all.'

Ian pulled at my arm: 'Better go round and see what is happening with Gary. I hope he's going to be all right.'

'So do I,' I answered. We rounded the end of the railway coach to find Gary sitting up with DS Kidd kneeling beside him. With great relief, Ian said: 'We thought you were a goner when you fell. Where's that blood coming from? Your face is covered.' Blood was running down Gary's face from a cut somewhere on his head.

DS Kidd said: 'He's OK. He's a tough nut.'

'I banged my head on the rail when I fell, that's all. It must have knocked me out, but I feel fine.'

'You might feel fine but you're coming with me, son.'

'Who are you?'

'They're ambulance men. You have to go to the hospital, Gary.'

'Why? I said I'm OK.'

'You might think you are, but we have to make sure.'

'Well, if I'm going, I don't want to travel in the same ambulance as him!' Gary pointed at Ted.

'Why not?'

''Cause he smells. He *stinks!*'

'So would you, Gary, if you had been treated like Ted for twenty-four hours or more! But I'll see what I can do.'

I turned to Gary: 'Put it on, Gary.'

'Put what on?'

'You know.'

'Know what?' We went round the end of the coach.

'What's that there?' Gary asked, pointing to a large object on the ground.

'That's PC Duggins,' answered DS Kidd.

'Why don't you arrest him?'

'No point, son.'

'Why not?' Gary stopped walking and looked at us, dazed and puzzled.

I answered: 'Because he's brown bread, Gary.'

'What d'you mean, Chris?'

Frankie spoke up: 'He's dead, Gary. Duggins, he's dead!'

Gary froze and felt decidedly weak. The most terrible thought flashed into his mind. Was he now a murderer?

***

Inspector Marshall was angry that two constables from his police station had been involved in a vile crime and that his own reputation could suffer as a result. He was also concerned about the bad publicity the police would get in the media. The inspector knew that this issue must now be dealt with to the very highest standard.

'Right, Montrose! I think it's time we had a chat, don't you?' Montrose had been brought up from the cell where he had spent the night. 'Have you any idea what this is all about?' Montrose looked straight ahead, stone-faced, but did not reply. 'Well, I'll give you some idea. Friday, there was a robbery at the bank in town and we think you might know something about it. I take it you know about PC Duggins.'

'Why, what's happened?' Montrose managed a sullen reply.

The Inspector leant close to Montrose: '*He's dead!*'

Montrose showed no reaction to this news.

'Since when?'

'Since yesterday afternoon.'

'What happened?'

'He was shot dead by one of our own marksmen!'

'Why?'

'Because he went to that old railway coach. That's where the hostage from the bank was taken. Duggins was checking on him but he took along his shotgun. He got cocky, fired off a few rounds, threatened to shoot us, wouldn't throw down his gun, took aim – but before *he* could shoot our man shot him!'

Montrose stared blankly straight ahead.

'So, Montrose, what do you know and what can you tell us about Duggins? You see, when the robbery took place and we finally got hold of you two, you said that you were rounding up horses down by the old mill, the one that is being pulled down.

But we have been in contact with the owner of the field. There haven't been any horses in there for about six months.' Montrose bottom lip started to quiver, just slightly. 'So you might as well tell us what you were doing down there!'

'It was us,' Montrose answered in a weak voice.

'What do you mean, it was us?'

'We did the robbery. But it didn't pan out as it was supposed to do.'

'Go on, Montrose.'

Chapter 15

Gary came out of hospital first to the roar of a crowd of onlookers, and he was whisked away in a police car. The only sign that he had been in the wars was a large bandage around his head. That was all for his troubles. Ted came out next.

'Can you make a statement?' a reporter asked.

'Sorry, my lips are sealed. No comment.' Joan was by his side, proud to say 'My Ted'. Ted and Joan were also whisked away in a police car but taken to the police station to be interviewed.

Sunday was very quiet compared to the last twenty-four hours. Dad said at lunchtime: 'It could have gone either way.'

'You shouldn't talk like that,' Mum spoke out. 'Ted's back where he belongs, with Joan.'

As Joan peered into Ted's eyes, I turned to her and said: 'Put him down. You don't know where he's been!'

Joan scowled at me: 'Oh, but I do!'

***

Roger Kidd couldn't wait to see the gang on Monday morning.

'Have you been here long?' Ian asked.

'About fifteen minutes. Where have you been? You're normally early.'

'Oh, Gary was doing his usual at the corner shop. But this time they insisted that he shouldn't pay for anything. Funny thing is, he doesn't anyway. Just nicks it. Anyway, what do you want?'

Roger told Ian: 'I overheard my dad telling Mum what had happened on Saturday afternoon.'

'Well, we were part of it. We were there.'

'Yeah, I know that, but I also know what happened after they took you lot home and Ted and Gary to the hospital.'

'Go on, then. What happened?'

Roger repeated what he had heard: 'They had to stop the trains while the police searched the area.'

'What were they looking for?'

'I don't know. I didn't hear what they were looking for. Anyway they took Duggins' body away.'

'Well, they would do. He was dead … brown bread. Put it any way you want, he was dead,' said Gary.

'Go on, what next?' demanded Ian.

Roger continued: 'You know Montrose was the other policeman involved with this robbery?'

'Yes, we saw Montrose and Duggins at the old mill twice,' Gary said.

'Three times,' Ian piped up.

'He went away on holiday Saturday morning.'

'We know that as well.'

Roger continued: 'By the time they realised what was happening, Montrose and his wife had taken off. Inspector Marshall asked the airport people if he could get the aeroplane brought back. They diverted the plane to Bristol, saying there was something wrong with the plane. When it landed they took Montrose off and arrested him but let his wife fly off to foreign parts. Montrose and his bag of money travelled back up here on Saturday afternoon. Montrose hadn't realised that they'd managed to get his luggage from the plane.' Roger paused.

'Then what?' asked Gary.

'While Montrose was travelling back up here, Duggins was playing out what he thought was the hostage's release, only Duggins thought he was the good guy. The police knew otherwise and a firefight took place. Unfortunately Duggins lost the fight.'

'Go on, then. What happened next?'

'Well, Dad decided that he wouldn't interview Montrose when he got back. He would let him stew in a police cell overnight. Dad interviewed him yesterday.'

'So what happened then?'

'Dad and Inspector Marshall interviewed Montrose!'

'So can you tell us more? Because everything you've told us so far we already know!'

'Right, well, they told Montrose what had happened on the Saturday afternoon. Dad told Mum that Montrose just sat there, no expression on his face at all, even when they mentioned that his sidekick had been shot. It was only when they produced his luggage and asked him to open it that they got a response. Dad and Inspector Marshall already knew what was inside the luggage because they had had it opened earlier, before they interviewed Montrose.' Roger leant against the wall.

'Then what?' Gary wouldn't let him stop now.

'At first he claimed that the money had been planted in his luggage. He was asked who would do that but he couldn't give an answer. But then he must have thought about it and decided to make a full statement. He told them what he and Duggins had planned but made no comment about the other two men until…'

***

Inspector Marshall said to Montrose: 'So you have decided to make a statement, thinking that you and Duggins would come clean, only Duggins can't. You are going to blame it all on Duggins. You just followed orders. That may be so, but what about the other two guys?'

'Which two?' came the reply.

'The two you met at the old mill, the mill they are pulling down.'

'We didn't meet anybody.'

'Well, we have it on good authority that you met these two guys at least twice. If you and Duggins planned the robbery between you, why did you meet someone down there on Friday after the robbery, then hand over the money and the hostage? So let's start again. Who are the two men you planned the robbery with?'

'I don't know,' Montrose repeated. 'Duggins met the one with the Jag about six weeks ago. He stopped them over something that was wrong with the car. He didn't book them, just had a word. Over the next couple of weeks we met them both at the old mill and they planned the robbery. We just had to carry it out.'

'What in?'

'That was the problem. On the day that the robbery was planned we had no car, so we had to put it off for a week. Last Friday was the only day left as I was going on holiday, so we had to do it then.'

'So what car did you use, and where is it now?' DS Kidd was quite expecting it to have been fired.

'It's back in the garage!'

'Which garage?' asked DS Kidd.

'The police garage.'

'It's your *police car*?' The detective couldn't believe his ears.

'No, not my police car, it's the *boss's*.'

'*What?*' shouted Inspector Marshall.

'It's your car, Inspector,' Montrose smiled inwardly at the irony.

'What do you mean, it's *my* car?'

'Our car broke down during the week. Something went wrong with the driveshaft and we had to be recovered. The only car available at the time was your car, sir, so we were told to take that one. Very comfortable and fast for its age! When we brought it back at night expecting ours to be ready it wasn't, so we were told to keep using yours. So we used yours to do the robbery.'

'You robbed the bank using *my* car!'

'Yes, sir.'

'No wonder we couldn't trace the car,' Kidd said, shaking his head.

'Well, the black Wolseley we put false number plates on.'

'And where did you put them after you, as you say, did the job?'

'They're in the back of your car, sir. We wrapped them up in a bit of cloth. Looked like an old coat.'

'That's my new golfing jacket!'

'Duggins wrapped the plates up in your old— sorry, golfing jacket, and stuffed them in the boot. Duggins was told to get rid. He contemplated firing your car to get rid of the evidence.'

'Firing *my* car!'

'Yes, sir, but I talked him out of it. If it had been any other car, he would have. But I said: "You can't fire the boss's car! How are you going to explain the car being burnt out?"'

Inspector Marshall was fuming, almost frothing at the mouth: 'Kidd, get someone over to my car in the garage and see if the number plates are there. Just say they are wrapped up in a coat. I expect if they are there my coat, old or not, will become evidence. *Old coat* my arse!'

'Sorry, sir, I didn't quite catch that.'

'Never mind. Also, while you're at it, get the fingerprint guys over. Tell them to go over the whole car. Let's see what prints are on or in it.'

'Yes, sir.'

Montrose interrupted.

'We wiped it clean, sir. The only prints or dabs in the car will be yours, I'm sure of it. We spent about twenty minutes going over everything.'

'So what you're saying, Montrose, is if the false number plates are, as you say, wrapped in my old – new – golfing jacket, and only my prints are on or in the car, then I'm in the frame for doing this bank job?'

'Yes, sir.'

'But I was sat at my desk last Friday morning when you did the job!'

'That may be so. But it was your car, and the lady did give a good description: black Wolseley, like a police car, number plate NJA 479.' Montrose felt very smug.

Just then the intercom buzzed: 'Hello, yes, Kidd speaking. The number plates? Yes, they are in the boot of the Wolseley, wrapped in yes an old coat. Right, got that. Anything else? Yes, the number plates are off a Ford Popular and belong to a car in Manchester. Right I'll pass the message on. What? The fingerprint guys are working on the car as we speak.' DS Kidd turned to the inspector: 'The number plates were in the back of the car, sir.'

'Anything else?'

'They have found out what car the plates are off and are following it up. They'll let us know the results.'

All this time Montrose stared straight ahead. No emotion passed over his face. Nothing, not even a bead of sweat. His hands were placed on the desk in front of him. Not a movement, not even a twitch.

'Well, Montrose, we have one thing – the number plates. Let's see what happens when we speak to the owner. You know we have recovered the money – well, part of it?'

Montrose hadn't known that. His mind raced to work it out. It must be Duggins' share. They'd have searched his place and found it.

'*It can't be mine,*' he thought. '*My share was put on the aircraft and will be abroad now.*' A wry smile crept across his face, then he went back to staring.

'Yes, Montrose, while you were waiting to reboard your flight at Bristol Airport the guys at Bristol found your bag and took it off the plane. When your wife and the other passengers reboarded the plane and took off, you were put into the back of a police van and the money you thought you were taking abroad was put in the front of the van. So you see, Montrose, we have *your* share of the takings! What have you got to say about that, then?'

Montrose's face suddenly turned from a motionless stare to one of sheer panic. What was he going to do now? His mate and big buddy Duggins was dead. He had been caught good and proper, and the other two robbers had gone. He couldn't talk his way out of this. How would he survive in prison?

'Montrose, we'll give you some time to think about it back in the cells. Right, PC Greenwood, take him down.' With that, Montrose was marched from Inspector Marshall's office. 'So what do you think, DS Kidd?'

'Well, sir, you could be in the frame for the job. If your dabs are all over the car and nobody else's are…' Kidd smiled.

'I know, like you know, that Montrose and Duggins did the job. Pity about your car being involved. But we really want Montrose to tell us who the other two are, the ones who used Duggins and Montrose as fall guys.'

'Well, we can't ask Duggins because he's dead, so it will have to be Montrose!'

Just then the intercom buzzed. It was one of the chaps from the fingerprint department.

'The car, sir, is covered with *your* prints, but the number plates have Duggins' prints on and Montrose's on the back one, as clear as a bell. The back one must have been a bit fiddly. One must have held the plate while the other one screwed it on.'

'Anything else?'

'No, nothing.'

'Thanks.' The intercom was turned off.

'At least we know that your car was used and had false number plates and that Duggins and Montrose did the job. I have asked the desk sergeant to get in touch with the boys at Manchester to get one of their plod platoon to interview the owner of the car that the plates came off. Let's see what that throws up.' DS Kidd shuffled some documents.

'Do you want to have another word with Montrose, Kidd?'

'No! Let him stew. We've given him something to think about. In fact, let him stew until tomorrow. He's ruined today. What do you say, sir?'

'OK. Fancy a pint?'

'OK, sir, then home for a spot of tea. It'll be better than what Montrose will be getting.'

∗∗∗

Monday morning, Roger had gone to school early, eager to tell Chris, Frankie, Ian and Gary what his father had told his mum. Roger, as his mum and dad imagined, had gone to bed. But Roger, being Roger, had listened to the conversation sitting on the stairs. Meanwhile DS Kidd had gone into work earlier than usual but had met Inspector Marshall coming out of the police station.

'Can I just have a word, Kidd?'

'Sir?'

'Montrose has only tried to top himself this morning!'

'When?'

'About forty-five minutes ago. I rang your wife but she said you had just left. Anyway I'm off down the hospital.'

'Do you want me to go?'

'No, I have to go see the mayor afterwards but keep in touch.'

'Right, sir,' DS Kidd replied and went into the station.

'Have we heard anything from Manchester?' Kidd asked the desk sergeant.

'I got this message about ten minutes ago. They've been round to see the guy who owns the car. He said he sold it to a garage in our area about two weeks ago, so I've just sent one of our plods over to have a word.'

'Right, let me know as soon as he gets back. Better still, ask him to come and see me.'

'Right, sir, I'll do that.'

Just as DS Kidd was starting on a packet of custard creams and a mug of hot steaming coffee there was a knock at the door.

'Yes, come in, lad.' It was the young PC who had gone round to the garage that had bought the Ford Popular from Manchester.

'So what have you to say, son?'

'The man at the garage said that he had taken the Ford in part exchange for one of these new Minis and put the Ford Popular on the forecourt last week. He noticed that the number plates had disappeared, thought it must be kids and replaced them later that day.'

'And where's the car now?'

'Still in the same place, sir, on his forecourt.'

'Thanks, son. Just one thing, what's the car like?'

'Rough, sir. Bloody rough!'

Later that day word came from the hospital that Montrose had passed away. The news brought disbelief and anger, as the police were no further forward. Duggins had been shot dead on the Saturday afternoon in some foolish attempt to prove he was a big man with a big gun and wouldn't take orders from anybody. Montrose decided he was going to keep quiet about the other two robbers, so now the hunt was on for the gang leaders: the Mr Bigs, the masterminds.

Nothing much happened during the next week or so. Ted went back to work. Joan was back in the Silver Salon, cutting and shampooing. Ted was the big hero at work. Mr Windle was still at home. He had taken quite a battering. His doctor had made sure that he wasn't going back to work until he was fully fit.

Gary, on the other hand, was the star turn at school. A lot of the girls in his class suddenly took a shine to him. Nothing like this had happened to Gary before. We would see him in the schoolyard, groups of schoolchildren standing around him and staring at him, taking in every last word he uttered. He would be telling them the way he fought to protect his fellow gang members, how he was hit on the head but survived to down the person who was attacking him. Gary certainly knew how to keep the kids entertained with a new story or a different line every day.

Just as he was about to speak to another audience he found a scrap of paper in his jacket pocket, all crumpled up. At first he was going to throw it away. He looked at it carefully – and lo and behold, there was a car number on it.

'Hey, Chris, look what I've found!'

'What is it?' I asked.

'You know when we were in the old mill, you said to write down the car registration numbers? Well, I did, but I only put down the Jaguar car number, then my pencil broke. What shall I do with this number?'

'Tell the police. From what Roger has been saying, they don't appear to be getting very far with their enquiries. Tell you what: I'll go with you tonight from school. We should be able to get a lift on the service my dad does.'

'Right, then. You never know, if we play our cards right they might take us home in a police car.'

'Since the other week all you ever talk about is riding around in police cars.'

'Yeah, well.'

'Yeah, well, what? You want to be careful or you'll be riding in one for all the wrong reasons!'

'What do you mean?'

'Mr and Mrs Cherry, corner shop. Does it ring any bells? Their profits are down, and who's that due to? You!'

'Well, I've been thinking.'

'Thinking what?'

'I'd better start paying for what I get.'

'How's that come about?'

'It's just something they've said since I became famous. They let me take what I wanted free of charge and it didn't seem right.'

'So you've finally got the message, then?'

'Well, yes.'

'That's good, Gary.'

'Ah, but it was great while it lasted.'

'And how long have you been doing it?'

'Since I started at school. I started when I was at junior school and just worked my way through.'

'It's a wonder they've not gone bankrupt through your activities!'

***

'Can we see DS Kidd, please?'

'And who might want to see him? I'll see if he's in.' The desk sergeant knew full well that he was in as he'd passed by the desk only moments before, holding a hot steaming mug of coffee and what looked like a bacon butty dripping brown sauce.

'Mr Hart and Mr Singleton want to see him.'

'I'll inform him that you would like to see him. Take a seat.' Gary spun round looked at the chairs and straight away said: 'Chris.'

'What?'

'How can we take a seat? They're fastened down.'

'Just sit on one. That's what he meant. Not what you thought he meant.'

'I'm not sitting next to him.' He pointed at an older man who was the worse for wear.

'Why not?'

'Look at him. He looks like he's pissed himself, and he's drunk.'

'Well, I'll sit there, then.'

'So where am I going to sit?'

'Just stand there. I expect we won't be long. Anyway, you should be used to sitting next to people like him.'

'Why do you say that, Chris?'

'When I've been with you and your dad and we've been round collecting scrap, we nearly always stop for a butty and a mug of tea at that place on the ring road. There's always two or three undesirables in there, so what's the difference? At least in here if they try anything on, the one behind the desk over there will stop them.'

Gary, being Gary and not very tactful, said quite loudly: 'He would never be able to jump over the counter, and it would take him a week if he had to walk round!'

'Shush, Gary! If you're going to talk about anybody, especially in the same room, keep your voice down so at least they won't hear you.'

'What do you mean?' Gary glanced at me.

'Tell you what, Gary, just shut up and then no one will be any the wiser.'

'OK. I'll just stand here.'

Just then DS Kidd pushed the door open, thinking he was going to see Mr Hart and Mr Singleton. He was taken aback to see Christopher Hart and Gary Singleton.

'Oh, it's you two. What do you want?'

'Can we see you somewhere else?' I said, looking at the drunk and the copper behind the desk, who appeared to be writing, but you could see was trying to latch on to our conversation.

'Follow me,' DS Kidd said. We went in single file through the door and up the stairs into the interview room. 'Right, what have you got to tell me?'

Gary let me talk: 'Well, you told us a few days ago if we remembered anything to come and see you. Gary went to school this morning wearing the same jacket he was wearing when we saw Duggins and Montrose by the Wolseley and the other two men standing by the Jag. I had asked Gary if he could write the numbers of the cars down and, luckily for you, he managed to scribble down the reg of the Jaguar. But the lead in his pencil broke before he could write down the reg of the other car. Like I was saying, he had that jacket on today and found the crumpled bit of paper stuffed in his pocket, and here it is.'

'You say this is the number. Just wait a minute. I must make a call.'

The intercom burst into life.

'Ah, Jackson, can you get in touch with the Ministry of Transport and find out who owns car registration number LTN 793E? I believe it's a Jaguar, but see what you can come up with. Thanks.' The intercom crackled, then went silent.

At that moment Inspector Marshall walked in.

'Hello, are you two all right?'

'Yep,' Gary answered.

DS Kidd spoke to his inspector: 'I think we might have a lead on the other car, sir. You know, the Jaguar.'

'How come?'

DS Kidd started to tell Inspector Marshall about what Gary had found.

'At least we appear to be getting somewhere now, Kidd.' The inspector looked pleased. The intercom spluttered into life.

'Sorry, can you repeat that?' DS Kidd said. 'Sorry, it's no good. I just can't understand what you're saying. Bloody intercom. I've been meaning to have a word about this. It's getting worse, sir. It's getting like that chap on the telly, the one that's on the programme called *The Comedians*.'

'Who?'

'I think he's called Norman Collier. You know who I mean. He comes on stage, taps the mic to see if it's working, then starts talking into the mic but it doesn't pick up all the words. So you get part words and part sentences. Well, sir, this bloody intercom is going that way!'

'Who?'

'Never mind, sir. I'll put it another way: the intercom is knackered!' and with that DS Kidd was through the door and halfway down the stairs before DI Marshall realised what was happening.

'So we have two stars in our midst,' Marshall muttered.

'One, sir,' I corrected. 'It has to be Gary. He's the one who kept coming from under the old coach and hitting Duggins with a lump of wood, sir.'

'Well, you both did a fine job.'

'But there was the other two, Ian and Frankie. They helped as well.'

'I'm sure they did.'

The door swung open again as DS Kidd made an entrance, puffing slightly and with a few beads of sweat running down his forehead.

'Must start doing more exercise.'

'You look bushed, Kidd.'

'I am, sir.'

'Well, slow down. We don't want to lose another.'

'Lose who?' Gary had to ask.

'Shut it, Gary,' I muttered. 'Just shut up and listen.'

'Nothing yet, sir.' Just as DS Kidd spoke, the intercom burst into life: 'Yes, yes, really! Thanks. They have been quick. Did you manage to hear all that, sir?'

'Yes, I did.'

Me and Gary sat with our mouths open, trying to take in what was being said and how things were moving forward so fast.

Kidd spoke: 'It makes a change that the Ministry of Transport have gone up a gear and have come up with this info so quickly.'

'It appears you two – especially you, Gary – did write the correct reg number down and I can confirm to you that it is a red- or burgundy-coloured Jaguar car. Well done, lads,' the inspector said. 'Well done! Right, Kidd, we'll get these two home before their parents start wondering where they are. You two go down to the front desk and I'll get someone to run you home.'

A few minutes later: 'Are you ready to go?'

We walked outside and down the steps. In front of us was the same car that we'd seen in the warehouse of the old mill.

'We are going home in the robbery car! Wow!' Gary said, excited.

'No, son, the car that was involved in the robbery is at HQ. They have let us borrow this one while the other is getting seen to.' Our policeman chauffeur burst the bubble for Gary.

Nothing more was said as we drove home. I sat in the back like a movie star. Gary sat in the front next to the driver.

'What does this switch here do?' he enquired. I leant forward, wondering what Gary was pointing at. 'This one.'

Before the driver had time to tell him Gary moved the switch, only to hear *'ee haw, ee haw'*.

'I guess you know what it is now.' The constable smiled as they drove along the road, siren blaring. Gary was in seventh heaven, grinning widely!

Chapter 16

'Is PC Greenwood still on duty?' DS Kidd was standing at the front desk, a mug of hot, steaming tea in one hand and a dripping bacon butty in the other.

'He should be coming through the door anytime, sir, as he's just finished his shift.' Then the door swung open.

'Ah, PC Greenwood, can I have a quick word? I take it you're going off duty.'

'I am, sir.'

'Good. Come with me into the office. What I am going to ask you is for your ears only.' DS Kidd shut the door behind them. 'The other week I asked you to go round to Auto Speed regarding a Ford car that had had the number plates stolen, as the owner put it. But the owner didn't report the theft. He said he thought it was kids. Is that right?'

'Yes, that's right, sir. I did, at the time, mention it was strange that kids would have taken the front *and* rear number plates, both at the same time.'

'And what did the owner say about that?'

'Nothing, sir, just, "Kids will be kids," and left it at that. I went past the other day. Same old cars there, nothing new in.'

'Well, Greenwood, I want you to go back and look around the place. Make out you're interested in buying a car from him. See what you can find out about him, see if anybody else works there – you know, do some digging. It might be better if you go in plain clothes, like you are now, going off duty.'

'I can go this afternoon. I was going to watch the local team play football but they aren't much good. So I'll go home, get changed into something more casual then go and call on Auto Speed.'

'Just one more thing, Greenwood. Don't make out you're a copper. And one more—'

Greenwood butted in: 'I won't be buying a car. They are all "sheds".'

The following day PC Greenwood was sitting in DS Kidd's office, waiting for him to come into work.

'My, you're bright and early, Greenwood. I take it you've managed to find, or should I say, dig some dirt on our local car salesman?'

'I think you're going to be quite surprised, sir.'

'So, what have you found out?'

'The chap I spoke to regarding a car that he thought took my fancy was called Bert Fry. He's worked for Auto Speed for about six months. I took him to be quite genuine and pleasant, and he seemed to know what he was talking about. Then I found out he wasn't the owner so I asked who the owner is. It's a man named – wait for it, sir – Drango Williams! It sounds Spanish but in fact he's Welsh. Comes from Abertillery.'

'Where the heck is Abertillery?'

'It's in South Wales, sir. His real name is Horace Albert Williams. I walked through the garage bit. The office is at the back. Stood in the far corner was what appeared to be a car under a cover, covered with a dust sheet. During my conversation with Mr Fry I asked him: "What's that?" He replied: "It's a car that came in for repair." "What, then sell it on?" "No, it's the boss's car. It's been in an accident." "What sort is it?" Mr Fry pulled back the dust sheet. I said: "My, that's some car," pretending that I was really interested.'

'And what sort of car is it?' DS Kidd asked.

'It's a red, or should I say, burgundy Jaguar, and it had wire wheels.'

'So what was the damage to it?'

'A bit of a scuff mark on the bodywork. Bert, Mr Fry, said the boss had caught it when he was leaving home. He also said: "We've been on to Jaguar to get a colour match, and they said they could supply us with a tin of the matching paint. So when it's been repaired and painted, the boss will be using it again." That's about all for now, sir.'

Kidd was impressed.

'Good work, Greenwood. By the way, I have put a request through the system and you have been transferred to me from pool duties. From now on you are DC Greenwood. Congratulations, and welcome to my team.'

'Thank you, sir. Many thanks.'

***

Meanwhile, Ted and Joan had been talking about getting a car. They had got the house sorted and they couldn't really expect to keep travelling for free on the buses. Not having to hang around at bus stops waiting for 'Dad Hart' to turn up would be an improvement.

'So what sort of car do you want, Ted?' Dad asked.

'Something cheap and cheerful,' Ted answered.

'Why don't you go down to Auto Speed? He has a lot of cheap cars.'

'Will you come and have a look with me?'

'OK, Ted. When do you want to go?'

'How about now? That's if you're not doing anything else at the moment.' Ted was keen to go looking.

Dad shouted through: 'Annie, I'm just going down to Auto Speed with Ted. He wants to have a look at some cars.'

'How long will you be?' Mum called back.

'A couple of hours. No longer, dear.'

'Tea will be on the table then.'

'OK, Annie. Come on, Chris. You tag along as well. Give Mum a bit of a rest from us.'

'OK, Dad.' The house shook as I slammed the door behind us.

'What are we going to do, walk it?' Ted asked.

'We are not. Ken is on my service today. He'll be along in about five minutes. We'll jump on that, and if we have time we'll walk back.'

'Right.' We all set off.

'What sort of car were you thinking of getting, Ted?' We stood in front of a long line of smartly polished gleaming cars – mostly black, but there were some multicoloured ones amongst them. But they were out of Ted's range.

'Can I help you gents? This one is a fine example for a car of its year.'

'And what year is that?' Dad asked.

'Registered in 1958 and one careful lady owner since then.'

Dad turned to Ted: 'They all say that, Ted. Don't believe a word. Make your own mind up. If that's the kind of car you want, don't just jump in. Car salesmen will try and pressure you into buying a car.'

'You say one lady owner?' Ted asked.

'Yes.'

'And what's the mileage on the speedo?'

'Come over to the office and I'll show you the logbook.' Bert Fry smelt a profit!

'OK.'

The three of us followed Bert Fry into the office.

'Now, here you are.' He handed over the logbook for the Morris Traveller. 'As you can see, one lady owner from new. Genuine.'

'But it says Francis Tweedy and I know Francis Tweedy!' Ted spoke out. 'Tweedy's Pig Farm at Four Lane Ends. You know where it is, Chris.'

'Well, it must be his wife's car.'

'I don't think it is. *He's* called Francis and I think his wife is called Carole, with an e on the end!'

Dad exclaimed: 'I thought there was a funny smell when I opened the back doors of the car. Now I know what it is – he's probably been carrying the odd pig or two around in the back.'

Bert Fry ushered us outside for another look at the Morris.

'I'll tell you what,' Mr Fry said quickly, 'I can give you a good deal on the car. Say I knock fifty quid off the asking price … that will make it *only* £450. What do you say?'

Me and Dad looked at Ted. Ted looked at us both.

'I don't think so.'

'Well, what about another fifty quid off, then?' Mr Fry wanted this vehicle off his forecourt.

Dad said: 'At this rate, Ted, you're going to get the bloody car for nothing!'

'I'll tell you what. Let me just give Drango a ring, see what he says.'

'Drango, who's Drango?'

'He's the owner of this place, Drango Williams.'

'Strange name, that.'

'His real name is Horace Williams, but with a name like that you aren't going to sell many cars so he came up with the name Drango.'

'It's certainly a catchy name.' I nodded.

'Won't be a mo.' Mr Fry dashed back into his office. Minutes later he was back to his victims. 'He says if you agree to have it right now, you can have it for £250. Deal?' He offered his hand.

Ted took a step back.

'Er, can I think about it until tomorrow morning?'

'OK, but no later. I've got other customers interested in this car.'

Dad spoke to Ted.

'Tell you what, Ted. If you decide to buy it, I'll ask the mechanics down at the bus garage to have a look at it, make sure it's OK.'

'What about a guarantee?' Ted shouted to the Bert Fry as we walked away.

'I'll give you a month, take it or leave it!' He walked back towards his office.

In the distance I could hear the distinctive sound of what appeared to be a police car. As the sound was getting closer – *ee haw, ee haw* – there seemed to be more than one.

'Come on, Chris, you know what Mum said. If we don't get a move on the dog will be having a good tea.'

I had only gone a couple of yards when a police car, closely followed by a police van, pulled up alongside me. Two cops got out of the van and out of the back came another one with a dog.

Bert Fry spun round: 'What's up? What you doing?'

'Put your hands on the boot of that car and don't move or the dog will have you! Where's the owner?' It was DS Kidd who was asking the questions.

'He's not here.'

'What do you mean he's not here? Is he hiding in the back?'

By this time Ted, me and Dad were onlookers, watching and wondering what was going to happen next. I shouted out: 'He's at home. That man there rang him not twenty minutes ago. Ted is thinking about buying this car.'

Bert Fry spluttered,

'He's not there, he's not at home!'

'He must be! The young lad says you rang him regarding the purchase of that car,' DS Kidd said.

'I made it up. He's been abroad for the last two weeks or so. I didn't call him!'

You could see in an instant that DS Kidd had worked out the connection.

'You claim he's been away for about two weeks?'

'Yes.'

'And you say you don't know where he is?'

'Yes, well, I think he might have gone to Spain!'

'Do you think or do you know for certain?'

'He's gone to Spain.'

'So when do you expect him back?'

'This weekend.'

DS Kidd moved in close to Fry's face.

'Now, are you sure?'

Fry felt the spray from DS Kidd's mouth as he spoke.

'That's what he said on the phone.' Fry realised he had given the game away.

'I think we had better carry on this conversation down at the police station, Mr Fry.' Fry was marched to the door of the garage. 'Where are the keys to the Jaguar car?'

Fry shook his head: 'We haven't got a Jag for sale.'

'The one at the back of the garage, the one underneath all those dust sheets. You know the one. The one belonging to the owner of this place. Or are you the owner of this business?'

Bert Fry was surrounded by policemen now. The police dog stood menacingly directly in front of him, saliva dripping from its mouth onto his shoes. Fry farted and the dog looked up towards the crotch of his trousers, growled, showed its fangs and licked its lips!

'*Better than licking its own arse*,' Fry thought. The police dog growled again. Fry whimpered and stiffened up. 'No, no, I'm his partner.'

'My colleague was in here on Saturday afternoon and he saw the Jag. Is that right, DC Greenwood?'

'Yes, sir.'

'In fact, this is the same car that DC Greenwood was invited, *by you*, to lift up one corner of the dust sheet to reveal a polished but scratched burgundy-coloured wing of a Jaguar. The keys, please, for that car.'

'But … but…'

'Never mind the buts, the keys! Now.' DS Kidd followed Bert Fry to the tiny office at the rear of the garage. 'I see you have a good filing system. Invoices, scraps of paper, an ashtray, butt ends everywhere, a waste bin nearly empty. What's this? When the floor is full you'll start putting waste paper in the bin?'

On Fry's paper-strewn desk lay a copy of the local rag showing a photo of a blood-splattered pavement outside the bank on the day of the robbery.

'Did this Drango fellow see this?' DC Greenwood pointed to the picture on the front of the paper.

'No, he left the night before.'

'Things are starting to drop into place, Greenwood.'

The trouble was that Greenwood hadn't a clue. He had only come on board at the weekend and wasn't quite up to speed.

Greenwood moved some papers.

'Got them, sir!' he said, whisking the keys into his hand. Bert Fry, thinking he would be in for a grilling at the police station, decided to make a move for the door. Greenwood went through and walked to the Jag. Bert Fry got to the door, turned and made a dash for the outside and freedom.

'Grab him!'

'Grab who?'

'Fry, you idiot!'

PC Newbould went to grab Fry and managed to get one foot on an oily rag. Oh, ah! One foot went forward, the other back. Newbould fell backwards – thud – and slid along the garage floor. He made contact with a tin with more oil in it. He knocked that over, his hand ending up inside the tin.

'Did you get him, Newbould?' DS Kidd was looking at the prostrate figure lying on the floor!

'Missed him by a hair, sir!'

'Well, get up and follow him.'

PC Newbould tried and tried again but he now had both boots covered in oil and grease and one hand stuck firmly inside an oily tin. The chances of PC Newbould ever reaching the dizzy heights of standing up were becoming more and more impossible as the seconds ticked by.

'Where's PC Jarvis, and the dog?' Kidd called out.

PC Jarvis was standing alongside the garage door, looking, and watching what was happening. The dog was having a lazy pee at the side of him and sniffing at some oily rags.

'*Jarvis, let the bloody dog off!*' Kidd yelled.

As Bert Fry thundered out of the garage, Jarvis didn't have time to let the dog off. The dog went into pursuit mode as Fry passed by. A sharp tug of the lead and PC Newbould was in hot pursuit as well.

Bert knew which way to go between the cars that were parked very close together. The police dog was only a few feet behind him.

Ted and me and Dad watched as these events started to unfold. PC Jarvis, on the other hand, realised that his dog was managing to get between the cars. He was going to have a problem. The dog stopped, unable to go any further. By this time the lead had become taut and PC Jarvis was stuck! He couldn't reach to let the dog off the lead. Another sharp tug from the dog – he wanted to get back to the chase. Unfortunately the second sharp tug pulled Jarvis off his feet and firmly wedged him between two cars!

Ted, realising that Bert Fry was getting away and the police dog wasn't going to go anywhere fast, shouted: 'Here, Chris, hold this. I won't be long!' He pushed the details of the Morris into my hand.

Ted started to run after Bert Fry. He made a flying tackle, with his hands and arm going round Bert's legs and bringing them both crashing to the ground. Thud, thud. Bert struggled to get away from Ted but he held on tight.

'I think you have done all your running for today!' Ted said, as he sat on top of Bert Fry. As he spoke, PC Newbould arrived on the scene, covered in oil and grease. His helmet was dripping oil and the back of his jacket and trousers were covered in a mixture of oil, grease and sawdust. He had managed to wipe his face, but that too was streaked with greasy oil.

'I'll take him now, son.'

'Son? Thanks!' Ted did not appreciate that police speak.

PC Jarvis was still stuck face down between the two cars, dog lead taut. One end was wrapped around Jarvis's wrist, the other end on the dog collar. The dog was lying down unable to move.

'Come on, Jarvis. You can't stay there.'

'Sorry, sir, I'm stuck fast!'

'Well, let go of the dog lead.'

'I can't, sir.'

'Why not?'

'It's round my wrist, sir.'

DS Kidd looked at DC Greenwood and rolled his eyes. In turn DC Greenwood just smiled.

DS Kidd turned to me and Ted: 'Can you give me a hand?'

'What do you want us to do?'

'If you can rock that car, me and Greenwood will do the same to this one and with a bit of luck it will free Jarvis. OK, go!' And with a couple of rocks, a thud and a groan, Jarvis was free.

'I'm free, but still stuck!'

'You can't be both, Jarvis, so what's it going to be?' Greenwood and Kidd grabbed hold of Jarvis's boots and in a couple of seconds he was dragged free. This time the dog got stuck between the cars!

'Now what, Jarvis?'

'The dog's stuck now, sir.'

'Just bend a bit between the cars. Don't get stuck again, and unclip the dog lead. Then no doubt it will be able to free itself.'

Once the dog was free it bounded round the cars and back to PC Jarvis, who by this time looked a bit the worse for wear. The dog ran up to him, wagging its tail.

'Next time, Jarvis, let the dog go immediately. He can run faster than you and probably catch the person he is chasing!'

Some of the other policemen had taken the covers off the Jaguar and manoeuvred it so that it could be loaded onto a recovery vehicle.

'Right, lads, make sure we have everything, and make the place secure before we leave.' DS Kidd walked over to Dad, me and Ted. 'Thanks once again for all your help. With a bit of luck, and if Fry sings, we should be a lot closer to getting the last gang member.' Kidd shook our hands.

'We'd better be off. You know what Mum said – tea will be on the table in two hours – and I think we've been here nearly two hours.' With that Dad, me and Ted started walking home.

The police van flew past, followed by the recovery truck loaded with the burgundy Jaguar. DS Kidd and DC Greenwood followed in a police car. They slowed to a halt.

'Do you want a lift?' DC Greenwood shouted through the open car window.

'Yes, please.' Moments later we were squeezing into the back seat of the car. 'Just like bugs in a rug,' Dad whispered.

'Are you all in?'

'Yer. Tight, but we're all in.'

The car sped off. Most of the bystanders had melted away and the road became its usual self. Within minutes the police car screeched to a halt right outside our front door.

'Here you are, gents. Home.'

We removed ourselves from the back seat of the car.

'Thanks.'

'Not a problem.' Within seconds the police car had vanished.

Mr Wilks arrived home just as Dad, me and Ted were stepping from the car.

'More trouble, then?' Henry enquired.

'No, no. Just had a lift home. We went and had a look at some cars down at Auto Speed, but it appears that the owner was involved in the robbery at the bank. You know, the one where Ted was taken hostage. Anyway, Mr Wilks, are you calling round?' All four of us went inside.

'Sorry we're late. We got held up,' Dad apologised. 'Not what you're thinking. We went down to Auto Speed and we were looking round a Morris Traveller when all hell broke loose.'

'What do you mean by that?' Joan asked.

'In the background we could hear police sirens but thought nothing of it. Bert Fry who was, as it turned out, part-owner and salesman, was discussing the car with us when in burst the police. You know, DS Kidd – Roger's dad – and several others.'

'What did they want?'

I spoke up.

'They wanted the car that was at the back of the garage, all covered up. In the end this Bert Fry decided to make a run for it and one of the policemen who had a police dog on a lead gave chase. But he didn't let go of the dog! They both finished up with one at one end of a car and the other at the opposite end!'

Dad expanded the story.

'Bert Fry must have thought his luck was in, but he didn't realise that Ted here had dropped everything and given chase.'

'What happened then?' asked Mum.

'Ted brought Bert Fry down with a bang!'

'I did,' Ted enthused. 'Rugby tackled him. He went down with one hell of a thud. Let's put it this way: he didn't bounce and he didn't try to get up!'

I joined in.

'Two coppers picked up Fry and threw him into the back of the police van. They got the car out and loaded it onto the back of a recovery truck and took it away.'

Now Dad.

'We started walking home, and Roger's dad stopped and asked if we wanted a lift.'

'So, Ted, what about the car you went to see?' asked Joan.

'I quite liked the Morris Traveller, but we'll have to wait and see what happens to this Fry chap with the police,' Ted answered.

Shelley came bounding in, tail wagging.

'Your dinner is in the dog' mum commented.

Chapter 17

Over the next week Roger kept feeding us with information about the robbery. This was conversation he had overheard his dad telling his mum, I suppose in confidence.

Roger was telling me, Ian and Frankie. Gary, as usual, was away with the fairies.

'I just gave them a false sense of security,' said Roger.

'What do you mean?' Frankie asked him.

'I tell them I'm off to bed. I leave the stairs door open just a couple of inches, then shout goodnight. When I get to the top step, I sit down and listen. It's only then that Dad tells Mum what was happening at work that day.'

'I see,' said Frankie. 'Out of sight, out of mind, and they never suspect anything.'

'Nope. Only one time my dad came up to use the toilet, but I beat him to it. That was a close-run thing!' Roger paused to think, then continued. 'Apparently, Bert Fry has protested his innocence since he was arrested. Mind you, if he hadn't tried to run but had gone into the police van of his own accord, my dad would have probably treated—'

Gary broke in: 'What, to an ice cream?' Gary, who was away with the fairies, had just landed.

'No, Gary, just listen to what Roger is telling us!' Frankie said firmly.

Gary turned and looked down at the football that had just hit him in the back. He took aim and, with a swipe of his left foot, kicked the ball over the heads of the young players. The ball was heading in the direction of the headmaster's windows. As it went further it seemed to go faster. Me, Frankie, Ian and Roger, who had stopped speaking, turned and stared at the ball as it whizzed through the air.

'You're for it now, Gary!' said Roger at the precise moment we expected to hear a crack and the tinkling of broken glass as it fell to the ground. But the ball went thud against the side of the Golden Grain bread van that was delivering our daily bread supplies.

The van jerked to a standstill. The driver got out and walked round to see what he had hit. The ball was still rolling about on the ground. The driver picked it up, started to walk back to his cab then noticed a large dint on the side of the van. The dint was right in the middle of the 'o', the second letter of 'Golden'. He smiled to himself, looked again at the dint and then at the ball, turned and drop-kicked it back to the young football players.

'That was a close-run thing, Gary. I was thinking you were for the high jump then.'

Gary turned and looked at me and Ian.

'It was planned!'

'Never.'

'I saw the van coming. I placed the shot to hit the side of the van.'

'And to hit the letter 'o'?' laughed Frankie.

'No, just hit the side of the van. The letter 'o' was a fluke. Well, you've either got it or you haven't, and it appears I have it by the vanful!' Gary looked at the ground and started to shuffle a few twigs around with his feet.

'Isn't it about time we went in?' Frankie asked. 'The bell will be going soon.' As if by magic the bell rang.

The week passed slowly to start with but, as the weekend loomed even closer, the days started to become shorter. The only real news that Roger had was that Albert, or Bert to his friends (and at the time it seemed he had none), kept on pleading his innocence. On the Friday morning Roger announced that his dad had told his mum that they were expecting to arrest someone 'within hours'.

'Who's that, then?' Frankie asked.

'Who do you think?'

'If I knew that I wouldn't be asking, would I, Roger?' came a sharp retort from Frankie.

'Dad's heard on the grapevine that Drango Williams is returning home this weekend from his holiday abroad.'

'So what?'

'So that's who they are going to arrest as he steps of the plane.'

'Gotcha.' We were all standing around Roger, taking in his latest revelations, except Gary. He was more interested in watching the ants at his feet trying to carry a leaf back to where their nest was. Their hard work was over in a trice.

Gary was getting bored with all this. I was watching him out of the corner of my eye and said: 'What are you doing Gary?'

Gary promptly stood on the ants.

'Nothing, Chris. What are we doing tomorrow?'

'Don't know,' I replied. 'Dad and Ted were going to have a look at some more cars. Ted liked that car at Auto Speed, but with Bert Fry still helping the police with their enquiries and the place all locked up and no sign of it opening for trade, well…'

'Well, what?'

***

Nothing much happened over the weekend. Roger lived on the other side of town. Gary was out with his dad on Saturday collecting scrap, getting used to working for a living. But he had done that most weekends and school holidays since he was about ten years old. Ian hung around with me most of the day.

Mum went and did half a day at Mr Wilks' shop. She seemed to run the shop better than he did: she could find anything, and everything had its place. Not like at home: she put things back, Dad put things back and me … well, I picked things up and just left them anywhere, much to the annoyance of my mother. Things would turn up in the strangest of places: a tin of shoe polish in the potato bin, a dishcloth draped over the back of the settee in the front room…

'How did that get there?' Mum retorted.

'Don't know.'

'Well, you must know, because it wasn't there ten minutes ago. You said you would wash up, then you wandered off. The thing is, Chris, why say you are going to wash up then wander off with the dishcloth in your hand and leave it in the front room on the new settee? Come on, Chris. Start getting your head together.'

There was a knock at the front door.

'Go and see who that is, Chris.' Mum walked back into the kitchen with the dishcloth to return it to its rightful place on the draining board.

'Mum,' I shouted out.

'What, Chris?'

'There's a man who wants to see Dad.'

'Ask him in. It's rude to have him standing at the front door.'

'Right, Mum.'

The man stepped inside.

'How can I help you?' asked Mum politely.

'I'd better tell you who I am first. My name is David Woods. I'm the managing director of the company that is pulling down the old Mars Mill and is going to put up the new houses on the site. I had a pleasant chat with your husband a few weeks ago regarding the mill lodge. He and a group of his friends wanted to fence the lodge off and use it for private fishing. I can now tell you that we have been given permission to carry on pulling the old mill down. The police have got everything they need. Terrible thing, the robbery.'

'Yes.'

'And that poor chap they took hostage! What his family must think!'

'We know what they are going through. Ted, the young man who they took hostage, is engaged to my daughter Joan.'

'How is he now?'

'He seems to have got over it, but who can tell what is going on in his mind?'

'*Nothing!*' I thought, but didn't say anything.

'Well, we should have the mill flat in a few days and most of the rubble will have gone in a week or so. As I am a keen angler, I've decided to fence the mill lodge off and have a small building erected, somewhere to go if it's bad weather. We don't all sit outside in the pouring rain trying to catch fish. I'll grass the area between the lodge and the fence. How does that sound? So, if you could tell your husband when he comes in.'

'If you'd care to have a cuppa, he shouldn't be that long.' As Mum spoke, the front door opened.

'I'm ho-ome, Annie.'

'There's a man in the front room wants to talk to you, Wilf. I'm going to make us all a cuppa.'

'Grand, Annie. Just what I need.' Dad put his slippers on and Ted did the same. They went into the front room to be met by Mr Woods. 'Pleased to meet you, Mr Woods. How can I help you?'

'Please, call me Dave.'

'OK, Dave, so how can I help you?'

'It's more how I can help you, Mr Hart. I've just been explaining to your good lady wife the reason I'm here.'

Ted turned to the guest.

'Would you like a tea or coffee or something?'

'If you don't mind, yes, I'll have tea, please.'

'Come on, Chris. I think they need to chat, and they don't want us hanging around.'

As Ted reached the door, Dave Woods spoke: 'I take it you're the famous Ted?'

'Yes, that's me.'

'You're the one that was taken hostage in that bank job a few weeks ago.'

'Yes, that was me.'

'How are you getting on now?'

'I still have flashbacks. Keep wondering what would have happened if Chris and the others hadn't come to my rescue.'

'So you are Chris?'

'That's me,' I replied with a smile. 'Me and Ian found Ted trussed up like a chicken waiting to go on the spit in that old railway coach. We couldn't free him then because when we were in the old mill we had overheard somebody telling PC Duggins and PC Montrose to go and check on him on the Saturday. Later on that night we heard PC Montrose tell Duggins that he was going away the next day, flying abroad. So PC Duggins would have to check Ted alone.'

Mr Woods sat in awe at what he was hearing. I had more to tell.

'We, that is me, Ian, Frankie and Gary, went down to the police station on the Saturday morning and managed to speak to DS Kidd. We told him what we had heard and witnessed, and you know what happened next.'

'Is it true what they reported in the papers, Chris?'

'Well, up to a point. The one thing they didn't manage was to stop the trains from running, but yes, most of it is true.'

'Have you heard anything more about what has happened since?'

'Only that a bloke called Albert Fry, who works for Auto Speed—' I was interrupted.

'Yes, I know the place. He was arrested.'

'Well, did you know that he tried to evade arrest?'

'No.'

'Yes, he got away from the police and we were there looking at some cars. Ted wants to buy one. Ted gave chase and rugby tackled him to the ground.'

'Right. Anything else?' Mr Woods asked.

'That bloke Albert Fry claimed he only worked there. But we have since found out that he is the co-owner with a man called Drango Williams, who has disappeared. In fact he disappeared the night of the robbery, and his car found its way to Auto Speed. The front wing had a scrape on it which matched a paint scrape found on the warehouse roller shutter groove – you know, where the door slides down.'

'I know what kind of fitting you mean. Go on, Chris.'

'Roger, that's DS Kidd's son who goes to the same school as us, told us yesterday that he had heard his dad talking. He said they were expecting to arrest someone when they returned from abroad this weekend and that only means one person – the owner of Auto Speed, Drango Williams. But me, Frankie, Gary and Ian won't hear any more until we go back to school on Monday.' And with that me and Ted left the room.

'Chris seems to be clued up about it all,' Mr Woods said to Dad.

'He should be,' Dad replied. 'It was Chris and his mates that overheard the conversation and saw four men in the warehouse loading bay at the old mill. They had the guts to go and report it to the police. The only thing they didn't know was the time, the day and the place where the robbery was going to happen.'

'Anyway, Lenny,' Dave said. 'I want to have a chat with you about what I propose to do, with your help, regarding the old Mars Mill lodge.'

Mum came into the room with tea and a few buns. It was nearly five o'clock when she heard the front door close.

'My, Lenny, that was some chat!'

'Yes, we have hammered some things out. At least we can get things moving. He really likes our Chris. He said he has his head screwed on right. He felt sorry for Ted after what he'd gone through, but at least Ted seems to be getting over it. I expect it will take some time yet, Annie.' They looked at each other.

'What's for tea then, love?' Dad asked.

'That's all you think about! How about a fry-up?'

'That'll be fine, Annie, just fine.' Dad slumped into the chair by the fire. It was just flickering. 'Better get some more coal on it before the damn thing goes out. Where's Chris gone now?'

'He's gone out,' said Mum.

'Where?'

'Well, Ian was going to meet his girlfriend, Sandra Williams. Chris decided he would go too, so they were off to see if Frankie would go with them. I think she must have. You know that Chris and Frankie are fond of each other.'

***

Monday morning came with no sign of Gary at Cherry's corner shop. Frankie spoke out: 'He's been nabbed stealing and hauled off to the cop shop—'

'Or,' I butted in, 'he's late and his old man's dropping him off. That's more like it.'

And who was at the school gate to meet us? Gary!

'I see you were late, Gary,' Ian said.

'Yep, but when I got here I was early. Dad said if he saw you lot walking to school he would pick you up.'

'I'm glad he didn't!'

'Why do you say that, Ian?'

'Remember the last time that happened? The only time we got a lift with your dad, we all had to ride in the empty skip he was delivering. We arrived at school and were promptly sent home because of the smell! God only knows what he'd been carrying in the skip. There was only Frankie sat in the front but she had to share it with your dog.'

'You're right, Ian,' Gary said. 'We were sent home. But we didn't go back until the day after.'

'Mum had to wash all my clothes. They just stunk!'

'What of?' Gary asked.

'I don't know, Gary, but it was a horrible smell.'

We all agreed that we were glad Gary's dad hadn't picked us up.

'Don't be offended, Gary.'

'Don't worry about that,' Frankie said. 'Gary and his dad will be used to any smells that come from the stuff they pick up in those skips. Where do you take the full ones, Gary?'

Gary said,

'The council tip! Saw Roger when I was getting out of the truck. He's gone into class. Had to see the teacher about something.'

'Did he say anything?'

'What about?'

'Well, what happened over the weekend.'

'Nope, but he did say Ringo was in the custard. I think it must be a new Beatles song. I was trying to listen to the radio in the truck on the way in but it crackles a lot and you miss what they are singing so I haven't heard it yet. Have you heard it, Frankie? You're always listening to it.'

'Listening to what?'

'The radio.'

'No, I haven't heard it. What did you say it was called?'

'I'm sure Roger said, "Ringo was in the custard".'

'That's a strange name for a record track!'

With that we all ambled into school.

***

It was lunchtime before anyone could have a chat with Roger.

'What's this new record out by the Beatles?' Frankie asked him.

'Which one's that, then?' Roger had no idea.

'Something about "Ringo in the custard". Strange title for a new record.'

Roger looked perplexed.

'I've never heard that one.'

'Well, you told Gary this morning while he was waiting for you at the school gate.'

'No, I didn't. What I said was, "Tell Chris, Frankie and Ian that Drango Williams is in custody now!"'

We all turned and looked at Gary, who in turn looked the other way.

'I can see,' Ian said, 'we are going to have to sort Gary out. It's funny. If you tell him something he gets it all wrong.'

'But have you noticed,' Frankie put in, 'since he became the school hero in the Duggins' affair, it seems to have gone to his head. He can't do anything wrong.'

'You mean he can't do anything *right!*'

'So Roger, what's the latest on Drango Williams, then? We heard Gary's version when we got to the school gates this morning and he had it that "Ringo was in the custard". We managed to figure that one out! We think that Drango is in custody. Are we right or is there something else we have missed?'

Roger told us: 'I overheard Dad telling Mum last night that they had charged Drango with masterminding the robbery. Apparently PC Duggins and Montrose stopped Drango about four months ago over a minor traffic offence. Shortly afterwards, Duggins became quite pally with Drango and that's when they started planning the robbery. They intended to snatch the briefcase from Ted's hands as he came from the bank but things started to go wrong from that point. They had no intention of taking a hostage but had to, as the briefcase was attached to Ted's wrist by a length of chain. To make it more convincing, Duggins carried a sawn-off shotgun but, as Drango put it, just for show and it was not loaded.

'But apparently Duggins had a different approach. He fired it twice, once into the air, killing a few pigeons – one of which dropped onto Ted's head. That made it look like he'd been hit because blood was running down his face. The other shot went into the front of Mr Windle's car, making it undriveable. By the way, how is Mr Windle?' Roger asked me.

'Ted told us that Mr Windle went back to work last week but Ted said he hadn't got over the shock of what happened. It's made him go really old. But you never know, he might get over it in time. What about the car, Roger?'

'What car?'

'The getaway car.'

'That became a bit of a problem. They had planned the robbery for the week before but had to change the plans because the car they were going to use, which was their own police car, had a problem with the driveshaft and was taken to the garage for repairs. Anyway, in the end they had to use their boss's car at work and that was the car they used for the robbery. Drango got a set of number plates off a car at Auto Speed, one he had on show for sale. When DC Greenwood went to see him regarding the number plates, he said kids had pinched them and he couldn't see the point of reporting it to the police.'

We were spellbound with Roger's story.

'What else do you know?' Ian asked.

'Nothing much. Duggins and Montrose were in a bit of a flap when they met up because they had a hostage. But as they were called back to the crime scene, they dumped Ted on Drango and he somehow managed to get Ted to the old railway coach. You know what happened after that.'

We looked at each other and asked Roger to tell us more. We were enjoying listening and reliving the events. So Roger, feeling important, continued.

'They all met up in the old Mars Mill warehouse and divvied the money up. Montrose was going away on holiday on the Saturday. He was flying somewhere abroad. It also turned out that Drango Williams went out of the country later that night, so that left Duggins and Bert Fry. Duggins turned up for work as normal on the Saturday morning, unaware that you lot had gone in to see my dad. Dad started the ball rolling. One thing they worked out was the car that had been involved in the robbery. They had gone through all the proper channels but they just couldn't trace it. That was until they had Montrose in the interview room. That's when the penny dropped!'

Gary then asked a sensible question for once: 'What about the other guy, Albert Fry. Where does he fit into all this, Roger?'

'Well, this came out the other day, even though he's always protested his innocence in this robbery. It turns out that Bert Fry was the owner of Auto Speed but ran into a few money problems. Basically he was going bust. Drango Williams bought into Auto Speed and, heigh-ho, things started to pick up.'

'So how did Fry get involved with the robbery?'

'He didn't. Windle came in to see Bert Fry one day, as he was having problems with his car. Fry asked him to drop the car in on the following Friday and he would have a look at it. It turned out that Windle mentioned that he had to pick up the wages on Friday from the bank. That's when the seeds were sown. Bert Fry was driving the Jaguar on the night before the robbery and managed to catch the offside front wing on the slide of the roller shutter door of the warehouse. That's how the Jag came to be in the back of the Auto Speed garage, covered up so no one would see it. I think you lot know the rest. Anyway, if there's anything I've missed you'll be able to fill in the gaps.' Roger took a well-earned breather.

I spoke: 'We all know what happened to Duggins. The police marksman fired two shots. The first one hit the railway carriage and missed Duggins but the second shot hit Duggins in the throat and killed him. My dad said the marksman was probably trying to disable Duggins but Duggins might have moved slightly as the shot was fired and that's what caused *Duggins' demise!*'

Ian asked: 'What happened to Montrose, Roger? Can you tell us?'

'They put him in the cells so they could question him the next day, and during the night he managed to hang himself. So Drango Williams has been charged, and I think by the end of the week Bert Fry will be charged as well.'

'Well, they can't ask Duggins anything – he's brown bread and so is his partner in crime, Montrose. He's gone to the same place as Duggins,' I said, feeling satisfied with this result.

Gary was half-listening, half-somewhere else in the universe. As soon as brown bread was mentioned Gary came back into the real world.

'Brown bread… Where is it?'

'What?' We all turned and looked at Gary.

'Where is it? Where's the brown bread? I haven't had anything to eat since breakfast!'

I took up the challenge: 'If it was a day like normal, and you were at your normal time, no doubt you would have called at Cherry's corner shop and bought something for a snack.'

Gary looked at me.

'I would have called, yes, but you know me.'

'Yes, that's the problem, Gary, we *all* know you. You would have made friends with something that wanted leave the shop and go travelling!'

Roger looked at Gary then at the rest of us.

'What do you mean by that, Chris?'

'He takes things without paying for them. He's done it for years.'

'I'm surprised Cherry's are still open,' Frankie added. 'And the fuss they made of him when they realised that he was the one who harassed Duggins at the shoot-out, by the old railway coach! You can't believe it, can you? Can you, Gary?'

Gary looked a bit sheepish.

Ian put him right: 'Anyway Gary, there's no brown bread. It's a figure of speech. Brown bread: dead. Got it, Gary? And there's no bread involved!'

'Well,' Gary said, 'I'm still going to have to find something to eat. I'm starving!'

'I've got a piece of toast with raspberry jam on it. Mum made it this morning for breakfast. I didn't have time to eat it so Mum wrapped it up in that paper the bread comes in. You can have it if you want it,' Ian offered generously as he was unwrapping the toast.

'But it's cold!' moaned Gary.

'Well, what do you expect? It's now about one o'clock and I've had it since about eight o'clock this morning.'

'It's all soggy.'

'Look, Gary, if you want it take it, but don't moan about it. In fact, Gary—'

'What?'

'I'm going to eat it!' And Ian took a bite of the toast and jam. Gary's bottom jaw slowly fell open. 'Go on then, Gary, you have the rest.' Ian offered what was left.

'Thanks, Ian.'

'Next time, Gary, don't go on about it. You would kick a gift horse in the mouth. And before you ask, I'm not explaining that either.'

Roger turned and faced Gary, who was munching a cold and soggy raspberry jam-laden slice of toast. 'Chris, Ian and Frankie, I've told you what I know about the robbery. It's supposed to be secret so can we all agree, and that includes you, Gary. Don't blab any of this information to anyone, not even your parents. If any of it gets around then my dad will know where it came from.'

'Got it,' we all agreed, even Gary, who by this time had nearly finished the slice of cold toast, with most of the jam on his chin.

'Right, I'd better be off. We'd all better be off into school for the afternoon session.'

Nothing further was said about what Roger had told us. On our way home Ian asked Frankie what she was doing that night, only to be surprised when she said she was going to town with me.

'You kept that quiet, Chris.'

'Why don't you ask Sandra if she wants to come along? There's no school tomorrow, and anyway we only have a couple of weeks before we leave for good. Then, as Dad says, we join the "real world".'

'OK, I'll give her a bell.'

'What on? You haven't got a phone at your house.'

'I know we haven't, but you have. Can I use yours, Chris?'

'If Chris won't let you use theirs, you can use ours, Ian,' Frankie chirped up with a smile on her face. 'We have been through a lot in the last few months.'

'You can say that again, Frankie,' Gary said.

'You know you don't have to, Frankie. It's only a figure of speech,' Ian blurted out.

That night me, Frankie and Ian went down to town on the bus and met Sandra outside the Regal Cinema.

'Are we going in?'

'Of course. *Whistle Down the Wind* is showing. We'll see that. Come on, I'm getting some popcorn before we sit down. Let's get tickets for the back row, the double seats.'

A good night's entertainment was had by all.

'What did you think of the film?' Ian asked.

'Not a lot. What did you?' I answered.

'I don't know. I didn't see much of it!'

'I know, Ian. All you were doing was snogging Sandra.'

'Well, you were doing the same with Frankie!'

The following Friday, Roger was waiting as usual. Even though it was a summer's day, it was chucking it down. Roger had moved from the school gates to stand behind the wall, hoping not to get wet. Standing outside the gates you were in collision course with a large pool of water that was just waiting for a car or truck or bus to dislodge it, sending a spray a couple of feet into the air towards an innocent bystander. Within seconds you would feel the full force of the water trickling down your once-dry legs.

Me, Gary and Frankie were approaching, ready to start another school day. Gary was splashing in the puddles like a little kid and singing in the rain. Ian was a little later than the others that morning.

Chapter 18

'Chris, Chris!'

'What?'

'Got something to tell you all.'

'What's that, Roger?'

'The trial date has been set for Drango Williams!'

'Good news. When is it, then?'

'Four weeks on Monday, 9.30 sharp. Manchester Crown Court. So you will all be getting letters to attend.'

'What's that?' Gary asked.

'We have to go to Crown Court in Manchester, four weeks from Monday,' I repeated the news.

'Can't go!'

'What do you mean you can't go?' I asked him.

'Can't go. I'll be on the cart with Dad. We leave school next week and I'm going working for me dad. So, like I said, can't go!'

Frankie tried: 'I think you will find out that you *have* to go, like the rest of us, including your dad.'

'So how do you work that out, that my dad has to go?'

'Well, wasn't it you and your dad saw the robbers down at the old mill? He will have to testify what he saw that night and so will you. Plus what happened at the old railway coach, you know, when you became a bit of a local hero.' Now Gary had got quite a smile on his face.

'So don't tell me you can't go. You will be going, like the rest of us. You never know, you might even be on the telly. And don't turn up in your working clothes. You will have to be smart and presentable, not like you are when you're working!'

Ian arrived, puffing from the rush not to be late for class.

'I had to help Mum move some furniture in the house. It's all done now. What's occurring?'

I told him the news: 'Have you heard? We have to attend Crown Court in Manchester, four weeks from Monday. It's Drango Williams's trial. I know what you're thinking but don't say it, Ian. Gary has already made that point. We'll all have to attend – we were all there at the old mill and at the railway coach.'

***

The four weeks to the trial went in no time at all. We had all left school and gone our separate ways to start this new 'adult' life. Me and Frankie were walking out together, as Mum put it. Ian was doing the same with Sandra. We didn't see as much of each other during the week but at the weekends, Saturday nights, we all met up and talked about what had happened the previous week. Sometimes we'd go to the flicks or Shakers Coffee Bar, then fish and chips later.

The Saturday before the trial Ian asked: 'What are the arrangements for Monday?'

Still 'gang leader', I answered: 'Well, Dad's managed to borrow a single-decker bus. He told Mum that Bill said he could take one of the new single-deckers, so long as he looked after it. He – Dad, that is – asked Reg Parks if he would drive the bus so Dad could ride on the cushions with us.'

'Has he agreed?'

'Yes. Well, he would. Reg and Dad go back years, and they are always going fishing together.'

'So go on then, what're the arrangements for Monday?' asked Ian.

'Reg will bring the bus to ours for eight o'clock so, make sure you're at mine for 7.45 prompt.'

'Why 7.45? I'll be round at 7.30.'

'Why 7.30?'

'Cos no doubt your mum will have a bacon sandwich for me!'

I smiled: 'You and your food. Is Sandra coming?'

'She wants to, but can you pick her up closer to where she lives? I'll tell her to meet us on the main road at the bottom of her street.'

'OK, Ian, that's good.'

'How many are travelling on the company's bus?'

I thought for a few seconds while I counted on my fingers.

'Well, there's me, you, Frankie, Sandra and Mr Wilks – he's shutting his shop for the day. He was round at ours last night and Dad asked him why he wanted to go with us to court. "Wouldn't miss it for the world," he said. "They're a grand bunch of kids, and they've done something good. Can't say much for the police, though. Shot one, another hung himself and your lad did most of the work. Him and his mates got information, following, listening. They did all the work. The police did nothing much." My mum and dad are going – what about your mum?'

'Yes, she's going.'

'I believe Frankie's mum's going.'

'Have you been round to see Gary?'

'Yeah, me and Dad went round the other night, told them what time. I think his mum's going as well. Mrs Cherry said she was coming. Mr Cherry is going to look after the shop.'

'What about Ted and Joan?'

'They are going on the bus on Monday. Dad's only having the bus for the one day. With us giving evidence first, we shouldn't have to go again, hopefully. So for the rest of the trial, Ted and

Joan are going with Mr and Mrs Windle. The only one who's not going is the dog!'

'So what's he going to be doing, making the dinner?' Frankie laughed at the thought.

'What do you think? Sleeping like he always does, lazy git!'

'Stupid!'

'John can't come. He's just had an operation.'

'What, to remove his wallet?'

'No, he's had something taken out. I don't know what. But anyway, he can't go and Roger might be going but he won't be giving evidence. He was never around when there was any action.'

***

The bus rolled to a stop right outside the front door of our house. Reg Parks was dressed in a grey suit.

'We are very smart today, Reggie,' Dad said.

'Well, it might only be a bus but we are off for something special, to the big city.'

'Come on, then, folks, all aboard.'

Most were standing on the pavement. Ian's mum was sitting in our back kitchen, talking and helping Mum. As Ian had said on the Saturday, most of the people who were travelling had gone through a bacon sarnie. Mum and Mrs Hogan had made a big pile of them. Ian was still eating leftovers.

'You know, Annie, you're more like a second mum to our Ian.'

'Well, boys will be boys,' Mum said as they both watched Ian eating away.

'Come on, Annie,' Dad was calling. 'We're ready to go.'

'Just a mo. I'm getting a sandwich for Reggie.'

Moments later they were off.

'Don't forget Sandra,' Ian shouted.

Within minutes Sandra was on the bus.

'How long is it going to take, Reg?'

'About an hour from here, Dunsford Parra to Manchester. We've been given permission to park the bus at the side of the Crown Court.'

Gary and his dad were travelling on the bus. They were going to take the truck but decided against it, as his dad would have been trying to collect scrap and with Mrs Singleton going with them it didn't seem right! All they had to worry about was the fashion police. Gary was wearing a jacket that was too big and trousers that were too tight, and the other notable feature was that his trousers appeared to be at half-mast with bright orange socks showing. He was wearing a light grey jacket, a dark-blue shirt and a brilliant yellow- and red-striped kipper tie.

'What do you think, Ian?' he asked as he gave a twirl down the middle aisle to a round of applause from the crowd.

'It's a bit of overkill, don't you think, Chris?'

'Well, yes,' Chris replied without hesitation.

Gary's father was a bit more presentable but he too had on a large kipper tie, bright blue with an awful green stripes running across it. Of all three, Chris's mother looked the best – more prim and proper.

We arrived outside court and went, like a procession, from the bus to the courtroom in single file, Dad in front. As he got to the big solid oak brown doors he stopped and we all stopped. Though some at the back, not realising that the front had stopped, carried on – only to bump into those in front. That followed through the procession until it got to the front, like a row of railway trucks.

'Right, all, pay attention,' Dad spoke up. 'The ones that are giving evidence, go to the left as we go through the doors. The remainder, go to court number one. I'll just make sure that the court ushers know we have arrived and where they want us to sit and wait to be called in.'

At nine thirty prompt, the trial started.

'Will you all rise.'

Ted was called first. He went in and was on the stand for about twenty minutes. Then it was the turn of Mr Windle. It seemed to take ages, as he had become quite frail since his attack and being manhandled onto the floor of his car. Next it was our turn.

The usher came over: 'They want you in court now. Follow me, please.'

We rose and followed him into the courtroom. I caught Dad's eye. He smiled and gave me the thumbs up.

The courtroom appeared small but at the same time very big. There must have been fifty to sixty people sitting around. The judge stared at us all as we entered. He was small, probably smaller then Ian. He had a big chubby face, ruddy in colour, and white hair – or that could have been his wig. He sat there. He could have been a dummy, except for his left hand moving to his mouth to stifle a cough.

We all stood on the witness stand and took the oath. From the back of the courtroom it must have sounded like a loud mumble. Our statements were read out and then we were questioned. This took some time, as they went right back to where it all started. I think we all gave a good account as to what we saw and heard.

Just before we left the stand the judge wanted to hear from Gary, who was by this time getting a bit fidgety, about the part he played in trying to rescue his friends from the old railway coach. At this point Gary came into his own. At one point I felt sorry for him, stood there like he should have been going to a fancy-dress party. His clothes didn't fit, and he had no colour-matching skills, but on the other hand I felt very proud of him.

He was the one who had put everything else aside to save his mates. At one point we thought he had bought it but Gary, being Gary, he'd decided that he couldn't do any more at that moment in time and decided to play dead! By the time that happened, PC Duggins was black and blue.

All the time we stood on the witness stand Drango Williams and Albert Fry sat motionless in the dock, staring at us. We hadn't seen Drango until we took the stand, only Albert Fry. He seemed quite nervous. He knew was on a lesser charge of trying to evade police arrest. He had cooperated fully with the police since Ted had rugby tackled him to the ground. His only wish was that he hadn't tried to make a run for it.

Meanwhile, Drango was taking everything in. What was going through his mind? It appeared that he was going to take the rap for everything. Duggins, gun-toting Duggins, had been shot dead. Drango had told him not to take – or think of using – a weapon, but Duggins knew best. Now that he wasn't there, Drango was going to take the rap for that. Duggins's so-called mate, Montrose, couldn't take the pressure but wanted the money to help start a new life.

Drango had masterminded everything but he couldn't have planned what was going to happen now. He had made his mind up: he was going to escape. At the first opportunity he would be gone. Let Fry take the full force of the law. He had been there, though he hadn't taken part. The only part Fry played was to hide his car.

'No further questions, your honour. You four are free to go.'

We had just gone through the door when we heard the announcement: 'Court adjourned until 9.30 tomorrow morning. All rise.'

We were all relieved that our ordeal was over. The usher told us that they didn't want us the next day. By the time we got to the bus Reggie had it started up and it was running.

'As you have all done really well today, how about calling in at the new McDonald's on the way home?'

By the time everybody had got something to eat and drink it was seven o'clock before we reached home.

'Thanks, Reggie,' everybody muttered as they got off the bus.

'Thanks, Reggie. Do you want a cuppa before you take the bus back?' Dad asked our driver.

'No, you're fine. It's been a long day and besides, I'm on earlies tomorrow morning. Thanks anyway.' With that, a crunching of the gears, a cloud of smoke and Reggie was off down the road.

'Good day, Annie?' Dad asked.

'Different, I'll say that!'

'What do you think about that Drango Williams?'

'Strange sort of man, Lenny.'

'Yes, and a strange name.'

'You could see when he stood in the dock he was working something out in his mind. What do you think about the name?'

'Well, there's one thing. It certainly makes you say "what?" The name will stay in your mind.'

'Drango Williams, second-hand car dealer. It's more catchy than Joe Bloggs, car dealer, don't you think?'

'It might be, but what a strange-looking bloke. I wouldn't trust him as far as I could throw him!'

'What?'

'You heard me. He's a strange, very strange man.'

***

The trial was expected to last until the Thursday. Ted and Mr Windle went every day to listen to the evidence, the police statements and further questioning. Drango Williams complained that the bracelets were getting too tight around his wrists, and could he have them a bit looser? The court officials had relented and removed them altogether.

Ted returned home each night and gave us a rundown of the day's events. He said: 'At one point it appeared Drango Williams would be going for a long stretch.'

'What do you mean? They are going to stretch him?'

'No, Mum, he will be in prison a long time! I was going to say—'

'Say what?'

'Never mind, Mum.'

We all looked at Mum. She shrugged.

The jury was sent out on Thursday afternoon but couldn't reach a verdict, so Ted and Mr Windle went back on Friday morning.

'Well, it should be over today, Ted.'

'It should be, Mr Windle.'

As they sat at the back of the courtroom, the judge entered the room.

'Be seated.' The courtroom was quite full. Not as many as there were for the start of the trial, but there again it was a hot morning. The sun was shining and it was the start of the town's holidays. People were getting away early for their well-earned summer break. Still, the courtroom was full enough for this important case.

'Has the jury come to a verdict?' asked the court clerk.

'Yes, your honour, we have.'

'And how do you find the defendant, Mr Drango Williams, guilty or not guilty?'

'Guilty, your honour!'

Drango Williams never heard the rest, or what the sentence was going to be.

The prison guard who was standing behind had just left.

'May I be relieved for a toilet call, your honour?'

Before the next guard got into position Drango Williams and Albert Fry were momentarily alone in the dock. Having heard the guilty verdict, Drango took a chance. He vaulted over the guard rail of the dock, landing on the table belonging to the defence lawyers. Paper, ink, pens … everything scattered. Another step and he was on the floor of the courtroom. This time he was really on the move, one arm stretched out along the desktop. Everything in his wake fell or flew into the air.

People in the gallery watched in awe. This was starting to look like the clowns had come to town! The usher by the door tried to stop Drango, but to no avail – she was just pushed aside. It seemed to take ages. People sat glued to their seats watching the melee take place.

Drango had gone. He had taken a chance and left the courtroom in total disarray, but he had fled.

Mr Albert Fry was found guilty of a lesser charge of aiding and abetting, and was given a twelve-month suspended sentence. The judge told Mr Fry that he knew what was going on and he could have told the police.

'But, as you didn't, most of the money has not yet been recovered, Mr Drango Williams has escaped, PC Montrose took his own life and, as for the other police officer, Duggins, he unfortunately lost his life to a police shoot-out. Mr Windle was injured in the robbery. I give praise to Edward Harker for trying to stop Duggins taking the money. He's the one other person who needs to take a lot of credit for the actions they took. When the others found Edward Harker tied up it was Gary Singleton who had the presence of mind to try and disable PC Duggins in any way he could.'

I was told at work that they had heard on the radio that someone had done a runner from a courtroom in Manchester. When I got home the television was switched on to the Friday night six o'clock news. Drango Williams had escaped from the courtroom in Manchester. His whereabouts were unknown, but the police had a warrant for his arrest. Then the newsreader carried on and described what had gone on and what sentence Albert Fry had been given.

'What do you think, Dad? Do you think they'll catch him?'

'Come on, you two. Your teas are out,' Mum shouted through.

'Aren't we waiting for Ted and Joan?' I asked.

'No, they've been and gone.'

Ian came round after tea and Frankie called: 'What do you think then, Chris?'

'Mum said on Monday night she thought that Drango looked a bit fishy. Dad reckons that it will be a while before they catch him.'

'We'll have to get a paper in the morning, see what it says in there about it. Gary's dad came into the bank this morning before Drango made a run for it and he said that the local newspaper reporter had been round. They interviewed Gary for quite a while, and on leaving they said it would be in tomorrow's paper. So don't forget, and spend a bit of your hard-earned cash on one.'

I couldn't wait and went down to the paper shop early.

'Now, Chris, what do you want?'

'Local rag, please.'

The newsagent handed over the paper: 'What about the rest?' he said, pointing.

'What do you mean?'

'The story might be on the front page of the local, but all the national papers have the story as well!'

'You're kidding me!'

'Take a look, Chris.' He wasn't kidding at all.

'Tell you what: you take a copy of all the papers.'

'But I can't.'

'It's OK. Have them on me.' He bundled up a copy of each paper.

'Thanks, thanks a lot. Wait 'til Mum and Dad see this lot!'

Around nine o'clock the phone started to jingle: 'Answer that will you, Chris?' Mum shouted from the top of the stairs. 'See who it is.'

'It's Gary.'

'What does he want?'

'He wants me to get hold of Ian and Frankie and go down to their place for ten o'clock.'

'What for?'

'He says the television people are going to be there. They want to interview us all.'

'Well, you'd better get a move on. Have you had a wash this morning?'

'Course I have,' I assured Mum. Just then there was a knock at the door. 'It's Frankie, Mum. Have you had a phone call from Gary?'

'Yes, we'd better go. Ian's mum hasn't got a phone, so we'd better go round and get him.'

We all managed to get to Gary's for ten o'clock, just as a big van pulled up outside. It was the television people. A man and a woman got out and walked over. Gary's dad walked across to meet them. Gary had used his brains for once and chained the dog up, who wasn't very pleased and carried on barking.

'I see the dog's barking mad, like the owner,' Ian laughed.

'What?'

'Forget it, Gary.'

'Well, I didn't know what you said, anyway.' Gary, as usual, was dressed for the occasion. He said he was quite smart, but to us he looked like he had just chucked the first lot of clothes on that he'd found.

Gary's dad, who had been talking to the TV people, came over and introduced us all.

'This is Christopher, Ian, Frances, or as she likes to be called, Frankie, and my son Gary. He was the one who tried to stop PC Duggins.' He was proud, to say the least.

'So you're Gary. Take some shots of Chris, Ian and Frankie while I have a chat with Gary. So, you're the one who everybody is talking about.' Gary's face turned from pinky-white to almost blood red. 'There's no need to be nervous,' the interviewer told Gary. 'Just tell me in your own words what you did when you realised that the others were in danger.'

The interview with Gary seemed to go on for ages. Once it was over, they took some film of us.

'I think that's a wrap,' the interviewer said.

'Just before you go, could you give a mention to one of our mates who spent quite a lot of time with us when we were in the old mill and when we were talking to the police? His name is John. He can't be with us today, as he's been in hospital for an operation.'

'I'll see what I can do about that, and thanks once again. Bye.' And they were gone.

'Did they say when it was going to be on the television, Gary?' I asked.

'This evening, I think she said.'

'That's you to a T, Gary.'

'Well, you know what it's like for Gary with all this fame! There's too much floating about in his head to take in what she said!'

'Well, that's it. We've had our day of fame. Some have had more than others.'

'Meaning?' Frankie asked.

'Well, Gary got praise from the judge telling everybody what a fine job he had done in saving his mates. He was interviewed by the local press, which went national, and now this!'

'You sound a bit pissed off with it all.'

'Well, I suppose I am. Would be nice to get back to normal, or as it was. Don't you think, Ian?'

'No, it will never be like it was!'

'Right, then, what are we doing tonight?'

'I'm meeting Sandra at seven.'

'Come round and we'll go down town with you. What are you going to do, Gary?'

'I've got a *date!*'

'Who's that with then, Gary?'

'She's called Norma Harbuckle.'

'Where's she from, then?'

'T'other side of town.'

'Tell you what, Gary, you come round to ours for 6.30 and we'll all go down town. Ian will hook up with Sandra and you hook up with your Norma.'

We all managed to watch the six o'clock news. There wasn't much on the national news but the local news that followed was full of it. Mum and Dad sat glued to the telly.

'There you are folks, fame at last!'

'Go on, you lot. See you later.'

It sounded as if a herd of elephants had charged out of the front door. The door slammed shut. Peace and quiet descended on Mum and Dad as they sat back. The door opened again: 'What have you forgotten?' Mum asked. But it wasn't me.

'It's me, Mum,' Joan said. 'And Ted.'

'It's just been on the news about Gary and his role in securing your release from your ordeal, Ted.'

'Yes, we were waiting for the bus in town. You know the stop by Visionhire. They had all the televisions on. You couldn't hear what they were talking about due to the thick glass window. But we managed to watch it, and so did quite a few other people that were waiting for the bus.'

'Who was driving the bus?'

'Reggie Parks.'

'Another free ride, then?'

'Yes.'

'By the way, Ted, I have to ask you… Can you be at the bus garage Tuesday night seven o'clock sharp?'

'Why?'

'Because Bill wants to see you, so make sure you're there.'

'Will you be there?' Ted asked.

'I'll be around somewhere. I come off my shift at 6.30 so yes, I'll be around.'

Ted and Joan went into the kitchen.

'What's all that about, then?' Mum asked Dad.

'Well you know that car Chris, Ted and me went to see down at Auto Speed, at the time when Bert Fry was there on his own?'

'Yes.'

'We all chipped in at work and we went down and took it off Bert Fry's hands. The lads in the garage have worked wonders. Old man Windle, Ted's boss, he paid for the respray and new upholstered interior. It looks brand-new – well, it looks better than brand-new. They are going to present it to Ted as a thank you for what he has done for the town.'

'That's another bus passenger you will have lost!' Mum remarked.

'Well, he wasn't a bus passenger, really. More like a bus employee.'

'How do you work that out?'

'He always rode free on the buses, like he does now. And Joan, she always rides free. More often than not you ride free as well. In fact, all the family ride for free!'

Tuesday night arrived. Since the Sunday it had rained and there were big puddles and little puddles. Cars whizzed past, splashing water onto the footpaths. Three double-deckers and a single-decker stood in a line waiting to enter the bus garage, all with their engines running, rainwater streaming down the sides.

'Come on, Joan. If we don't hurry up we're going to be late.'

'What do you think it's about?'

'Don't know. I expect I'm going to be told I'll have to start paying or I'll be in trouble. Has your dad said anything?'

'No, not a word.'

They entered the garage. Everywhere buses stood in lines.

'Where do we go, Ted?'

'I don't know. Over here. Follow me.' Ted and Joan walked towards a room where people were moving around. Ted pushed the door open.

'Come in, Ted, Joan as well.' The room was big but made smaller by the number of people. Ted could see Lenny and Reggie over in the far corner. Everyone was smiling.

'Can I have a bit of hush, please?' Bill announced. The room fell silent, except for a few coughs now and then. 'I've asked Lenny to get you here tonight because of what you did during the robbery and also the citizen's arrest of that chap Fry at Auto Speed. We – that is all the staff and your boss, Mr Windle – have got you a present.'

One of the drivers shouted out,

'*Handcuffs!*'

'Shut it, Smithy! Well, Ted, if you look outside you will see what it is.'

Ted and Joan turned and looked through the window to see a shiny green Morris Traveller. It was standing in front of the new Bristol single-decker bus that had taken them all to Crown Court the previous week.

'What do you think about that, then?' Bill asked.

'I just can't believe it. It's the car that was at Auto Speed!'

'You're right, Ted. But we all chipped in and now, after being restored, it's *yours*.'

'What can I say, Joan?'

Joan spoke up: 'Thanks, and thanks again to you all.' As she spoke, tears of joy came to her eyes.

'Well, aren't you going to get in it?'

Ted walked over to the car, opened the door and sat in the driver's seat. As he turned the key in the ignition, the car burst into life.

'Come on, Joan.'

The car set off out of the bus garage and everybody stood and cheered as it disappeared into the dark, rainy night. The car now has its own garage right next to the one with the new roof panels that Ian had managed to drop through.

The following Monday morning Mr Windle made an announcement that Ted Harker was, from that day, a director of Windle and Son. Ted was getting all the attention, or it seemed that way.

We four had heard everything, informed the police of what we had heard, rescued Ted, seen Bert Fry's attempted escape and Drango Williams's departure from the courtroom. Oh, and I almost forgot, we witnessed the shoot-out and poor Duggins' demise!

What did *we* receive? Well, that's another story.

See you soon,

Chris.

About the Author

I entered this world in 1946, born in Blackpool. After leaving school I joined the British Army, serving in some far away places. I eventually retired from my civilian job in the transport industry. Using my experiences of life and a vivid imagination I have written this, my first novel of the series for young (and older) people to read and enjoy.

Forthcoming Duggins' titles

Duggins' -
The Green Stuff Is Gone

Duggins' -
Blast Off

Duggins' -
Tomorrow It's Back To The Real World